SCORCHED BY MAGIC

THE BAINE CHRONICLES, BOOK 7

JASMINE WALT

DYNAMO PRESS

Cover illustration by Judah Dobin

Cover typography by Rebecca Frank

Edited by Mary Burnett

Electronic edition, 2017. If you want to be notified when Jasmine's next novel is released and get access to exclusive contests, giveaways, and freebies, sign up for her mailing list here. Your email address will never be shared and you can unsubscribe at any time.

AUTHOR'S NOTE

Dear Reader,

If this is the first book you've picked up in the Baine Chronicles series, I've included a glossary in the back of the book to help illuminate the backstory. If you've already read the previous books, this glossary will help reacquaint you to the people, places, and things introduced to you in earlier volumes. You can either read the glossary first to familiarize or re-familiarize yourself with Sunaya's world, or you can plunge into the story and refer to it as needed. The guide is in alphabetical order, and characters are listed last name first.

To the new reader, welcome to the Baine Chronicles! And to those of you who have read the previous books, welcome back and thank you! Your support allows me to continue doing what I love most—writing.

Best,
Jasmine

"You did a wonderful job organizing this party, Sunaya."

"Thanks." The approval in Iannis's deep, slightly musical voice sent a little thrill of joy through me, and I smiled. Surveying the ballroom from our seats at the head table, I had to agree the praise was deserved, even if I hadn't done it all on my own. The place looked resplendent in the state colors of blue and gold, which were featured in the Canalo emblem hanging from banners draped along the walls, echoed in the linens on the round dining tables, and even in the uniforms the servants wore as they went around serving food and refilling champagne glasses.

Chandeliers boasting hundreds of magic-fueled, dripless candles glittered above us, illuminating the ballroom, which was packed to capacity. Every seat at every table was filled with shifters and humans alike. Relatively few mages were present aside from the guards flanking the entrances. It was an unusual state of affairs for the Solantha Palace ballroom, which usually hosted mage-only events, and I took it as a good sign that neither the Mage Council nor the Secretaries seated at the high table with Iannis and me were being particularly snooty tonight.

Captain Galling should be up here with us, too, I mused, my eyes surveying the crowd. This was his farewell reception, and he was the guest of honor. But Galling had wanted to sit with his enforcers, and I couldn't really blame him. He would be much more at ease celebrating amongst his own, rather than up here with a bunch of mages he barely knew. He was sitting at a table near the front with Deputy Captain Skonel, Foreman Vance, and a bunch of other Main Crew enforcers with their spouses. And at his elbow was Mrs. Galling, fully recovered from her liver disease, her cheeks glowing with health and her eyes sparkling.

The sight did my heart good, and I reached beneath the table to squeeze Iannis's hand. He'd healed Captain Galling's wife some months earlier in exchange for his cooperation during the Uprising, and after word had quickly spread of the miraculous recovery and its cause, many others had come to the Palace requesting a healing as well. Rather than rebuff them, Iannis had decided to devote every fourth day of the week to healing terminal cases. He would spend all day at the Maintown Hospital, then come back to the Palace and collapse into bed, exhausted. The healings took a toll both mentally and physically, but they had done wonders to help repair relations between the Mages Guild and Maintown.

As I reached for my glass, a tremor shook the walls and floor, causing water to slosh onto the tablecloth and over my half-eaten steak. Gasps of surprise and dismay echoed throughout the room, and servants rushed over to assist guests who had accidentally spilled food or drink on their clothing. My aunt Mafiela, holding court at a table toward the middle with the rest of the Shiftertown Council and Inspector Boon Lakin, looked particularly incensed at the large red wine stain on the bodice of her peach-colored gown. Inspired, I surreptitiously pointed a finger at her, and muttered the Words to a cleaning spell Iannis had taught me during our travels. The stain magically disappeared, and Mafiela's head jerked up, shock in her beautiful face. Those yellow shifter eyes met mine, and I gave her a knowing grin. She inclined her head to me, a small smile playing on her lips, then turned back to her food.

From her, it was high praise indeed.

"I do hope that tremor isn't a sign of worse things to come," Cirin Garidano, the Finance Secretary, said from Iannis's left. "The last major quake here was nearly two hundred and fifty years ago. Judging by the stories, I wouldn't like to experience an event like that."

"We get tremors like this on a regular basis, Cirin," Iannis reminded him, clearly unwilling to discuss the subject during a celebration. "This is Canalo, where the earth is never entirely silent."

Iannis wasn't nearly as blithe and dismissive as he sounded —I knew the subject had already cost him some sleepless hours. Upon our return to Solantha a few weeks ago, Fenris had presented us with a letter he'd received from Lord Faring, an ancient mage who'd lived in the area during Solantha's last major earthquake. After narrowly escaping death, he'd made studying tectonic events his life's work. He'd warned that another big quake was likely imminent, and that the city was not well prepared for it. Iannis had made an appointment to consult the old mage further—in fact, he'd gone to see him this morning. I was very interested in hearing what he'd learned, but there hadn't been a chance to talk to him about it, what with the banquet preparations. Despite his calm, stately demeanor, I could sense that Iannis was worried about whatever he'd been told.

When the servants were about to serve the dessert course, Iannis stood. A hush instantly settled over the room, shifters and enforcers turning their attention toward their Chief Mage. As Iannis launched into his farewell speech for Captain Galling, giving a rundown of the captain's career and accomplishments, I let my eyes drift over the crowd again. Most of the guests were relaxed and in a good mood, but there was still tension in many faces and shoulders. There might not have been very many mages in the room, but shifter and human relations were still strained since it had come out that the Resistance had been planning to backstab its shifter members.

That news had poisoned race relations everywhere, including within the Enforcers Guild. During the three months Iannis and I had been gone, several crews had broken up and new ones had been formed. And all this time, Father Calmias's fervent followers were still stirring racial tensions.

Not wanting to look like I was bored, I turned my attention back to Iannis just in time for him to bring Captain Galling up to the podium for the obligatory speech. The captain had been working for the Enforcers Guild for over thirty years, and while he had gone soft and sloppy toward the end of his career, he was still well respected. Many of the enforcers present seemed genuinely sad the captain was leaving. There was much stomping and cheering from them as he made a few enforcer in-jokes, the raucous behavior drawing appalled looks from the stuffy Mage Council members.

"I know that some of you are uncertain about the future of the Enforcers Guild," Captain Galling was saying, a grave expression on his face now. "But my successor, Acting Captain Skonel, is more than man enough for the job." He raised his glass to Skonel, who was still seated, and the crowd cheered again. Skonel had been Foreman to the second largest crew for a good ten years before he was promoted to deputy captain. Clean-cut, handsome, and with a fair but militant air about him, he was a far a cry from Garius Talcon, his sleazy predecessor who'd secretly been working with the Resistance and had tried to press me for sexual favors more times than I could count. I didn't know Skonel very well, but I expected he would manage the Enforcers Guild with a firmer hand than Galling had-.

"I will never truly stop being an enforcer, and I will be here to assist with this transition as Captain Skonel settles into his new role. But I am getting to be an old man now, and I would like to spend what's left of my time here on Recca with my lovely wife." He raised his glass to Mrs. Galling, who beamed at him. "Her restored health is entirely due to Lord Iannis's abilities, and I will always be grateful." He turned toward Iannis, his steely eyes brimming with emotion, and bowed. "Thank you, sir, for all you have done for Solantha and Canalo. You are the finest Chief Mage this state has seen for some time."

I could tell by Iannis's slight hesitation that he had not been expecting the compliment, but he smiled and inclined his head graciously. There was a second or two of silence before the room erupted into thunderous applause. It took everything I had to dim down my grin into a more sedate smile. Iannis worked far harder with the shifter and human populations in Canalo than his predecessor had, and it was often a thankless job due to the animosity toward mages that had built up over centuries. I was thrilled to see he was finally getting some genuine recognition.

After the speeches were finished, the tables were cleared away to make room for dancing and general mingling. I took Iannis's offered arm and we made our rounds throughout the room, taking the time to speak to Captain Galling and his family, the Shifter Council members, and various prominent figures from Maintown and Shiftertown.

"Sunaya," a throaty, accented female voice called, and I turned to see Elania weaving through the crowd toward me. The talented witch looked sexy and elegant in a black sequined sheath dress, her thick dark hair piled up in one of her elaborate up-dos, and amber dangling from her ears and throat. "You look wonderful."

"Thank you." Smiling, I smoothed my hands over the silk skirt of my emerald-green dress. I would never look as graceful and mysterious as Elania, but I was getting more comfortable dressing in finery, even going so far as to request certain hairstyles and outfits rather than just letting my maid decide as I had in the beginning. My thick black curls had been braided and twisted into an up-do of their own, secured with tiny diamond pins that caught the light.

"Where is Comenius?" I asked. I had been too busy to notice his arrival. Even though Nelia, my secretary, had helped with the preparations, it had been my first time organizing an event on this scale and I'd been too stressed to keep track of all attendees.

Elania's full mouth tightened almost imperceptibly. "He is at home with Rusalia. The babysitter we used last week refused to come back, and we have not been able to find another on such short notice."

"Well, that sucks." I pursed my lips at the thought of Rusalia, Comenius's estranged daughter who had come to live with him after her mother's unexpected death. I hadn't met her yet since Iannis and I had only been back from our travels for a few weeks, and the one time I'd managed to stop by Com's shop, Rusalia had been in school. "Is she having a rough time settling in?"

"I'm afraid so." Elania sighed heavily, and my heart sank at the wave of despair coming off her. It unsettled me to see Elania looking anything but self-assured and wise—her confident and mysterious aura always made her seem as though she had the secrets of the universe locked behind those dark beguiling eyes. But apparently, those secrets did not include how to tame an unruly child. "I cannot blame the girl for being out of sorts," Elania said, trying hard to be fair, though it was clear to me that she was not so altruistic in her own thoughts. "Her mother did die very suddenly, and she is living in a foreign country with a father she can barely remember. We're trying to be understanding of her situation, but Comenius is taking it very hard. He has always wanted to be there for his daughter, and now that he finally has the chance, she is pushing him away as hard as she can."

"I'm sorry." I couldn't imagine what Com was going through right now, and I was damn sure I'd be handling it with a hell of a lot less grace than he probably was. "Is there anything I can do to help?"

Elania shrugged one shoulder. "No, but I'm certain Comenius would appreciate another visit. We have been looking forward to hearing more about your travels." She smiled, banishing the shadows lurking in her gaze. "We have missed you."

"I promise I will visit soon." I hugged Elania, my insides squirming with guilt. One hurried visit in three weeks was not nearly enough, but there had been so much to do after being gone for several months that I hadn't made the time. I'd take Rylan with me tomorrow to see Com, I vowed, no matter what else I had on my plate.

Speaking of Rylan, it was a shame he couldn't be here with his mother tonight. Like the other Shiftertown Council members, Mafiela had brought her children, and Rylan should have been amongst that number. But he'd been stationed outside the ballroom in his guard uniform, since he was still officially serving as Lanyr, my tiger-shifter bodyguard, as punishment for fighting for the Resistance. As long as he wore that disguise, he couldn't be with the Baine Clan even if he wanted to.

Glancing to my left, I noticed Iannis had moved off to talk to some other official. Rather than join him, I drifted through the crowd on my own. Maybe I'd go find Inspector Lakin—we were still friends, after all, and I wanted to catch up with him.

Most of the enforcers gave me polite smiles and nods as I passed, but a few outright ignored me. None of them seemed to know how to approach me, and it struck me that I wasn't really sure how to approach them either. I'd always considered myself an enforcer first and a mage second, but after everything I'd been through, was that still the case? As the Chief Mage's fiancée and apprentice, I no longer answered to Captain Galling —or rather, Acting Captain Skonel. Socially, I outranked them all, even though within the Guild, I was still just a lowly "lone-wolf" enforcer.

By Magorah, when was the last time I'd taken a bounty? Could I even call myself an enforcer anymore? I still wore my enforcer bracelet, but as I glanced down at my wrist, I was struck by how much it clashed with my finery. Sadness filled me as I realized I was slowly, inexorably, drifting away from my roots.

"Enforcer Baine," a male voice on my left said, and I blinked, startled from my thoughts. I turned to see Wex Ursini, a bear-shifter enforcer from one of the smaller crews. He was nearly seven feet tall, his massive form crammed into a brown and gold tunic and pants. His normally shaggy brown hair had been slicked back from his handsome face, leaving his dark amber eyes unframed. "Or is it Miss Baine, or Lady Baine? I'm not really sure how to address you," he admitted with a sheepish smile.

"Sunaya is fine," I said, partly because I wanted to try to establish friendly relationships with the enforcers again, and partly because I didn't really know how I should be addressed either. Did I have a title? I'd ask Iannis later. "How are you enjoying the party?"

"Very much," he said, raising his glass. "I'm guessing I have you to thank for making sure we have *teca* here tonight?"

"Hell yeah." I grinned. Teca was a spicy-sweet alcoholic beverage made by fermenting the fruit of a plant by the same name, and it was pretty much the only thing strong enough to get shifters drunk. It was being served by request only, because a single drink could kill a human. "I don't see why the mages and humans should be the only ones to have a good time tonight."

Wex grinned back. "I appreciate it," he said, then took another drink. His amber eyes found Iannis in the crowd across the room, and he nodded. "I know that some of the enforcers still aren't sure how they feel about you, but don't think a bunch of us haven't noticed the Chief Mage has been more involved in the community since you've shacked up with him. My father has high hopes that things will continue to improve for us."

"They will. I'm happy that the Shifter Council has become more open to working with the Mages Guild." Wex's father was the Chieftain of the Bear Clan—Wex was the youngest of five sons, which was why he could get away with working as an enforcer instead of joining the family's successful welding business.

"You know," Wex said, his easygoing expression growing pensive as he looked toward Iannis again, "I do wonder if Lord Iannis will ever truly be able to deal with the corruption in Solantha, and all the favoritism that's still occurring. He's a busy man, and unless he finds someone suitable to delegate these issues to, he may not ever have time to address them."

"Is there something specific you're referring to?" I asked, even though I already knew there was. I could tell by his body language that he'd been working his way up to whatever he was about to say.

"Well..." Wex leaned in, dropping his voice a little, "it's recently come out that the mages have been getting double bounties for their captures, and the rest of us are pretty resentful about it. A bunch of enforcers are even threatening to quit. I've approached Captain Galling, along with a few others, but he refuses to do anything about it. 'Take it up with the new captain' is all he says, as if he's been absolved of all responsibility now that he's retiring." Wex rolled his eyes, and I could sense his ire —he was far more upset about this than he was letting on.

"Are you serious?" I gaped, trying to wrap my mind around the idea that this had been going on for my entire career without my knowledge. "*All* the mages are getting double bonuses? Just because they've got magic? By that logic, shifters should get double bonuses too for our extra abilities!"

"Right?" Wex shook his head. "I wonder if the new captain will be more open to dealing with this, or if he'll just let the mages roll right over him. He seems to have a backbone, but I know the Guild isn't willing to let the few mage enforcers we have go." He pressed his lips together. "As far as I'm concerned, they can fuck off—we don't need them *that* much."

I nodded in agreement. "Thanks for bringing this to my attention. I'm going to talk to Captain Galling and see if I can find out more."

"Good luck," Wex said. He hesitated, then clapped me on the shoulder. "Whatever you're doing with the Chief Mage, keep it up. It's clearly working."

He walked off, leaving me wondering how a compliment could leave me feeling accomplished and anxious at the same time. My reputation was outgrowing me, and if I didn't get big enough to fill those shoes, I was going to drown in them.

DESPITE THE PROBLEM Wex had dumped on me, his compliment boosted my mood, and I was able to approach Captain Galling calmly instead of stalking over as I'd originally intended. I found him standing off to the side with Foreman Vance, already half drunk—his eyes were too bright, his stern face flushed, and the glass of champagne in his hand was nearly empty.

"Excuse me," I said smoothly, interrupting what looked like a jolly, spirited conversation. Foreman Vance gave me a thinly veiled look of contempt, and I ignored him completely. "I'd appreciate a word alone, Captain."

"Of course." The captain looked a little startled, but he recovered quickly despite his intoxication. "We'll catch up later, Vance."

Vance shot me one last look before disappearing into the crowd. I knew he hadn't forgotten the way I'd humiliated him during the silver murder investigation. Knowing him, he'd probably hold that grudge to his grave. He'd been seriously taken to task after it had been discovered that Brin, Nila, and several other Main Crew members were secretly working for the Resistance, and he'd been running the Main Crew with an iron fist since. I was okay with him hating me, as long as he actually did his job.

"What can I do for you, Enforcer Baine?" Captain Galling asked, sounding a little impatient now. It was clear he didn't appreciate being cornered at his own farewell reception, but I didn't care. He could endure a five-minute conversation before going back to being the center of attention.

"I was just talking to Enforcer Ursini," I said, dropping all pretense of pleasantry now that Vance was gone. "He told me it's recently come out that you've been giving the Mage enforcers double bounties. Is this true?"

Captain Galling scowled. "Yes, it's true, and it's not likely to change anytime soon. I wish people would stop pestering me about it, especially since I'm officially retired as of today." He gave me a pointed look, as if to say *Why are we still talking about this?*

But I wasn't about to let it go. "Why are you giving the mages double bounties?" I demanded. "You're not even a mage, Galling, so I don't understand the favoritism."

He sighed. "It's been this way since before I came into office," he admitted. "The mages struck a deal with the former captain, claiming their expertise and magical abilities warranted a higher pay rate, and since there are so few mages willing to be enforcers to begin with, I've honored the agreement. But it isn't as though I haven't tried to be fair!" he added, sounding defensive now. "The year-end bonuses are more than enough to make up for it."

"*What* year-end bonuses?" I demanded, folding my arms over my chest. And more importantly, why hadn't I ever gotten one?

Captain Galling's gaze flickered, as if he was having a hard time not looking away. "I've been giving the crew foremen the budget surplus at the end of the year, having them dispense the money to their crewmen as they see fit. It's been a perfectly workable system."

"Uh-huh." I couldn't believe what I was hearing. So on top of the mages getting double bounties, only the foremen and their cronies were getting bonuses? That meant "lone-wolf" enforcers like Annia and me were getting shafted. How the fuck had this been going on for so long without my knowledge? Was I really that oblivious? Of course I'd noticed that some enforcers always seemed to have more cash than others, but I'd just assumed that was because they were bringing in more bounties.

"Look," Captain Galling said, his demeanor softening a little. "I completely understand that you're upset about not getting the double bounties yourself, but there's nothing I can do. I'm sure if you speak to Captain Skonel, he'll reclassify you as a mage, too."

I stared at Captain Galling. Was *that* what he thought this was about? That I was upset because I hadn't been getting the mage bounties? By Magorah, I had more money than I knew what to do with now. It wasn't about the gold—it was about the principle. "Thanks," I said, successfully managing to keep most of the sarcasm out of my voice. "I'll be sure to talk to the new captain at the earliest opportunity."

And I would, I told myself as I walked away from Galling. But it would be about reforming the bonus system, not cashing in on it myself.

Determined not to spend the entire reception stewing, I put a smile back on my face and sought out Iannis. He was by the refreshment table, discussing something with Lakin, and I was very curious as to their topic of conversation. I'd been worried that Lakin's crush on me would prevent him from wanting to work with Iannis, but I was pleased to see that was not the case. He was the Shiftertown Inspector first and foremost, and even though he wasn't native to Solantha, he took his job very seriously. I knew he and the volunteers who worked with him were overloaded since the town was in the middle of a rebuild, and I made a mental note to make time in my schedule to help him out.

As I made my way to the refreshment table, I caught sight of a group of well-dressed humans crowded off to the side. Iannis and I had talked to them earlier—the Mendles and the Goraxes, two wealthy human families who ran the largest construction companies in Canalo. They had offices all over the state, I'd learned, and they'd built most of the newer buildings here in Solantha. I found it interesting that the two families were huddled together, talking like allies—they were supposed to be fierce competitors.

"It's very unfortunate about your hair," Mrs. Gorax said to Mrs. Mendle. She touched a hand to her own red locks, which were thick and lustrous. "It's curious that it has affected your whole family. Are you sure it's not something contagious?"

"Of course it's not contagious," Mrs. Mendle said, her voice sharp with annoyance as Mrs. Gorax subtly edged away from her. Her blonde hair was very thin indeed, and what I guessed was normally a pretty face was haggard despite the makeup she'd caked on. Her husband, a tall, lean man, was almost completely bald, only a little bit of mousy brown hair left on the sides and back of his skull, and their son, who looked barely twenty, was sporting a comb-over. "It must be some kind of mold or bug in the new house that's causing an allergic reaction. We're having an exterminator come tomorrow to take a look."

Not wanting to be caught eavesdropping, I moved on, even though I was very curious. I'd never heard of a bug or mold that could cause hair loss, or of an entire family suffering from the condition at the same time. The thought of losing all my hair sent a shiver through me, and I raised a hand to my own curls to reassure myself they were still there. Thankfully, Iannis could heal me if whatever the Mendles had was contagious, but I'd rather not find out either way. Honestly, what had they been thinking, coming to an event like this if they were sick? It was clear by their sallow complexions and sunken cheeks that they were suffering from more than just hair loss.

"Sunaya," Lakin cried as I finally approached, his reddish-yellow eyes lighting up with delight. "Lord Iannis and I were starting to wonder if you'd ditched the party."

I laughed, embracing Lakin briefly. "I wish, but that would make Iannis look bad, and I'd never do that to him." I slipped my arm into his and leaned against him, soaking up his calming presence. His sandalwood-and-magic scent soothed my still slightly ruffled feathers, washing away the bad taste in my mouth from my conversation with Galling. "How are things in Shiftertown?"

"The rebuild is going fairly smoothly; there's hardly any trace left of the Uprising," Lakin said. "But I've been thinking that repairing the buildings isn't enough. Lord Iannis and I have been talking about shoring them up with magical defenses as well. Some of the older buildings are developing cracks from the recent quakes."

"That's an excellent idea," I said. "I've been meaning to ask if you need any help dealing with local cases, or with any of the rebuild projects. I know you're really shorthanded."

"We do need all the help we can get," Lakin said. "There have been a lot of civil disputes and small crimes, and having you around would help a ton. But I know you're busy, Sunaya, and you have bigger things to worry about."

"Oh, it's no trouble at all—"

"*Trouble*," my ether-parrot squawked, materializing in a flash of blue light. Lakin jumped as the bird settled on top of his head —he wouldn't feel the weight, but the blue glow and the magical hum were bound to be disconcerting. A laugh burst from my lips before I could help myself, and it was echoed by the mages in the crowd around us.

"Come here, Trouble," I commanded, holding my arm out. The parrot squawked again, then flapped his wings and launched himself off Lakin's head. He landed on my arm, sending a magical tingle through me.

"What is that thing?" an elderly mage in the crowd asked, too far away to be addressing me.

"I think it's supposed to be an ether pigeon," a mage apprentice I'd met a few times said, a scathing note in her voice. "But Miss Baine bungled the spell, and now she has an obnoxious parrot instead."

"Really? The ether pigeon spell is so simple," the first mage said. "I had it mastered before I even started my apprenticeship. How is Miss Baine supposed to stand by Lord Iannis's side if she can't master Loranian?"

"*Don't*," Iannis said in mindspeak, just as I was about to break away from him to confront those insufferable bastards. "*They aren't worth your attention. Power-wise, you are already running circles around those cretins."*

I relaxed. *"Can't I at least sic Trouble on them? I could use the comic relief."*

"You could," Iannis said, sounding amused, *"but you would only prove their point."*

Trouble chose that moment to vanish, which was probably for the best because I was half tempted to ignore Iannis. The parrot had taken very well to the name Fenris and Rylan had given to him—too well, in fact, because every time I said the word "trouble," he appeared.

"Where'd he go?" Lakin asked, sounding confused and a little disappointed. "I was just getting used to having him around."

"Magorah knows." I had no idea if Trouble disappeared into some other reality or dimension, or if he simply went flying around the city. Ether pigeons made themselves invisible while flying, and I imagined Trouble could do the same thing. He could still be hovering about the ballroom for all I knew. I wondered how long he would stick around before the spell wore off, or if he was a permanent addition to my life. If so, I was either going to have to stop using the word 'trouble,' or figure out how to train him better.

Iannis and Lakin resumed their conversation about magical defense, and I did my best to contribute. It was an important topic, after all. But the words of those mages stung more than I wanted to admit, and I kept coming back to their disdainful attitude about my progress. I was doing very well considering I was only a few months into my apprenticeship and I didn't have the privilege of being raised by a mage family, but I still had at least ten years to go. Ten years of being looked down upon as a lesser being, ten years of mages whispering behind their hands that I wasn't truly Iannis's equal, and ten years of them placing bets as to how long he would hold out before choosing a mistress.

The very idea of people placing bets on our relationship filled me with fury, yet I couldn't help but wonder if they were right. I didn't think Iannis would ever cheat on me, but would the disparity in our power eventually take a toll on our relationship? He was one of the strongest mages in the Federation, and I wasn't just an apprentice, but a hybrid to boot.

Somehow, someway, I was going to need to speed up this apprenticeship. But damned if I could figure out how.

2

By the time the banquet was over, I was thoroughly exhausted. Leaving the Palace staff to handle the aftermath, Iannis, Director Chen, and I retired to Iannis's sitting room for a nightcap. Since I was unlikely to encounter any danger in Iannis's quarters, I allowed Rylan to sneak off with Nelia, my social secretary. She had a huge crush on him—I wasn't entirely happy about Rylan indulging it, but he promised not to take things too far. My shifter senses detected no lie, so I took him at his word, though I wasn't convinced I wouldn't regret it. Just because Rylan promised to toe the line didn't mean he wouldn't slip up.

Fenris, who had elected not to attend the banquet, was already sitting on a leather armchair by the hearth, swirling a glass of brandy in his hand as he stared into the roaring fire. Fall had settled in, and though the castle did have a magically powered heating system, the fires were still a welcome addition.

"Ah, you've returned." Fenris set his brandy down on a marble side table, then stood to greet us. I noticed his glass was half empty, wondering if brandy had been a favorite in his days as Polar ar'Tollis, Chief Mage of Nebara. Like me, he couldn't get drunk off alcohol—shifter metabolisms were simply too fast. "How was the banquet?"

"You wouldn't have enjoyed such a large crowd," Iannis assured him as we settled into the chairs and couches around the fire. Iannis used his magic to open the liquor cabinet across the room, and then floated a bottle of port toward us. Chen politely declined his offer of a drink, but I took one—I liked the sweet, fruity notes, and the way port heated me up from the inside, however briefly. "Everything went off without a hitch, thanks to Sunaya's excellent planning and management." He smiled, lifting his glass to me.

I chuckled a little. "Thanks, but Nelia and the servants deserve more credit than I do." I took a sip of my drink. "I wouldn't say that things went completely smoothly, though. There was a lot of tension in the room tonight."

"That is to be expected, with all three races mingling," Director Chen pointed out as she leaned back on her end of the couch. She was still dressed in her gorgeous green silk robe, but she'd pulled the pins from her long, dark hair so that it hung straight down her back. "Despite all that alcohol, no fights broke out, so I would consider it a success. Aside from keeping an eye on the acting captain to assess his performance, I see no reason for concern."

"That's true," I acknowledged, deciding not to tell them about my encounter with Wex or Captain Galling. That was something I could take up privately with Iannis later. "Were you terribly bored while we were gone, Fenris?" I asked, changing the subject.

He shook his head. "I have my books, as always."

It was strange to think of this rugged yellow-eyed shifter as a magical scholar, but even though Fenris was no longer a mage, he still had the soul of one. Besides, he did still have some magical talent left to him and could wield all but the most difficult spells, so he had reason to continue to expand his knowledge.

"How was your consultation with Lord Faring?" Fenris asked, turning his gaze to Iannis. "I know that the two of you meant to meet this morning."

Iannis nodded. "We did. After studying scientific calculations and measurements that he expounded at great length, Lord Faring is convinced that a severe quake is imminent, perhaps even bigger than the previous one."

Director Chen blanched. "I looked into historical accounts of that quake. The records show that nearly half the city needed to be rebuilt. How is he so certain?"

"Natural disasters have become somewhat of an obsession for him since that quake," Iannis said. "He barely survived it, after being caught off guard by a landslide when he thought the worst was over. He has traveled extensively to study quakes, tsunamis, tornadoes, and other such phenomena over the last two centuries, and invented various magi-tech instruments to measure their depth, strength, and frequency. I trust his judgment on the matter." He pressed his lips together. "Lord Faring informed me that after the last big quake, an official had been appointed to oversee the safety and solidity of all new structures. However, the office was disbanded over a century ago, shortly after my predecessor came into office. Faring protested at the time, but he was ignored."

"Most buildings in Maintown are a lot younger than that," I said, unable to keep the worry out of my voice. "We're going to have to inspect them and make sure they're quake-resistant."

"Yes," Iannis agreed. "However, that is not a simple task. The city is significantly larger than it was two hundred and fifty years ago, and it is no longer feasible to protect every building with magic. Even if we had hundreds of mages trained and ready for the task, it would take us months to implement the necessary protection spells. The way Lord Faring is talking, we may have weeks at best—in fact, the large quake he predicts could happen at any moment."

"Thankfully, the Mages Quarter is properly protected," Chen added with a self-assured tone that made me grind my teeth. "But of course, we need to assure the rest of the city is safe as well. It would be a shame for Shiftertown and Maintown to be destroyed while we are still in the middle of rebuilding."

"No kidding." I decided not to mention that this was another example of class disparity—we all recognized that the problem needed to be dealt with. The Mages Quarter had barely been affected by the Uprising—if we were hit by a quake and the rest of the city was left defenseless while the mages were safe, it would just reinforce the idea that the mages only cared about themselves.

"It is growing late," Iannis said, glancing to the grandfather clock in the corner, which pointed to a quarter past three. "We should adjourn for tonight. Let's have a working dinner in the Winter Garden room tomorrow night to discuss this further. We need to come up with a solid plan quickly, if we truly do only have days or weeks."

We agreed to meet tomorrow evening, and Fenris and Director Chen left, Fenris for his own room, and Director Chen for her townhouse in the heart of the Mages Quarter. I didn't bother with the pretense of going back to my own quarters— Chen and Fenris knew I slept here with Iannis every night.

"All right," Iannis said once we were alone. He pulled me tight against his body and pressed a kiss to my temple. "Tell me what's been bothering you."

I sighed, leaning my cheek against his strong chest, and told him about the mage bounties and the unfair distribution of bonuses at the end of the year. "This isn't about me," I said once I'd finished. "I really don't care about the money, not anymore.

But we can't allow this kind of blatant favoritism to continue, not if we want to repair the relationships between our communities."

"Agreed." Iannis stroked my hair as he gazed into the fire, a contemplative expression on his face. "To be fair, I can see both sides of the argument, but as you said, if mages are being paid more for their abilities, then so should the shifters. I will speak to the acting captain about re-negotiating the bonus system. It should be according to individual merit, not race."

"Thank you." A weight slid off my shoulders, and I relaxed more fully. The last thing we needed was for the Enforcers Guild to fall apart over something as stupid as money. With the threat of a big quake looming, we needed as many hands on deck as possible.

"Now, why don't you tell me about the other thing that's bothering you?"

"Eh?" I lifted my head, meeting his iridescent eyes. Those shimmering violet depths were so easy to fall into, but I did my best to focus. "What do you mean?"

Iannis's lips curved as he lightly gripped my chin. "I sometimes think I know you better than yourself, *a ghra*," he murmured, brushing his thumb against my lower lip. His eyes darkened with desire, and need blossomed hot and fierce in my core as it always did when he touched me like this. "You are still not quite...settled."

"Yeah, well, that look in your eyes isn't helping things," I teased, swatting his hand away. Biting my lower lip, I turned my attention inward and realized he was right. There was something still bothering me.

"There it is," Iannis said as I sighed.

"It's just..." I felt silly saying it out loud, but I knew Iannis wouldn't give up until I did. "I'm changing."

"We all do. Adaptability is a key component to survival. Those who do not change do not grow."

My lips quirked. "I didn't realize I was about to get a lesson in philosophy." But the smile quickly faded. "I know that change is inevitable, but I just feel like it's happening so fast. I made a promise to myself that I wasn't going to lose touch with my roots, and yet I feel like that's exactly what I'm doing. I still wear this enforcer bracelet—" I brushed my thumb over the charm as I spoke "—but I haven't been to the Guild or taken on a bounty in months. I still think of myself as a shifter, but I spend more time in human form than I used to, and I certainly don't interact with the shifter community as much as I have in the past."

"Those sound more like life changes, not personal changes."

I frowned. "Are the two not the same? We are talking about my life here."

Iannis cupped my chin again, forcing me to meet his gaze. "It matters not that you wear dresses and robes rather than leathers —the package inside is still the same, Sunaya. What was the reason you decided to become an enforcer?"

"To help those in need, fight corruption, and ensure justice is delivered," I said without hesitation.

"And is that not what still drives you?" Iannis challenged. "What motivated you to find homes for Tinari and Liu, what pushed you to shut down the Resistance even though you once thought you supported it? What drove you all the way to another country to assure our people remained safe from Thorgana's deadly weapons? What pushes you, even now, to fight for equal pay for enforcers, even though many of them still mistrust you, and, as you said yourself, you are hardly there anymore?"

His words stunned me into silence. "You may be wiser and less hotheaded than the girl who was dragged to my audience chamber in chains," Iannis continued softly. "But your essential self has not changed, Sunaya. You still burn with all the passion and fire that made me fall in love with you."

He finally kissed me, and I flung my arms around him, tears stinging my eyes. Emotion swelled in my throat, and I poured it into our passionate embrace. Growling, Iannis deepened the kiss, and I moaned at the taste of him as he slid his tongue into my mouth. His strong arms banded around me, large hands sliding around my ass to lift me against him. Suddenly, he was lowering me onto the big canopy bed that I'd begun to think of as *ours*.

"Let's see if we can find an outlet for all that passion," he said before covering my mouth with his again. And I was more than happy to oblige.

3

I awoke bright and early the next morning, full of energy and excitement. As usual, Iannis's side of the bed was cold —he always woke earlier than I did, since he didn't need nearly as much sleep. He was probably downstairs in his Guild office already, reading reports and compiling his list of tasks for today.

Under normal circumstances, I would have snuggled back under the covers with one of Iannis's pillows and let his scent lull me back to sleep since the idea of watching him do paperwork was boring. Unfortunately, I couldn't do that today. I had a busy day ahead of me, and I wanted to look my best, so I hopped out of bed and headed straight for the shower.

During our voyage back from Garai, I'd convinced Iannis to let me set up a sort of consulting office, where once a week I would hear complaints and dispense advice to humans and shifters about any magical problems they ran into. We'd decided it wasn't good enough to administer the yearly school testing— magic often awoke in children before the testing began and led to accidents when left unchecked. Offering a time and place where families could come and consult helped prevent unfortunate incidents. As it turned out, in the two sessions I'd had so far, there were lots of other problems I would never have learned about otherwise. As well as one or two scam artists I'd quickly thrown out. *That* had been the highlight of my day.

Deciding it would be best to look as approachable as possible, I forewent my enforcer leathers and my dressier outfits in favor of a black sweater, a pair of slacks, and a stylish dark red leather jacket. I left my hair unbound, but put on light makeup, making sure my weapons and harnesses were strapped on and secured. Yes, they made me look more intimidating, but I still had people out there who wanted me dead. It would be stupid to walk around defenseless, even if I did have a bodyguard now.

"Rylan," I called via mindspeak, wanting to make sure he was awake. *"Get your furry ass in the shower."*

"I'm up," he grumbled, though his mental voice sounded a bit fuzzy. *"Why exactly are we getting up so early again, if the Consulting Hour doesn't start until ten?"*

"Because I want to visit Com and Elania. Now get going."

I met Rylan in the hall twenty minutes later. He stood outside my door, showered and dressed in his blue-and-gold Palace guard uniform. The gold pin on his collar held his illusion firmly in place—Rylan walked around as Lanyr Goldrin, a tiger shifter with golden-brown hair and a lean frame. But the illusion couldn't hide the trademark wicked grin that he used on the ladies to great effect, or his swagger as he fell into step with me.

"I trust you kept your promise last night when you were with Nelia?" I asked as we headed for the dining hall to grab some breakfast.

"Sadly, yes. Nothing but a few stolen kisses." He huffed out an exasperated breath. *"I find it supremely unfair that you're lecturing me about sex when you're rolling in the sheets with Lord Iannis across the hall."*

My cheeks colored as his point struck home. *"I'm not a prude, and you know it,"* I protested. *"But Nelia doesn't know who you really are, and it's not fair to her to let her fall in love with you under false pretenses. Besides, you're not actually in love with her, or am I mistaken?"*

"No," Rylan admitted. *"I'm not. Perhaps I should break it off with her. But she's adorable in her way, and it's not like I can go roaming about Solantha looking for other conquests in the meantime."*

True. He was a prisoner under supervision, and I wasn't about to become Rylan's wing woman, not when I had bigger things to deal with. I had no doubt I would be called upon to assist with earthquake preparations, and between that and my apprenticeship, there wasn't time for much else.

We ate a quick breakfast of eggs, bacon, and muffins, then hopped onto my bike and headed to the Port. The sun was hidden behind thick, iron-grey clouds, and a chill wind ripped through my leather jacket. Fall was here, in the turning leaves of the trees lining the streets and the pleasant scent of cedar and pine smoke rising from chimney stacks. Pedestrians were bundled in warm coats and scarves, and they hurried along a little faster than usual in an effort to get out of the cold.

Traffic was heavy at this time of the morning, so it took us a good twenty-five minutes to get to Comenius's shop. Since it wasn't open for business, we went around the side and up the stairs to knock on the door.

An uncharacteristically scruffy Comenius answered the door, his cornflower-blue eyes bleary from lack of sleep.

"Well, hello!" he exclaimed, a smile blooming on his face despite the desperation in his eyes. "What a pleasant surprise."

"Hey, Com." I embraced him, hugging him a little tighter than normal. By the looks of him, he needed it. He let us into his apartment, where Elania was busy cleaning away the dishes from breakfast. My eyebrows rose at the sight of a pile of eggs and shattered ceramic dishes on the floor that she was sweeping up, and she gave me an apologetic smile. At least, I thought that was what it was—it came out more like a grimace.

"Sorry about the mess," she said, straightening up. "We had a rather...eventful breakfast this morning."

"I see." I looked around the apartment. It looked the same as always, but there was an edge of resentment in the air. "Where is Rusalia?"

"In the bedroom," Comenius muttered. "I banished her there after she refused to clean up the mess." He scooped a hand through his ash-blond hair. "Her temper isn't improving at all, I'm afraid."

"I can hear you talking about me!" a girlish voice called in a thick Pernian accent. Little feet stomped across the floorboards, and Comenius's bedroom door flew open to reveal a girl of about ten with strawberry-blonde curls to her shoulders, dressed in a flannel frock and stockings. Her large blue eyes, identical to Com's, flashed mutinously, and her rosebud mouth was turned down into a fierce scowl.

"Hey there," I said, in as friendly a tone as I could manage. After all, I knew what it was like to lose a mother at a similar age, though I'd never been allowed to express my grief in tantrums and broken dishes. "I'm Sunaya Baine, and this is my friend Lanyr."

"I know who you are," Rusalia sneered, tossing her hair over her shoulder. "You're my father's *hybrid* friend. I don't want to talk to *you*." She spun on her heel and made to storm back into the bedroom.

"*Rusalia*," Comenius thundered, but Rusalia acted as if she hadn't even heard him. His eyes glittered with rage and despair —I'd never seen him so angry before, and I couldn't blame him. This kid had a chip on her shoulder the size of Garai! Unwilling to let it go, I spoke the Words to a spell I'd tried out once or twice and flung out my hand.

Before she could take another step, a golden rope shot from my outstretched hand and coiled around her waist, pulling her to an abrupt halt. A shriek of anger and surprise tore from her throat as she tried to both pull away and turn toward me, but before she could, I jerked hard on my magical lasso, pulling her off her feet and causing her to come sailing toward me.

As terror flashed across her face, I reached out and grabbed her by the shoulders, arresting her fall and stopping her in her tracks.

"Now listen here," I said sternly as the fear on her face turned to anger. She struggled, trying to pull away, but it was no use. I was way stronger than she was, and even if I wasn't, my magic would hold her tight. "Your father is a good man, and he's doing his best to take care of you. I don't like the way you're treating him, and he doesn't either. What are you going to do if he throws you out onto the street?" I raised an eyebrow at her.

"If he does that, then he's just as bad as Mother always said," Rusalia spat defiantly. For a moment, I wondered if she was trying to push her father far enough to confirm her suspicions about who she thought he was. "Let me go!"

"Not until you apologize," I insisted, ignoring her struggles even though part of me wanted to shake her for being so unreasonable. Didn't she know how good of a person her father was?

"You can't leave me tied up like this forever." Rusalia smirked up at me, all petulant defiance, practically daring me with her eyes to do just that.

She was right, of course. I couldn't leave her bound forever, but I could do something else. Something she'd never see coming.

As I released my hold on her shoulders, I retreated two paces, leaving her bound by my spell. Confusion instantly replaced Rusalia's triumphant look as I reached for the beast inside me. As the familiar white glow enveloped me, my body stretched and shifted, reshaping itself until I stood not on two legs, but four. Fangs, claws, and fur replaced my clothing and weapons, and I opened my mouth wide, letting out a fearsome snarl.

Rusalia shrieked, darting behind her father for protection while she struggled against my binding spell. "Get her *out* of here," she cried, huddling behind Comenius as best she could with her arms bound.

"I think Sunaya's still looking for an apology," Rylan said, and Rusalia stiffened at his words. "She's a lot more dangerous in this form. I mean, have you seen those fangs? Practically big as daggers," he said, swallowing hard as he looked from me to her and back again. "You know how shifters are. She might not listen."

That was a total lie, of course, but it worked. Rusalia turned her wide gaze to me, still angry, but full of fear also. "I'm sorry," she muttered, not bothering to look at me as she spoke. "Now let me go!"

Knowing that was the best I was going to get, I cut the ties to my magic, releasing her in a flare of light and sound. As the remains of my spell shattered into ethereal shards, Rusalia was left standing there, eyes wide. She took a deep breath and stared at me like she was trying to decide what I'd do next. Then, obviously deciding I wouldn't chase her down, she took off running into Comenius's room.

"Well, that went well," Rylan said as the door slammed hard behind her.

I sighed, shaking my head as I pulled my beast back inside me and returned to human form. It was going to take a lot to teach that girl, and I felt for Comenius. He shouldn't have to deal with that kind of shit.

"Thank you for trying to get through to her," Comenius said, weariness filling his voice. "But I'd appreciate it if you didn't interfere like that again. She probably just hates me more now."

"I'm sorry." My heart ached for Comenius's predicament—I truly didn't know what to do to help him. "Hopefully she'll keep her head down for the rest of the day, at least."

"Perhaps we should consider taking her to a specialist," Elania said from behind the kitchen counter. Her lips were pursed, her elegant black brows drawn together into a frown. "Someone who knows how to treat children who have suffered trauma. She needs professional help, Comenius."

"You'd have me hand my daughter off to someone else to take care of?" He shook his head. "Rusalia will hate me even more if I do that."

"Yeah, but it might be good to have a third party to help mediate between the two of you," Rylan pointed out. "It's clear you both have issues that need resolving."

Comenius scrubbed a hand across his face. "I will consider it. But money has been tight recently."

"You know I'm always happy to help you out with that," I offered, but Comenius shook his head.

"I appreciate that, Naya, but I am a grown man." He gave me a faint smile that didn't quite reach his eyes. "I have run from this problem long enough—I must face the consequences and deal with it on my own." His expression softened a little. "Still, it means very much to me that you came over."

"I should have come sooner," I said as helplessness filled me nearly to bursting. I wanted to do something, only I didn't see what I could do other than be there for him. Knowing it wasn't enough, I embraced Comenius and Elania once more. "If you change your mind, or if there's anything else I can do, let me know."

They nodded to me as I left Com's place. While my heart was

heavy, I had to respect their wishes to stay out of it. I'd just have to let them do their best and trust that things would work out.

So even though it weighed on me, I tried to put the problem out of my mind as we sped back to Rowanville. Maybe I couldn't help Com right now, or his equally unhappy child. But there were other people coming to me for assistance today, and I was determined to give them my best.

4

I t only took us a few minutes to get to the consulting office —a small corner house in Rowanville that used to host a dental practice. I'd chosen to rent the place rather than buy it because the project was still experimental, but if it turned out to be a success, I would look for a permanent location and regular staff.

Rylan went in ahead of me to check for any intruders or hidden bombs—he took his bodyguard duties very seriously, for which I was thankful. I followed once he gave the all clear. The inside of the house was clean and simple—there was a waiting room with comfortable chairs, magazines, and a few toys for children. A twenty-something receptionist, on loan from a nearby office for this part-time gig, sat behind the utilitarian wooden desk to receive petitioners. I greeted her, then moved past the waiting room and down the hall. There were two more rooms—the first door on the left was my audience chamber, and the second, further down, was a sort of cell that Iannis had insisted on setting up in case any criminals or unruly petitioners found their way in and needed to be detained.

After Rylan performed one final safety check, I went into the audience chamber and settled in behind the wooden desk. Like the waiting room, it was a simple space with a single desk supplied with stationary, a small filing cabinet, and visitor chairs. A window to my left looked out onto the side street, and a magical mirror located in my desk drawer allowed me to peek in on the waiting room. I was also wearing my heirloom ring, a treasured gift from my father, which would alert me if anyone entering the premises harbored ill will toward me. Between my bodyguard, the mirror, and the ring, I was perfectly safe.

I pulled the mirror out from the desk. To my surprise, there was already a couple sitting in the waiting room with a small, dark-haired young boy. *That was fast,* I thought, a ball of nerves suddenly forming in my stomach.

"You've got this," Rylan assured me, scenting my change in mood. He patted me on the shoulder. "You want me to bring them in?"

"Yeah." I straightened my shoulders. I was only here for the morning. Might as well make the most of it.

Rylan came back a minute later with the family in tow. The couple was in their late twenties, the husband dressed in a clean but slightly faded suit, the wife in a dress that had been mended once or twice. The child, on the other hand, sported a brand-new woolen coat and shiny shoes. Not a rich family, but one that skimped and scraped to provide well for their child.

"Miss Baine, this is the Barning family," Rylan said. He introduced them by name—Leo and Rana, and their son, Durian. The parents were polite, but reserved, whereas the boy stared at me with open curiosity, his golden-brown eyes bright with questions.

"Very pleased to meet you all," I said, smiling. "Please, have a seat."

They did as I asked, the mother scooping her son into her lap as there were only two chairs. "Can you really turn into a panther?" the boy asked eagerly before the parents could say anything.

"Hush, Durian," his mother scolded, her cheeks coloring. "I'm so sorry," she said to me, her tone apologetic. "He's very rambunctious."

"As boys should be." My smile widened as I looked at him. "I can turn into a panther," I confirmed. "Normally, I would be happy to show you, but I'm afraid I don't have a lot of time today —there are other people coming here to visit me."

"Oh." The boy looked disappointed, but he quickly bounced back. "Will you take me back to the Palace with you if I have magic?"

I laughed, then turned my gaze back to the mother. "Your son is eager to be a mage, is he?"

"It would appear so," she said, and she didn't sound entirely pleased about it. "Since he was old enough to talk, he's been fascinated with mages and magic. We didn't think anything of it, of course, but recently..." She trailed off, looking at her husband.

The husband picked up the conversation. "There have been some strange incidents," he said, his expression grave. "Objects appearing and disappearing around the house—the icebox appeared in the bedroom once. Another time, I was looking for the radio only to find it in the front seat of my car. I thought Durian was simply playing pranks, but one day while we were entertaining guests, our coffee table rose straight up into the air and floated into Durian's bedroom."

My eyebrows rose. "That definitely sounds magical to me. Have these incidents ever occurred outside the home?"

The mother shook her head. "No, not yet." She stroked the top of her son's head. "And Durian has denied these incidents are his responsibility, but you know how children are." She tightened her hold on him a little. "We just want to be sure."

"It really wasn't my fault," Durian said earnestly, squirming against his mother's iron grip. "But I do want to do magic! Please tell me I have some."

I wasn't sure whether to laugh or shake my head. This poor family! It was clear the parents didn't want Durian to be a mage, but Durian wanted it more than anything. Then again, he was only seven years old, with a wild imagination, so of course the idea of having magic appealed to him.

"I'll have to test you to find out," I said gravely. "Can you please come over by my side of the desk?"

Durian probably would have jumped straight across the desk and into my lap if his mother hadn't restrained him. He hurried around the desk to my side, and I turned my chair to face him. Despite his wish, I really hoped he *didn't* have magic. His parents clearly loved him, and it would be better if he was raised with his own family rather than in a mage household with strangers.

"All right," I said, settling my hands on his shoulders. "I need you to hold very still. Can you do that?"

He nodded vigorously, then stilled completely.

"Good. Now close your eyes."

He did as I asked, and I placed my hands on either side of his head, making sure my thumbs were pressed against his temples. Closing my own eyes, I murmured the Words of the testing spell Iannis had taught me, then allowed my magic to flow through Durian. It raced through the little boy, searching for the source of power that existed within the soul of every magic user. But though there were a few sparks that every living creature possessed, there was no burning core of power within.

"I'm sorry, Durian," I said, gently lowering my hands. "You don't have any magic. You're a perfectly normal human."

The boy opened his eyes, and I cringed inwardly as his lower lip wobbled. His mother instantly snatched him up as he began to cry, murmuring soothing words, but it was clear from her expression that she was relieved. The father thanked me profusely, and I promised to send someone to check on their house—someone had probably just hexed their property.

The next petitioner was ushered in—Lamar Vestes, a market vendor I recognized from Rowanville's Market Street. He was a rotund, bearded man with ruddy cheeks, a white apron, and a smile for everyone, but right now, his eyes were narrowed with anger, his lips compressed with frustration.

"My hams and sausages were set on fire yesterday," he complained, his back ramrod straight and his hands folded behind his back. "An entire day's worth of work, gone up in flames because of some pesky mage! Please, Miss Baine, these setbacks could wreck my livelihood. I need your help in apprehending the culprit."

I pulled out my notepad and pen. "Can you give me a description of the person who set your wares on fire?" I couldn't blame the man for being upset—his meats were delicious and fetched a pretty penny on Market Street.

"No, unfortunately," Lamar admitted, sounding very put out. "It was very crowded yesterday, and the person who did it was not close, so I couldn't figure out the source." Even so, he gave me as many details as he could about the incident, and I wrote it all down with a promise to investigate further into the matter.

"It may take some time," I finally said, closing my notebook. "In the meantime, I suggest you write up a list of damages and mail it to me at the Palace. As soon as the culprit is caught, you will be compensated for your loss."

The man didn't seem entirely pleased with the idea that he would have to wait, but he thanked me nevertheless and took his leave. I really did feel bad for him, and part of me was tempted to just compensate Lamar myself. I could easily afford to. But if word got out that I was personally compensating damages, I would be inundated with an endless series of fictitious claims.

I checked the mirror again and saw there was another person waiting patiently in the lobby—a male human clutching a large cardboard map.

"Some kind of artist, maybe?" Rylan asked, looking over my shoulder.

"Not sure. Let's bring him—"

Something crashed into the front wall of the house, rocking the very foundations of the building. I grabbed the edge of the desk with one hand and watched, absolutely horrified, as the tall rollers of a huge road-paving machine burst through the drywall, whirring madly and spraying chunks of brick and plaster everywhere.

In the next second, I was out of my chair and down the hall, Rylan hot on my heels. He went for the receptionist, who was huddled fearfully behind the desk, and I grabbed the male petitioner and flung him toward the back of the house and out of harm's way.

"My *map*," he shouted, eyes wide, but I only shoved him.

"Run! There's a back entrance—get out of here!" Not waiting to see if he obeyed, I turned my attention back to the machine and conjured a magical barrier. The machine halted halfway into the waiting room, its wheels spinning loosely, but I knew it wouldn't hold for long—the barrier was really meant for magical attacks.

"Get to the humans, Naya," Rylan shouted as he took a flying leap toward the machine. He passed through the barrier easily, landing on the rollers, and scrambled upward to the cab. He wrenched the door open, threw the driver—a human male— out, then jumped down into the street after him.

The barrier failed, and the machine lurched forward, still in gear. My heart leapt into my throat, and I sprinted for the back door. The vehicle belched thick gusts of steam as it rampaged through the house behind me, crushing the thin walls as though they were made of straw. I flung open the door, then grabbed the hands of the two humans and dragged them across the street, well clear of the machine.

"By the Ur-God," the man breathed, his mouth agape as he watched the machine roll out the back wall of the house, toward the neighbor's backyard. The structure was completely destroyed. "It's still running!"

Before I could respond, the man dashed across the street, back toward the huge steam engine. I shouted a warning, but he ignored me, jumping onto the metal ladder on the side of the machine. I watched with no small amount of admiration as he hoisted himself into the open cab and fiddled with the controls. Just a few yards from the neighboring house, the vehicle let out one final belch of steam, and then died.

"Are you all right?" I turned my attention to the receptionist, who nodded numbly. Her blue eyes were glassy, her cheeks pale —she was in shock. I took her face in my hands and asked her some questions—her name, what day of the week it was, where we were. It took her a few seconds to shake off the initial shock, but once she did, she answered normally, allaying my fears that she might have a concussion.

Rylan approached from around the side of the demolished house, his expression grave. "The driver is dead," he said grimly. "Broke his neck in the fall."

"Dammit." I clenched my jaw. I'd been hoping to interrogate the bastard, find out who'd put him up to this. But I wasn't going to berate Rylan—he'd just been doing his job. There hadn't been time to think about subtle nuances like making sure our attacker didn't get killed.

"Looks like our new friend here saved the day," Rylan remarked, turning toward the man climbing down from the cab. I had to admit that with his tousled chestnut hair and his red coat flapping in the wind, he looked rather like a dashing hero from a romance novel. As he approached us, I took note of his tanned skin, sapphire-blue eyes, and symmetrical features, which were currently drawn tight with worry.

"That was a close call," he said, brushing his windswept hair out of his eyes. He gave me a tight smile. "Thank you for getting me out of harm's way, Miss Baine. I would have been crushed if not for you."

"You're welcome," I said, ignoring the pang of guilt in my chest. I had little doubt that attack was meant for me, and that if this man hadn't come to see me, he never would have been in harm's way. But there was no point in dwelling on it. "And your name is…"

"Kardanor Makis, at your service." He bowed. "I'm an architect, and I came to see you regarding a matter of public safety."

"Oh?" I had been about to tell him that we should reschedule, but his words stopped me in my tracks. "Is this about the quakes?"

"Not exactly, but it is related." He ruefully glanced back at the ruins of the house. "I wish I could have saved the map—I was planning to present it to you so I could give you a better visual of the problem. But the long and short of it is that many of Solantha's public buildings have not been built up to code, and they are safety hazards in and of themselves even without the recent rash of quakes. I have been writing to both the Maintown Council and the Mages Guild about this for over a year now, but they've ignored my letters. Now that there are rumors that a big quake might be imminent, it is urgent I get an audience with the appropriate officials, to make them face up to the scale of the problem. I was hoping you might be able to speak to the Chief Mage for me, and perhaps arrange something."

"I can do one better." I smiled at him to hide my outrage. Why had such an important issue been lost in the shuffle? I could understand Argon Chartis stuffing Kardanor's letters somewhere out of Iannis's line of sight—he cared nothing for humans, and the Mages Quarter was well protected. But why wasn't the Maintown Council interested in this? "We're having a working dinner at the Palace tonight to discuss quake-proofing the city. Your expertise is relevant, so I'd like to invite you. Eight o'clock. You can make your case personally to the Chief Mage then."

Kardanor looked taken aback. "Really? You would do that for me even though we've only just met?"

I smiled again. "I trust you." My heirloom ring hadn't reacted to Kardanor's presence, so I knew he meant no harm. Pulling my notepad and pen out of my inner jacket pocket, I scribbled a note on it, then folded it up and handed it to Kardanor. "Just show this to the front desk receptionist when you come in. He's a bit of a grump, but if you give him this, he'll make sure you're admitted."

"Thank you." Kardanor tucked the note into his coat pocket, then bowed again. "It was a pleasure to meet you, Miss Baine."

"If I didn't know better, I'd say you had a crush on him," Rylan teased as I watched the architect walk away. "Does Iannis have some competition?"

I chuckled. "Hardly. I'm just impressed at how quickly he reacted in the face of danger." I dealt with dangerous situations on a regular basis, but as an architect, he probably wasn't used to facing down death. Even so, he'd handled himself with remarkable composure. I had a feeling that he'd be an asset—once Iannis and the others got over the shock of sharing their evening meal with a human.

Rylan, the receptionist, and I went back around to the front of the house to wait by the body of our would-be assassin. The enforcers arrived a few minutes later, a male-female pair from the Main Crew, and even their hardened faces slackened in shock as they surveyed the damage.

"You're very lucky that you all made it out unscathed," the male said as he crouched by the body, which he'd pulled from the rubble. The receptionist let out a tiny sob, and Rylan took her in his arms, turning her face away from the ghastly scene. The dead man's face was badly bruised, his neck lolling at a strange angle—as Rylan had said, it had been broken. He stared at me, unseeing, but even in death, fear and anger marked the lines of his face. It was as though his spirit still lingered, silently glaring daggers at me and cursing me for not dying neatly as I should have.

Well, fuck you, too, I thought, crossing my arms over my chest.

"Any idea who this asshole is?" I asked aloud.

"Got an ID." The male enforcer flipped open a wallet. "Aerin Yolas," he read aloud. "Forty-five, lives in Maintown." He rifled through the man's wallet, then pulled out a business card. "Works for Gorax Construction."

"That explains how he got hold of that road paver," I muttered. The Goraxes had been at the reception last night. Did they have anything to do with this, or was this man acting alone?

"I recognize this guy," the female enforcer said suddenly. "Took me a minute with his face so bashed in, but I've seen him at the Maintown Temple. He's a follower of Father Calmias."

I ground my teeth at that. That fucking pastor was determined to be the death of me, even behind bars. "That means he could be working on Father Calmias's orders." Just because the bastard was locked up didn't mean he couldn't slip messages to his followers.

"Maybe, maybe not." The female enforcer shrugged. "A lot of these guys are happy to commit any kind of crime in the Ur-God's name. Just means more bounties for us." To my annoyance, she seemed somewhat disappointed, and I had a feeling it had to do with the fact Aerin was dead. If he'd been alive, she could have brought him in for a bounty. And I sensed that she wouldn't have cared one iota if he'd killed me.

"Well, have fun with this one," I said, giving them a sarcastic salute. I turned my back on them, no longer feeling quite so nostalgic about being an enforcer. I had bigger things to worry about than whether these guys liked me. Like making sure I stayed alive, for one. And as soon as this quake thing was under control, I was going to deal with Father Calmias once and for all.

5

I annis was busy handling state matters when I returned, so I didn't bother telling him about the attack in Rowanville. He didn't need to spend the rest of the day worrying about it since Rylan and I had handled it well enough. I'd tell him about it before dinner, if I had a chance.

I spent the early afternoon on my Loranian lessons with Fenris. He was a patient teacher and explained well, but I kept mixing up the eighteen different tenses, so I was relieved when I finally moved onto practicing spells in the training room. Iannis had deemed me sufficiently advanced that he was comfortable leaving me alone to practice, so long as I didn't leave the warded room. At the moment, I was working on changing a block of wood into a living rosebush, and then back again. I'd already become proficient at changing one inanimate object into another—I could turn brass into stone and wood into gold. But changing a non-living object into a living one was a much tougher challenge.

Focusing my attention on the wood block, I turned my palms toward it, then spoke the transmogrification spell. I envisioned the square of walnut stretching and transforming, carving itself into trunk and roots potted in soil, branches reaching out to the world around it. To my delight, the block complied.

"*Yes,*" I crowed as leaves began to sprout from the branches, followed by rosebuds. They quickly blossomed, petals unfurling into brilliant shades of red...and then began to shrivel and blacken.

"Dammit, no!" Panicking, I shoved more magic into the plant, willing it to blossom and grow. But that only seemed to accelerate the decay—the trunk and branches crumbled until all that was left was the clay pot with a heap of ashes inside.

Disgusted with myself, I buried my face in my hands and groaned. How the hell was I going to speed up my apprenticeship if I couldn't master this technique? Iannis could probably do this with his eyes closed from a different room. How would I ever be seen as his equal?

A knock at the door dragged me from my pity party. "Miss Baine, are you almost finished?" Rylan called from outside. I'd ordered him to stay in the hall, so that I didn't have to worry about accidentally hurting him with a spell gone wrong. "Dinner's in less than an hour."

"Coming." I gave the pot of ash a dirty look, then turned it back into a block of wood. Humph. *At least that part was easy*, I consoled myself, picking up the object. It looked exactly the same as it had before I'd changed it, right down to the trio of tiny knots on its side.

"*You look like you were just slapped by a porcupine's tail,*" Rylan remarked in mindspeak as he escorted me back to my room. "*Everything okay?*"

"*I'm just...frustrated,*" I replied, exhaling heavily. "*Iannis and I are getting married in less than nine months, and I'm still just a rookie apprentice.*"

"*No, you're not.*" Rylan playfully punched me in the shoulder. "*You're Sunaya Baine, champion of the underdog and royal pain in my ass. You've never been 'just' an apprentice, and you'll never 'just' be a mage or 'just' Lord Iannis's wife, either. Your titles, or lack thereof, don't define you."*

The tension bled out of my shoulders at the familiar words, and I smiled a little. "Iannis said something similar to me the other day."

"He's a wise man." Rylan paused for a moment. *"You know, when Fenris offered me that deal to reduce my sentence in exchange for helping you, I came very close to refusing. I was Captain Rylan Baine, an officer of the Resistance, and I didn't work with the fucking enemy."* He snorted, and I grinned a little. *"But I felt really shitty about what happened with the forgetting spell I'd put on you, so I agreed mostly because I wanted to make it up to you. It's taken me a little while to get used to not running a company of soldiers, taking orders from colonels and commanders and working day in and day out to undermine the very establishment I'm now working for. And it's been really fucking hard to come to terms with the fact that the organization I've worked for these past seven years has always intended to wipe my kind from the face of Recca."*

I took my cousin's hand and squeezed it briefly. I'd been outraged enough when I'd found out Thorgana's true plans for the Resistance. I couldn't imagine how betrayed Rylan must have felt. His whole world, his entire purpose for the past seven years, had been ripped out from under him.

"But, like I was saying to you, I began to realize if I didn't want to sink into a funk, or drive myself insane, then I had to learn to define myself as something other than a captain of the Resistance. I have to figure out who I am—which is a challenge, by the way, considering I have to pretend to be someone else all the time," he added dryly.

I winced. *"That won't last forever,"* I assured him as we stopped outside my bedroom door. *"No matter what, I promise you won't have to live your days out as my tiger-shifter bodyguard."*

"Thanks." He hugged me swiftly. *"Now hurry up and get ready*

before we're late. You don't want Kardanor walking into the meeting without you there to explain his presence."

A QUICK SHOWER and change of clothes was needed after this morning's excitement—my clothing still had bits of dusty drywall on them, and it was probably in my hair, too. But instead of dressing for dinner in finery, I put on a pair of fresh leathers and strapped on my weapons. Though I wouldn't admit it aloud, I was still a little rattled from the attack this morning, and I'd been attacked on the Palace grounds before. I wasn't willing to walk around unarmed and encumbered by a frilly dress, even if that meant offending someone's sensibilities.

All the mages were already assembled around the dining table when I arrived, snacking on bread and butter while they waited for the first course to be served. Iannis and Director Chen sat at the head of the table, with Cirin to Director Chen's left, and an empty chair next to Iannis for me. Fenris was there, too, sitting on the other side of my chair, and I sat down between him and Iannis.

"There seems to be an extra setting," Director Chen remarked, looking at the empty space at her side. "Are we expecting anyone else?"

"Yes," I said. "I told my guest eight o'clock, so we should wait the few minutes till the hour."

They all stared at me, even Iannis.

"Who did you invite to join us?" Fenris asked with an encouraging smile, before someone could gather their wits about them enough to reprimand me.

"A human architect named Kardanor Makis," I said, giving him a grateful smile "He has some important information for us that is relevant to our discussion tonight."

"That is most unorthodox," Director Chen said stiffly. "I understood this was to be a working meeting amongst the top mage leadership. At the very least you should have given us warning—"

"I am fine with it," Iannis said mildly, cutting her off. "Sunaya will have her reasons for inviting this architect, and I, for one, am curious to hear them. How did the two of you meet?"

I took a deep breath, then gave them a rundown of the attack this afternoon. By the time I finished, Iannis's eyes were glittering with fury, and Director Chen looked pale.

"You are lucky to be alive," Cirin said, breaking the tense silence. "Your bodyguard ought to be highly commended, and your architect friend as well."

"Father Calmias again," Fenris said thoughtfully. "His followers are really getting out of hand. Something must be done."

"It will," Iannis said, his expression stony. "This persecution of Sunaya cannot be allowed to continue." He conjured a pen and paper, then quickly scribbled out a letter, which he handed to a servant. "Make sure this gets to Dira, right away," he ordered.

"What are you doing?" I asked, a little alarmed at the rage rolling off him in waves.

"I'm having Father Calmias transferred to the Palace. I plan to have a long conversation with him tomorrow." His tone was ominous.

The doors swung opened before I could ask any more questions, and Rylan stepped inside. "Your guest is here," he said, then moved aside so that Kardanor could come in. He wore the red coat from earlier, but as he shucked it off and handed it to a servant, I noticed he wore a decent grey suit and red tie, and silver cufflinks glinted at his wrists. A man with a sense of style, and not poor, though he didn't seem to be particularly wealthy either.

"Thank you for coming, Mr. Makis." I rose from my chair to greet him. Shaking his hand, I was careful not to brush against his cufflinks. "I appreciate you coming on such short notice."

"It's an honor," he assured me, bowing over my hand with a charming smile. Hiding my grin, I turned and introduced him to the others. The men greeted him politely, but Director Chen was a little frosty in her reception. Kardanor, on the other hand, stole more than a few admiring glances her way as he was seated and served at her side, despite the self-assured way he conducted himself around the other mages. He probably viewed her as an exotic beauty, with her ivory skin, almond-shaped eyes, and delicate features. In fact, her chilly demeanor would only make her more alluring, since confident men like him would take that sort of thing as a challenge. I had to wonder where he got his balls from, though—most human men wouldn't dare look at the Director of the Mages Guild the way he was.

"Well," Chen said coolly once our appetizer course had been cleared from the table. She fixed her dark gaze on Kardanor's face. "Now that you are finally here, I am interested to know what information you have that Miss Baine found so pertinent. Please tell us what you think we need to know."

"Certainly," Kardanor said, responding to her chilly tone with another charming grin. Oh, man. He was definitely going to give Director Chen a run for her money. "I am an architect, as Miss Baine may have already explained. Public buildings are my specialty. I went to school at the University of Alacara, and assisted in the rebuild when a highly destructive hurricane struck our coast some seven years ago."

"Ah. Then you have experience with natural disasters," Cirin said, looking mildly impressed. Alacara was located on Northia's southeastern coast, which was notoriously prone to hurricanes.

"Yes. I moved to Solantha a few years ago, and found work here quickly enough. I'd always wanted to experience life on the West Coast." He smiled, but the expression faded quickly. "A year and a half ago, I worked on plans for a new school in Maintown. The contract was given to Mendle Construction. I make a habit of checking in on projects that I design, even when I'm not directly involved in the execution, and I was very dismayed to find out that the company was deviating from my plans to save money. They cut corners by making pillars less sturdy, and using cheaper, shoddier materials than I had specified."

"Resulting in a building that would not stand up to an earthquake?" Iannis asked, his eyes narrowed.

"The roof would very likely collapse even in a moderate quake, killing the teachers and students within." Kardanor's square jaw tightened. "I immediately brought the matter to the attention of the Maintown school board, insisting my designs were not being properly followed and that they were putting the students and staff in danger. For whatever reason, they decided to take the builder's word over mine, and I've had difficulty finding work ever since." His blue eyes glittered with ire now. "I discovered that Mendle and Gorax, the other large construction company, had gone about spreading rumors that I was overpriced and difficult to work with. Being new in town, nobody wanted to hire me after that."

"Well that's fucked up," I commented. Director Chen shot me a scandalized look that I completely ignored. "Did you consider filing a lawsuit against them for slander?"

Kardanor shrugged. "That would have been very costly, and Mendle and Gorax have high-powered lawyers on retainer, who no doubt would have ground me into the dust. I've lived frugally off my savings, hoping for things to improve, though lately I've been seriously considering relocating once more. In the meantime, I have done an informal survey on the schools, hospitals,

and other government-owned buildings in Solantha. I've identified some fifty-odd buildings that are in a perilous state, though
with most you would never know from the outside. Many of
them are structurally unsound, with the foundations inadequate
to bear the building load. With additional stress like a quake, the
factor of safety would be zero."

We exchanged looks of shock and dismay as Kardanor
continued. "What's just as bad is that I've discovered numerous
buildings where fire hydrants are merely decorative and not
properly connected to the water mains." He pulled a map out
from his jacket pocket and spread it out on the table. "You can
see for yourself right here."

Everyone leaned in close to get a good look at the map. It
was drawn with thick black ink on white paper, and the buildings in question were marked in red. I was not surprised to see
that the Enforcers Guild was listed amongst these endangered
buildings, and an alarming number of other buildings were
marked down as well. Maintown had the largest concentration
of red marks, while Shiftertown had the least, since the town's
few newer buildings had been constructed by shifter companies.
The buildings that didn't have their hydrant lines connected
were marked with an additional X, and I was dismayed to see
how many there were. If a fire broke out in the city, those buildings would burn to the ground, and the flames would engulf the
entire neighborhood very quickly.

"This is unacceptable," Iannis finally said, leaning back in
his chair. His violet eyes simmered with annoyance. "Solantha's
building inspectors are clearly not doing their job. I find myself
very surprised that the Maintown and Shiftertown Councils
have not done anything about this. Did you contact them?"

"I have attempted to gain an audience with the Maintown
Council numerous times," Kardanor said. "The Shiftertown
Council would not see me because I'm human, and barely toler-

ated my survey efforts as it was. But the Maintown Council inspectors have likely convinced them that I am raving mad, so they refuse to see me. I am certain they have been bought off by Mendle and Gorax."

"I recall hearing about a large earthquake in Naraka some thirty years ago," Fenris said, speaking up for the first time. He stared at the map, his yellow eyes tight with concern. "The quake was quickly followed by a devastating fire, which ended up tripling the overall damage. In fact, from my reading, almost all serious quakes cause fires, since stoves, furnaces, candles, and electric lines are shaken up and will inevitably find fuel here and there. These buildings must be made both quake and fire resistant, if we hope to escape the impending earthquake relatively unscathed."

"I wish we had known about this predicament sooner," Director Chen complained, studying the map as well. Her lips were pursed, and I was surprised to scent anger radiating off her —she usually had an even cooler head than Iannis. "If Lord Faring's prediction is anywhere close to correct, there is not enough time, or mage power, to magically secure these structures before the big quake hits."

"At the very least, we must ensure the schools and hospitals are protected," Kardanor countered. "Can you really magically protect buildings from fire?"

"Yes," Iannis said tersely. "However, it takes a lot of energy and manpower to keep up such spells. It would be impractical to keep up fire protection for the entire city at all times."

"I wish I'd known about this," Kardanor said. "Inadequate resources simply mean that priorities must be set. To stop fires from engulfing the whole city, barriers of protected buildings might help, perhaps adjacent to open spaces—something that should have been included in city planning from the outset," he pointed out.

"There is little point in dwelling on what should have happened," Iannis said firmly. "We must move forward, and do what we can to protect the city. Director Chen, I would like you to draw up a plan with Mr. Makis as your advisor, and present it to me tomorrow night."

Chen nodded. "I will send teams to the public buildings Mr. Makis has marked off, according to priority, to verify their condition and apply provisional protection spells."

"I believe the situation warrants a state of emergency," Cirin said. "All local mages should be summoned to the Palace for refresher courses on fire protection and shielding against falling debris."

"That is an excellent idea," Iannis said. "I will teach some of the courses myself. We cannot afford to take any chances."

We spent the next thirty minutes tossing ideas back and forth as the servants brought out the main course, and then dessert. Kardanor suggested organizing extra earthquake and fire drills in the Rowanville, Maintown, and Shiftertown neighborhoods—the schools did them every so often, but he insisted they be extended to businesses and other government buildings as well. I proposed that we should prepare large, army-style tents and start pre-positioning food and water supplies outside the city, in case an evacuation was necessary. I was very pleased to see that everyone was fully engaged in the discussion, and that the mages had all seemed to accept Kardanor as part of the team, now that they'd gotten over the initial shock of working with a mere human.

Eager to start work, Chen and Kardanor left right after dessert to pick out an office big enough to spread out his detailed city maps, which he would be bringing up to the Palace as soon as possible. Cirin went back to his own office so that he could review the finances and increase the disaster-relief budget and order the tents and supplies, as per my suggestion.

"I think I will retreat to the library," Fenris said as he, Iannis, and I rose from our seats. "I'll dig up some of the more relevant spell books, and draw up a list of the most effective protection spells that will help us secure the city."

"That is a good idea. I may well join you—" Iannis began.

"Excuse me," a servant said, opening the door. "Lord Iannis, I apologize for the intrusion, but you have visitors."

"Yes, and we come on urgent business," said Garrett Toring, the Director of Federal Security. Iannis stiffened and the hair on my nape rose as Garrett entered the room right on the heels of the servant, a younger mage dressed in dark grey at his side. He looked around the room as we stared at him in shock, and my stomach dropped as his glance lingered on Fenris for a long moment.

"Good to see you again, Chief Mage, Sunaya. Pity you've already finished dinner. I don't suppose there's any left for us?"

6

"**D**irector Toring," Iannis said coolly, recovering from the shock well before I did. "What an unexpected pleasure."

"Yes, I suppose it is," Garrett said, a faint smile playing on his lips as he held Iannis's gaze. The two stared at each other for a fraught moment, tension crackling in the air. Despite Iannis's deadly calm façade, I knew he was very displeased Garrett had showed up without so much as a phone call beforehand. Garrett gestured to the other mage, who looked around thirty, with dark brown curls and an air of superiority. "This is my assistant, Harron Pillick. I apologize for not sending word of our arrival, but the Minister and I agreed that for security reasons, it would be best not to do so."

I clenched my jaw at the lie. Garrett might have been on some urgent mission, but there was no sincerity in his apology —he had meant to arrive without notice, to throw us off balance. What was he here for? Did the Minister really know and choose not to tell Iannis? My mind instantly went to Fenris, standing on my right. I couldn't see his expression, but panic and rage rolled off him at the sight of his deadliest enemy, in a way that deeply unsettled me. Fenris was always so even-keeled, but I could sense his fight-or-flight response kicking in, and the urge to flee was intensely strong in him right now.

Garrett turned to him, his hazel eyes gleaming with interest and calculation. "You must be Fenris," he said casually, eyeing Fenris up and down like a wolf might a particularly juicy steak. The irony wasn't lost on me that of the two of them, *Fenris* was the actual wolf in the room. "I have heard much about you."

"Surely nothing of interest," Fenris said calmly, and I was both astonished and proud to see that he was smiling cheerfully, as if he hadn't a care in the world. That would piss Garrett off for sure. "I am a mere shifter, after all."

"Ah, but you are being too modest," Garrett said, and his own smile didn't waver one bit. "A shifter who studies magical theory is quite rare in Solantha, or even the entire Northia Federation. What prompted you to delve into an esoteric subject that is useless to your kind?"

"Director Toring," I interrupted, sparing Fenris from having to respond. "Surely you didn't take the trouble to come out all this way—"

"*Trouble*," my ether parrot squawked. He materialized between Garrett and me, his glowing blue wings throwing off sparks of magic as they flapped in the air.

"What *is* that thing?" Garrett snapped, moving out of the parrot's way.

"A little experiment of mine," I said breezily—no way was I going to admit to Garrett that Trouble had been the result of an ether pigeon spell gone wrong. "His name is Trouble, and he appears every time I use the word. I'm still trying to smooth out that particular quirk."

"*Quirk*," Trouble squawked, and he sounded highly offended. The parrot turned his back on me and sailed over to

Garrett, settling his glowing, feathered body onto the Director's gilded head of hair.

"Well, I really must be getting back to the library," Fenris said, stepping past Garrett, who was unsuccessfully trying to shoo the bird off his head. Trouble wasn't corporeal, so no amount of shaking or swatting affected him. "I will come find you later, Lord Iannis, if I learn anything pertinent to these quakes." He flashed me a grateful smile behind Garrett's back before slipping out through the double doors.

"Quakes?" Garrett demanded, abandoning his attempts to dislodge the parrot from his head. "What quakes?"

"I fail to see why I should answer that, when you've yet to tell me the reason for your visit," Iannis said, letting some of his annoyance seep into his voice.

"Oh, how rude of me," Garrett exclaimed, and I nearly rolled my eyes. "We are here about Thorgana Mills. My office has been working around the clock since the day of the prison fire. We now have proof that not only did Thorgana survive the conflagration, but her confederates are the ones who caused it."

"Shit." I'd known that was a possibility, even strongly suspected it. But to hear confirmation... Dammit. I'd really hoped she was dead. "So she's on the loose again? What is she planning?"

"We don't know," Garrett admitted, displeasure coloring his voice. "But we did catch one of the arsonists. After a lengthy interrogation, he confessed that he overheard she might be heading to Solantha. Something about 'squaring accounts'."

A chill went down my spine at that. Was I one of the "accounts" Thorgana intended to square away? She had every reason to want me dead, and Iannis as well—we'd thwarted her plans at every turn, and were the ones who had finally taken her down. I tried to catch Iannis's eye, but his shimmering violet gaze was firmly fixed on Garrett.

"Not now," he said to me in mindspeak. *"We'll discuss this later."*

Aloud, he said to Garrett, "While I do appreciate you taking the time to relay this information, I don't see why you had to come out all this way. A simple phone call or telegram would have sufficed. We are more than capable of handling Thorgana, as we have proven in the past."

"I don't doubt that," Garrett said, sounding thoroughly unimpressed, "but I am under strict orders from the Minister to find and capture her myself. Her compatriots killed dozens of mages during the breakout, never mind her other crimes. He will not be satisfied until she is back behind bars, and if she happens to be killed while resisting arrest, so much the better. Besides," he added silkily, "if Solantha is about to be hit by an earthquake, I imagine your hands will be full with preparations to secure the city. You could use my eyes and ears, Lord Iannis. I am very good at what I do."

There was a long silence, and even though I hated the idea of Garrett being here, I couldn't find any flaw in his argument. We really were stretched thin right now, and Thorgana needed to be taken down. It would be just like her to use the commotion of an imminent earthquake as a cover while she cooked up some plot to hit us hard and take down the Mages Guild in Solantha.

"Very well," Iannis finally said. "I cannot argue with your logic, though I will bring the matter of your jurisdiction up at the next convention. But as you say, we are very busy preparing for a possible big quake, and I will not be able to spare significant manpower to assist you with this search. Now is really not the best time for a manhunt," he said ruefully, and I knew then that he really would have preferred to go hunt for Thorgana himself, if only so that he could get Garrett out of here as quickly as possible.

"I'll help," I said, drawing the gazes of both men my way.

"There will be little time for my usual magic lessons, and I have a personal stake in finding Thorgana. I'm not going to sit on my ass while waiting for her to come and kill me."

"Perhaps we can devise a plan to draw her out, with you as bait?" Garrett's assistant suggested, his eyes gleaming eagerly as he studied me. From his expression, his mind was no doubt racing, chewing on calculations, studying all angles.

"It might be worth considering," Garrett agreed. "Although—"

"Absolutely *not*," Iannis snapped, his eyes blazing. "Sunaya is my fiancée, Director Toring, not a tool for your personal use."

"She's also right here in this room," I said irritably. "And although I don't love the idea of being bait, I wouldn't be opposed to it in the right circumstances." Iannis opened his mouth to argue, but I cut him off. "That's not going to be my first plan of attack, and I definitely will not do anything like that without discussing it with you first. But I'm a trained enforcer with intimate knowledge of this city, including possible allies and suspects," I pointed out. "I even knew Thorgana before we identified her as the Benefactor."

"Did you really?" Garrett asked, sounding intrigued. "In what capacity? I can't imagine a wealthy, pampered socialite like her rubbing elbows with an enforcer."

"I did a couple of security gigs for her," I said coolly, not appreciating the insinuation that I was riffraff. Garrett flinched slightly, as if realizing how offensive his statement was, and I wondered a little at that. Did he actually care about my feelings? I'd scented interest from him once or twice during our return trip from Garai, but lust didn't necessarily translate to affection.

"*I don't like this,*" Iannis said in mindspeak, simmering with ire. "*However, someone needs to keep an eye on Garrett while he's here—to make sure he doesn't go poking into things he ought not to.*"

"No kidding." I held in a sigh. *"I'll do my best to deflect any questions about Fenris, and keep his focus on Thorgana."*

"Sunaya makes valid points," Iannis said to Garrett. "She would be an asset in this search, and I can think of no one better to assign as your liaison. The two of you will work together to find Thorgana, but you will keep me informed every step of the way." His eyes narrowed, and his voice turned dangerously soft. "I will not overlook another slight, Director Toring."

"Understood." Garrett said stiffly, his scent changing subtly —he was wary of Iannis's power, if not outright fearful. I wasn't sure how powerful Garrett was, but clearly, he did not want to provoke an actual conflict. "Shall we meet for breakfast tomorrow to discuss our plan of action, Miss Baine?"

"Yes." I paused for a moment, considering my options, then said. "We'll meet back here, in the Winter Garden room, at eight." I didn't want to invite him into my suite for breakfast, nor was I interested in going to his—that would be all kinds of inappropriate. "In the meantime, let's get you settled in for the night." I rang a bell, summoning the Palace staff.

"Excellent." Garrett smiled, his hazel eyes glinting. "I look forward to seeing what we might accomplish together."

I don't, I thought as I handed Garrett off to a servant who would show him and his assistant to appropriate guestrooms in the East Wing. By Magorah, we didn't need this. But I met Iannis's eyes again, and they were surprisingly steady.

We'll find a way through this, his gaze said. *We've been through worse.*

Nodding, I slipped my hand into his, and we hurried down the hall to find out where Fenris had gone off to.

7

Unsurprisingly, Fenris wasn't actually in the library. We checked there anyway, but I figured he wouldn't want to risk Garrett seeking him out. His scent lingered near the entrance, as if he'd been here recently, so he must have stopped by to grab some books to continue his research elsewhere.

"You're back faster than I thought you'd be," he said by way of greeting as we entered Iannis's suite. Fenris's room was farther down the hall, but I'd smelled him right outside Iannis's door, so we didn't bother going any further. He was settled into the wing-backed chair by the fire, a thick leather tome in his hand and several more stacked on the side table by his left elbow. "How was your chat with Director Toring?"

"Unsettling," Iannis said, sitting down on the end of the couch closest to Fenris. He snapped his fingers, and the scent of magic tickled my nose as the eavesdropping wards he'd set into the walls were activated. I kicked off my boots, then stretched out on the remainder of the couch and settled my calves across Iannis's lap. "Thorgana survived the fire, and Garrett strongly suspects she has fled here."

Fenris sat straight up in his chair, setting the book aside. "That woman is like a blasted cockroach," he growled, his yellow eyes narrowing to slits. "How did she survive?"

Iannis relayed to Fenris what Garrett had told us—that the fire had been orchestrated to break Thorgana out, and that one of the arsonists had heard she was headed to Solantha for some payback.

Fenris's bearded face was drawn so tight by the time Iannis was done, I half expected his tanned skin to start cracking. "I wish there was some way I could be of more help," he said, "but with Director Toring here, I am severely limited."

"We'll be fine," I assured him. "You just need to lie low until he's gone. I'm going to be working with him to apprehend Thorgana, and I intend to find her quickly so that we can send him on his way."

Fenris nodded. "As soon as he is gone, I shall be on my way as well."

Iannis stiffened, and I stared at Fenris in shock. "What do you mean? Where are you going?"

"I don't know yet," Fenris admitted. He scrubbed a hand over his face, and my heart began to ache—he looked so brittle, as if a well-placed blow would shatter his soul and send it scattering to the winds. "But it is clear that I can no longer stay here. My shifter nose has much improved since you came to the Palace, Sunaya—I could smell Garrett's ill will quite clearly during his brief interrogation attempt. He will not be content to focus his energies exclusively on Thorgana, and I believe Thorgana may only be an excuse. Now that he and Iannis are contenders for the Minister's position, he will use any means at his disposal to eliminate the competition. I may well be the perfect weapon. If not for the fact that it would confirm Toring's suspicions, and my guilt, I would leave right now."

"I concede the point," Iannis said reluctantly, looking troubled. "If I could, I would simply tell Garrett to his face that I care nothing for the position, and that he is welcome to it. But he would not believe me, and besides, he will not be satisfied until he solves the mystery of how you slipped from his grasp as Polar ar'Tollis."

"That's all well and good, but Garrett doesn't have any proof that you and Polar are the same person," I argued. "We don't even know that is what he suspects—we only know he sees a mystery in Fenris." Anger bubbled in my chest—I wasn't going to accept this! Fenris had been my only friend when I'd first come to the Palace, bridging the gap between Iannis and me with his calm, compassionate manner. If not for him, I might never have become Iannis's apprentice. "We'll just have to make sure he walks away empty handed."

Fenris shook his head emphatically. "Director Toring will not suffer to be made a fool of twice," he growled, his yellow eyes gleaming as the fire in the hearth reflected off them. "He and his assistant will be watching me very closely, and questioning the servants and staff about me. He is very intelligent and highly motivated, so there is a distinct chance he might discover the truth before Thorgana is apprehended. Even if he doesn't, he will find another excuse to come back and keep searching. No, I must not tempt fate. As soon as he leaves, I will depart."

"But what are you going to do?" Tears stung at my eyes. "You can't go back to Nebara."

"No," Fenris agreed. "I would not endanger my parents by returning there, just as I will not continue to put you or Iannis in danger by staying." His rugged features softened—he must have seen the anguish in my face. "I may have been the one who escaped a death sentence, Sunaya, but Iannis did not just help me get away—he also used forbidden magic to turn me into a shifter. If Garrett finds out the truth, Iannis's life will be forfeit as well."

"If worst comes to worst, we could all leave the country," Iannis suggested, but I shook my head.

"No. You've fought too hard for your people, and have made more progress uniting the three races than any Chief Mage of Solantha has before you," I said firmly. "We can't abandon them now, especially not with this earthquake on the way. As much as I hate to say it..." A lump swelled in my throat, and I had to force it down. "Fenris is right. The easiest thing is for him to go."

But it's not fair! A voice in my head howled. *He's family.* He was supposed to be the best man at our wedding. To be the godfather to our future children. How could Fenris do any of that, if he was on the run?

"I will not miss any of the important events in your lives," Fenris said, seeming to read my thoughts. He met my tearful gaze with a valiant smile. "Even if I have to do it in disguise, I will be there when you two are married, and when your children are born."

I couldn't take it anymore. My heart brimming with emotion, I stepped over Iannis, then knelt in front of Fenris's chair and threw my arms around him. "You must tell us where you've relocated to," I whispered fiercely as I squeezed him tight. "I want to be able to come and visit you, to meet your own wife and children when you have them."

Fenris started a little at the mention of wife and children. "I don't know about that," he said, a wry smile in his voice as he embraced me in return. "But I will send messages as I can, so that you know I am still alive."

"You'd better." Pulling back, I wiped my sleeve across my teary eyes. "And I have no doubt that you'll meet a fine woman someday and have a whole brood of children. You deserve to live a full life, Fenris, with all the joys and pitfalls that go with it."

"Yes," Iannis agreed, wrapping his arms around me as I returned to sit next to him. "And while we will miss you, I fear that staying here in the Palace has not truly done you any favors."

"No," Fenris agreed ruefully. "I have appreciated the opportunity to lie low and absorb as much magical theory as I have been able to these past few years. But living in a Palace, surrounded by mages, has not prepared me for life as a shifter. If I am to truly become Fenris, and make the most of my new existence, I must go seek my fortune in humbler surroundings. I have a good bit of gold saved up, and I will be able to settle comfortably wherever I choose, so do not worry about me."

We discussed the particulars of Fenris's departure for a little while—he was going to pack in secret, ready to depart at a moment's notice should Garrett come too close to the truth. In the meantime, Fenris would spend as little time in Garrett's presence as possible, and if they did have to be in the same room, he would do it in wolf form. Garrett couldn't use mindspeak, and he wouldn't be able to question Fenris as a wolf.

"Fenris will be fine," Iannis said as the two of us burrowed beneath the blankets in his huge bed, long after Fenris had left for his own room. "He may no longer have all of his magic, but he is very clever and resourceful, and his shifter senses are much more developed than they were when I first brought him to the Palace. He will be fine on his own, and there are many places in the Federation where he can live a comfortable life so long as he keeps his head down."

"I know." Laying my head against Iannis's bare chest, I tried to comfort myself with the steady beating of his heart. But I couldn't help fearing that despite all our careful planning, we were teetering on the brink of disaster.

8

I tried to sleep, but though Iannis's arms were snug around me, his powerful body wrapping me up in a cocoon of warmth and safety, I found myself restless. Even though I'd told Fenris that I understood and accepted his decision, turmoil continued to writhe and roll around in my chest, churning my thoughts into a muddled mass of worry.

What if Fenris didn't manage to get away in time? What if Garrett and his assistant found enough evidence to arrest and convict him? Iannis would be stripped of his role as Chief Mage, and he might very well be executed alongside Fenris.

No way, a voice in my head argued. Iannis wasn't a victim, and he wouldn't meekly submit, either. He was clever and resourceful enough that he might be able to flee the Federation. But what kind of life would he have after such public humiliation? I would also lose any prestige and favor I might have gained in the mage community. I didn't know if they could execute me after all I'd done for the Federation, but I would no longer be in a position to help the shifter and human communities. And that was unacceptable.

Careful not to wake Iannis, I slipped from the bed as quietly as I could. He mumbled a little in protest, but dutifully curled his arms around the pillow I pushed against his chest. I took a moment to admire the way the moonlight filtered in through the window above the headboard, highlighting his alabaster skin and making his dark hair, the color of cherry wood, shimmer. Long lashes fanned out against high, razor-edged cheekbones, and his full mouth, normally so firm and stern, was slightly parted. The sheets had slipped down to his waist, baring broad shoulders and a strong back that tapered into lean hips. Scratches marred the pale skin beneath his shoulder blades, left over from our lovemaking last night, and I was filled with a sudden urge to lean over and kiss the small wounds. Wounds that he'd chosen to leave rather than heal. But I didn't want to wake him, so I turned away, then quietly returned to my room via the secret passage in the corner.

I dressed quickly in a pair of jeans and a sweater, then strapped my crescent knives to my right thigh. I debated putting on shoes, then decided against it—my footfalls would be silent if I went barefoot, relieving me from having to use a silencing spell. Mages could detect if a spell was in use if they were paying attention, so I wanted to rely on magic as little as possible. My shifter senses would be enough.

It was a little eerie walking through the Palace halls at this time of night. There was absolutely no one else about—not even a maid. Guards were strategically stationed by the entrances, but none were near the guest rooms in the East Wing. Powerful wards had been set up to protect against intruders, so there was no need for anything more than a patrol.

Speaking of a patrol...footsteps sounded on the stone floor around the corner. Quietly as I could, I darted into a broom closet, wedging myself behind a forest of mop handles and buckets as far back as I could go. The footfalls grew closer, and flickering torchlight seeped beneath the crack in the door as the guard made his rounds. He paused outside the closet, and I held my breath, praying to Magorah that he wouldn't open it.

He moved on, and I held in my sigh of relief until his steps had faded completely. I really did *not* want to have to explain to him why I was hiding in the broom closet. Strictly speaking, I didn't have to—I was the Chief Mage's fiancée, free to come and go as I pleased. But I didn't want any guards to catch me snooping outside Garrett's room—they would inevitably talk about it, and I didn't want them discovering there were conflicts among the mages. As far as the staff knew, Director Toring was here to apprehend Thorgana—they didn't need to know that he was also interested in Fenris, or why. The fewer eyes on Fenris, the better.

Once I was absolutely certain no one else was around, I left the closet, then crept down the hall. My bare feet sank into the plush carpet that ran the length of the chilly stone floor. I didn't know exactly which room Garrett was in, but I didn't need to— my nose led me right to him, following his masculine scent to a corner suite. Dammit. I couldn't very well press my ear to the door out here—guards would see me coming down either of the two corridors that crossed here.

Good thing I brought my picks, I thought, moving to the room next to Garrett's sitting room. My shifter eyes needed no additional light, and I was inside within seconds. I closed the door behind me as quietly as I could, then hurried over to the wall adjoining this room to Garrett's so I could listen in.

"You may not be aware of it, Pillick, but there's an ancient law forbidding mages to teach our lore to outsiders," Garrett was saying, and I grinned a little—they were still up, just as I thought. Mages didn't sleep much as a general rule, so Garrett must have decided to stay up late and plot with his assistant. "Lord Iannis, who is older than I by a considerable margin, must be perfectly aware of it. Yet it looks very likely that he has been teaching this pet shifter of his Loranian or magical theory. We came here to catch Thorgana Mills, but that does not mean we should simply overlook any other crimes that come to our notice."

"Even if we could prove exactly where Fenris acquired his knowledge," Harron said, sounding skeptical, "it would be a misdemeanor at best. Indicting Lord Iannis for such a small offense would only make us look petty, Sir. He is practically a war hero. Unless we find something much worse to charge him with, I would advise against it, from a public relations perspective."

"Agreed," Garrett said, though he didn't sound happy about it. I was sure it rankled the hell out of him to hear his rival referred to as a war hero. "Let's keep our eyes open, though. Lord Iannis may be perfectly innocent, of course, and his courage is beyond doubt, but I have a gut feeling that this foreign-born Chief Mage may not have the Federation's best interests at heart, or respect our laws as much as he ought. The Minister is considering him as a possible successor, and we would be remiss if we did not exercise due diligence. We cannot afford to have a traitor holding the reins of our country."

I clenched my fists as rage heated my blood, fighting against the urge to punch through the wall and grab Garrett by the throat. If I thought violence would solve anything, I would have already broken down his door. But Garrett was a powerful mage, and although I was strong, I was still an apprentice. I wouldn't be able to beat him in a duel, and even if I did, the Minister would punish me for injuring or killing one of his highest officials. No, I had to outsmart Garrett, not out-muscle him.

"Of course, Director," the assistant said smoothly, no doubt catching onto the undertones of Garrett's statement. The bastard wasn't really concerned about Iannis's loyalties—anyone with half a brain could see that Iannis had the Federation's best interests at heart. Garrett just wanted to eliminate him as a rival, and Pillick would be more than happy to assist, as it would put him that much closer to a position of power as well. "While we are here, I will do some digging into our host's background and confirm there is nothing untoward."

"Make sure you're discreet," Garrett warned. "It would be awkward if Lord Iannis or his staff were to learn that we are looking into him. I still feel we should focus our efforts on our host's wolf-shifter friend to start with. I believe he spends a lot of time in the library, so perhaps the head librarian can tell us more about this highly unlikely scholarship of his."

"I will interview her tomorrow, after our breakfast with Miss Baine," Pillick declared, and my stomach sank. By Magorah, they were going to drag Janta into this?

They retired shortly afterward, and I slipped out of the guest room. I desperately wanted to run to the library and leave Janta a note on her desk, warning her not to give away any information about Fenris, but the library was too close to where the guards were stationed. I wouldn't be able to get in and out unseen. And there would be no sneaking out to warn her—the guards would definitely see that.

Riding the edge of exhaustion now, I snuck back into Iannis's room, then stripped off my clothes and cuddled into bed next to him. He grumbled a little in his sleep, but his long arms tucked me against him, my back to his chest, and he pressed a kiss to my shoulder. Sparks skipped along my bare skin, and I relaxed, a smile coming to my lips despite everything. With a deep sigh, I forced myself to let go of my problems and finally sink into sleep. I'd need all my wits about me to deal with Garrett tomorrow.

9

"So," Garrett said as he slathered cream cheese and lox onto his onion bagel at breakfast the next morning. "Do you have any idea what Thorgana may be planning, Sunaya? You have spent more time with her than I—what sort of revenge would she be plotting?"

I was silent for a moment as I chewed on my mouthful of bacon, considering. "She's not one for silent strikes in the night," I finally said, reaching for my glass of orange juice. "She'll want to make a big splashy statement with her strike, and take out as many mages as possible. Shifters, too, if she can, but mages are her priority. She'd destroy all of us if she could."

"Do you think she still has any of those dangerous viruses?" Pillick asked. He'd ordered steak and eggs, and I'd done my best to avoid enviously eyeing his plate. "I know the labs in Osero and Garai have been destroyed, but some of their products may have been shipped out before you got there. She might have stashed them in other locations."

"She did have some deadly concoction around her neck when we captured her," I said, a chill running down my spine as I remembered the thick, bright red smoke that had exploded from the shattered vial. Iannis had contained it before it could touch us, but a sense of *wrongness* had pervaded my being at the sight of that stuff. I knew if it had touched us, we would have died. "I sincerely hope that she doesn't have more, but that would be wishful thinking."

"Indeed," Garrett agreed, his golden-brown eyebrows drawing together. "It's a pity Lord Iannis wasn't able to collect a sample of it to study."

I ignored the subtle dig, and instead launched into a discussion of our plans for the day. We agreed that visits to the Enforcers Guild and the Shiftertown Inspector were necessary, to enlist their assistance and offer bounties for useful information. We also decided to visit the Herald and the Shifter Courier, and question Thorgana's known associates. If there was time left in the day, we would take a trip to Prison Isle and interview the few high-level Resistance members languishing there who had worked with her personally.

"This is a good start," Garrett said, scanning the list of names I'd compiled of those I believed to be part of Thorgana's social circle, "but a woman of Thorgana's status would have more friends and associates than this. We should pass by the library and check the archives of any society magazines that would have reported on her many parties."

My shoulders tensed at the mention of the library, but I only nodded. "That's a good idea. I can go ahead and do that, then meet you at the Enforcers Guild a little later."

"Nonsense," Garrett said, waving his hand. "I've a fondness for libraries, and we'll get through the task faster if all three of us work on it together."

My stomach sank—I'd hoped I could find a way to stall them, so I could get to Janta first. But Garrett was chomping at the bit to get going, and he was right—it really didn't make sense for us to split up right now. My appetite gone, I finished up the few morsels left on my plate, then forced myself to escort Garrett and his assistant to the library.

As we passed the main entrance lobby, a small commotion at the front door caught my attention, and we paused. My eyes widened briefly in surprise as four mage guards brought in an old man dressed in clerical robes. He'd lost a little weight, his white hair was thinner, and there were circles beneath his eyes, but there was no mistaking him—it was Father Calmias, brought back from Prison Isle.

"How interesting," Garrett said, his eyes gleaming as he studied the prisoner. He would recognize him from the photos in the press—articles demanding his release appeared nation-wide, almost every day. "That such an old, frail-looking human could be the cause of so much trouble."

"You have no idea," I growled under my breath as I watched the guards herd Father Calmias past us. Our eyes clashed, and he lifted his chin, somehow managing to look down his nose at me despite the heavy manacles dragging at him. As if *I* were the scumbag who'd preached violence and genocide. "Iannis is going to interview him this morning."

"That is something I wouldn't miss for the world," Garrett said. To my supreme annoyance, he turned to follow Father Calmias and his escort. "Harron, you and Miss Baine can go on to the library without me. I will meet you later to go to the Enforcers Guild."

"Yes, sir," Pillick said, and if he was annoyed at being left behind, he didn't show it. The two of us continued on to the library, and the tension in my gut grew heavier with each step of the way.

Maybe Janta won't be there today, I thought fervently as we approached the library doors. *Tinari could have gotten sick, and she might have had to stay home with her.* Not that I would wish that on the little girl, but she would recover from a cold. Fenris would not recover from an execution.

Unfortunately for me, not only was Janta in the library, but so was Tinari, the sweet little girl who'd been rejected by her human parents when she'd tested positive for magic. Janta was quietly talking with a mage who was seated at one of the tables, piles of old tomes obscuring much of him, but she straightened up as soon as we came in. Tinari, who was comfortably curled up in a corner with pillows, blankets, and a stack of books, waved cheerfully to me. But her smile immediately dissipated at the sight of Pillick, and she ducked her head back down behind the leather-bound book she was reading. I would have to find some time to talk to her later.

"Sunaya," Janta said warmly, coming to greet us. "What a pleasant surprise. What can I do for you?"

"Hi, Janta." I smiled, pleased with the genuine happiness in her tone. Janta had been coolly professional when we'd first met, but as time had gone by, we'd become friends and allies. "This is Mr. Harron Pillick, from the Department of Federal Security." Though my smile didn't waver, I did my best to convey a warning look with my eyes. *He's not trustworthy,* I tried to say without speaking, and Janta's eyes briefly flickered before she nodded ever so slightly. "Mr. Pillick, this is Janta Urama, our Head Librarian. She provided invaluable help in identifying Thorgana Mills as the Benefactor."

"Pleasure to meet you," Pillick said, inclining his head. He sounded as if he meant it, but then, Janta was a fellow mage. He had no reason to look down on her.

"Mr. Pillick and I are here to look at the magazine archives," I said, before Pillick could get in a word about Fenris. Lowering my voice, I briefly explained about our investigation into Thorgana. "We're specifically looking for high-society magazines that would have reported on her parties and particular friendships."

"I can certainly help you with that," Janta said, a note of disdain entering her voice. "I used to believe that woman made a career out of throwing parties. Of course, I know better now," she said as she led us back to the magazine archives, "but I still find it hard to change my image of her as a vapid socialite whose only purpose in life was to spend her father's money."

I wish that was all Thorgana was, I grumbled to myself as we began searching through the drawers full of magazines. Luckily, they were organized by publication date and title, but finding the ones we wanted was still a time-consuming task.

"Miss Urama," Pillick said in a faux-casual tone as we sorted through the magazines, "I had the pleasure of meeting the resident shifter scholar, Fenris, last night. I assume the two of you are well acquainted?"

"He spends much of his time here," Janta said, her tone carefully neutral. "And often comes to me when there is some obscure reference he has trouble tracking down. So yes, we are acquainted."

"How long has he been studying magical theory here?" Pillick asked. "It seems like such an unusual occupation for a shifter."

"I'm a shifter, and I study magical theory," I said coolly.

"Yes, but you are also a mage," Pillick said dismissively. "Fenris, on the other hand, cannot actually use any of the magic he studies, which is why I find his interest so curious."

"He has been studying it the entirety of the three years he's been here," Janta said, interrupting us, "but it was obvious to me from the very start that he was already quite advanced. The esoteric titles he was asking for when he first came here, plus the level of knowledge he regularly exhibits in our conversations, indicate he must have been studying the subject for decades."

"I see." Pillick looked a little disappointed, but I wasn't about to feel relieved. Janta had done well, steering Pillick away from the idea that Iannis had been teaching Fenris magic, which wasn't true anyway. But knowing that Fenris had already been studying magic for decades might push Pillick and Garrett toward the truth—that Fenris and Polar were one and the same. I was banking on the knowledge that such a concept would be completely outlandish to them; that would hopefully keep them from going down that path for as long as possible.

Pillick attempted to pry more details about Fenris's former life out of Janta, but she deflected his questions easily by saying that Fenris was a very private person. As we carried our stacks of magazines back to the common area so we could sit them on one of the tables and begin sorting through them, I noticed Tinari was still in the corner, her nose buried in that same leather-bound tome she'd hidden behind earlier.

"The books keep her company," Janta said quietly, sounding a little sad. "I wish I could send her to school, so that she could be around children her own age, but for the present, I must keep her with me constantly in case she suffers a magical outburst. She is of the appropriate age—it could happen any day now."

"That's too bad." I frowned, studying the little girl. "Is she really reading those huge tomes?"

"Oh, yes," Janta said proudly. "Tinari is quite the reader. She might well become a librarian herself someday."

Tinari made a face, and I bit back a laugh—I hadn't realized she'd been listening. "Why don't I take her off your hands for a little bit?" I suggested. "There's another little girl in the kitchens who is about Tinari's age who could use some company, too. And besides, it doesn't look like I'm needed much here," I added, gesturing at Pillick. He was already busy going through the magazines, marking appropriate articles with pieces of paper and setting them aside, while discarding others that were useless. He didn't seem to want to share the task, and I got the feeling that he didn't trust me—he wanted to scour each piece with his own two eyes.

"Yes, I think that's an excellent idea," Janta agreed. "Tinari, why don't you accompany Miss Baine for a little bit? You can come back to your books later." *I'll keep an eye on Mr. Pillick,* she mouthed, and I smiled in gratitude.

Tinari held my hand as we walked to the kitchens, practically skipping in excitement—despite her love of books, she must have been awfully bored being confined to the library all the time. I knew I would be. She chattered a mile a minute as we walked, asking me about my travels to Garai and telling me about the new things she was learning every day with Janta. She might not have many friends yet, but Tinari was well cared for, and it did my heart good to see her that way.

As we descended the stairs to the kitchens, the heavenly scent of baked apple pies wafted up to greet us, and my stomach growled in anticipation. We entered the kitchen to see Mrs. Tandry barking orders to the rest of her kitchen staff, who seemed to be baking up a storm. There were sweet and savory pies, breads, rolls, huge roasts of ham and beef, and more.

"Oooooh," Tinari exclaimed, her eyes going starry as she beheld a stack of chocolate tarts. "What are these for?" She reached for one with her small hand.

"They're being sent to Shiftertown and Maintown, for the volunteers assisting with the rebuilding," Mrs. Tandry said, swatting Tinari's hand away before she could grab a tart. Her dark hair was secured beneath a white cap, her rounded cheeks were ruddy from the heat of the ovens, and her apron was coated with flour. "Got to keep those men and women well fed if we want them to continue working at full strength."

"I agree," I said, looking around at the piles of food with astonishment. I noticed several of the kitchen staff were already wrapping the food and packing it in boxes. "Did you come up with this on your own, Mrs. Tandry?"

"I sent a letter to Lord Iannis with the suggestion, and he seemed to think it was a good idea," Mrs. Tandry said proudly. "He allocated us enough gold to allow us to provide food to the volunteers for several weeks."

Liu chose that moment to pop out from behind one of the islands, and I grinned at the sight of her. She looked adorable in her apron-covered frock with flour smudged over her cheek. Her long dark hair was secured beneath a white cap, leaving her thin face unframed. "Miss Baine!" she cried, rushing over for a hug. "Have you come to visit me?"

"I have," I said with a chuckle as I returned the embrace. "And I've brought you a new friend, too."

Liu pulled back to inspect Tinari. The two girls stared at each other for a few seconds, assessing. "I'm Tinari," Tinari spoke first, sticking her small hand out for Liu to shake. "I live with Janta, the librarian."

"I'm Liu." Liu looked confused about the hand for a moment, and it occurred to me that Garaians always bowed. But she figured it out quickly, then shook Tinari's hand. "I work here in the kitchens with Mrs. Tandry."

"Do you really get to stay here and make cookies all day?" Tinari asked, her eyes wide with wonder.

"Yes," Liu said proudly, grinning. "I even get to eat them sometimes." She grabbed a tart off the plate before Mrs. Tandry could stop her, then broke it, offering half to Tinari. "Here. I know you want one."

Mrs. Tandry rolled her eyes, but a smile twitched at her lips as the girls instantly began chattering away. "You'd think she'd be the size of Hawk Hill by now, with the way Liu eats," she said, turning to me. "I'm not sure where she puts it all."

"I'm glad to see she's filled out a little," I observed, smiling.

"You've taken good care of her." When Iannis and I had bought Liu from her father, a poor Garaian farmer, she'd been little but skin and bones, dressed in rags and dirt. Now she was clean and well-fed, her skin glowing with health and her eyes shining.

"It's no trouble at all," Mrs. Tandry said, blushing a little. "She's a joy to have in the kitchens, and whip smart. In fact, she's quite gifted as a cook, and I suspect she'll be giving me a run for my money in a few years." She let out a little sigh.

"But?" I asked, suspecting there was a downside here.

"Well, it's just that Liu doesn't know how to read, and it's an important skill to have as a cook." Mrs. Tandry brushed some flour off her apron, spraying my leathers with a fine cloud of the stuff. Oh well, it wasn't as though Liu hadn't already gotten it on me. "I would teach her myself, but I don't have the time. She has an excellent memory, so once she learns a recipe, she doesn't need to refer to it again, but she needs someone to read everything aloud the first time."

"Hmm." I stared at the two little girls for a moment, and a lightbulb went off in my head. "Tinari, what do you think about teaching Liu how to read? I know you've got a lot of time on your hands in the library."

"I've never taught someone how to read before," Tinari said, biting her lip. But Liu's eyes were shining with hope, and she relented. "But I could probably do it, and Janta can help me if I we get stuck."

"I would *love* that," Liu said, bouncing up and down with excitement. "You can teach me to read in the library, and I can teach you how to cook here in the kitchens. Then you can make your own chocolate tarts at home, every day!"

I couldn't help it—I grinned at their twin expressions of enthusiasm.

"I don't know that Miss Tinari will need to learn how to

cook," Mrs. Tandry said dubiously. "Mages tend to hire help for
that—they certainly never lack the gold for servants."

"Perhaps," I allowed, "but cooking is a good skill for anyone
to have, mage or not. If we hadn't found Liu, Lord Iannis and I
might have starved during our trip to Garai."

"Yes, and besides, I can spend more time with my new
friend!" Tinari grabbed Liu by the hand, and the two began
dancing around the room together. Mrs. Tandry shrieked when
two cast iron pans unhooked themselves from the ceiling rack
and began dancing along with them...to the same tempo, I
noticed in shocked amusement.

"Magic!" Tinari shrieked, her eyes going wide, and a set of
plates launched themselves from the drying rack and began
spinning about the room.

It took a few minutes for me to get everything under control.
Mrs. Tandry worked on calming Tinari down, while I used my
own magic to return the dishes to their rightful places. Luckily,
Tinari only managed to break two of them, which Mrs. Tandry
assured me was nothing—she'd seen much worse. She
promised to send Liu up to the library after lunch tomorrow, for
her first lesson, and the two girls hugged and made their
goodbyes.

"I can't believe it," Tinari gushed as I brought her back to the
library. "I did magic!"

"You sure did." Smiling at her enthusiasm, I squeezed her
hand. She chattered excitedly about Liu, and how much she was
looking forward to her cooking lessons, right up until we got to
the library again.

After briefly explaining what had happened to Janta—who
was disappointed at having missed the episode, but relieved it
had been relatively harmless—I went off to find Garrett. Pillick
was still hogging the magazines, and if Iannis was interrogating
Father Calmias, I wanted to catch the tail end of it.

A quick check-in with Dira, the Mages Guild receptionist, confirmed that Iannis was in his office with Garrett. I knocked briefly on the door, then let myself in. Iannis and Garrett were seated at his desk, in deep discussion, while Fenris was curled up in wolf form on the floor by Iannis's feet, well away from Garrett's keen gaze.

"Miss Baine," Garrett said, sounding a little surprised as he twisted in his chair to face me. "Did you and Mr. Pillick already finish up at the library?"

"Mr. Pillick is still going through the magazines," I said, settling into the visitor's chair next to him. "He seemed unwilling to share the task, so I thought I would come here and see what you two were up to." I turned to face Iannis with a smile. "How did your interrogation with Father Calmias go?"

"Not as well as I'd hoped," Iannis admitted. "Time on Prison Isle has not dulled his will or his wit—he has a very clever tongue, and no matter what line of questioning I took, I was unable to prove any direct complicity between him and Thorgana. His combination of stubbornness and charisma is very dangerous—he will not renounce his beliefs, and his followers will continue to champion him."

"Pity we can't just kill him," Garrett noted dispassionately. "But that would only make him a martyr."

"Indeed," Iannis said, "and that is the last thing I want. We must find a way to break him, and the hold he has over his followers. I have him under guard in one of the guest rooms, and I will tackle him again tomorrow." He glanced toward the clock. "For now, I have a disaster-planning class in the ballroom that's about to start any minute." He stood up.

"Let me know if you need anything," I said, rising from my chair as well. I caught him by the hand before he could leave, then pressed a kiss to his lips, heedless of Garrett and Fenris's presence. Truthfully, I was hoping to annoy Garrett a little with the display of affection—mages disapproved of that sort of thing. Catching on, Iannis slipped an arm around my waist and kissed me back, brief but hard. I could taste his frustration. Looking up at him questioningly, I silently inquired as to what was bothering him.

"Later," he promised in mindspeak, letting go of me. "Good luck today," he told Garrett over his shoulder before sweeping out of the room, Fenris on his heels.

Garrett watched them both go, his eyes glittering with some undefinable emotion. "I suppose we should head out," he finally said, sounding disgruntled. "I'd like to get something done before lunchtime, and Pillick will no doubt be busy for hours with the magazines."

"Sure thing," I said, my mind dancing with other ways to annoy or unbalance Garrett throughout the day. "What do you say we go for a ride?"

10

I shot out of the Palace grounds on my steambike, Garrett clinging to my waist. I'd left Rylan at the Palace, much to his disappointment, because there wasn't really any need to bring him with Garrett accompanying me. Besides, if the three of us went, we'd have to take a steamcar, which I wasn't keen on. It was a lot faster to get around Solantha's narrow, winding streets by bike.

To my surprise and annoyance, Garrett adapted to the steambike far better than Fenris had when I'd first ridden with him. After learning that Fenris had spent the bulk of his life as a mage, I'd assumed all mages would be uncomfortable riding this way. But though Garrett pressed his body closer against mine than I would have liked, he seemed otherwise completely at ease astride my shiny, steam-belching beast. In fact, I strongly suspected he was enjoying the ride.

"You were correct," Garrett said, pulling off his helmet once we'd come to a complete stop. "Your steambike is a most efficient means of transportation." He eyed the bike with no small amount of admiration gleaming in his eyes. "If it were suitable for an official of my status, I would be tempted to get one for myself."

I bristled at that. "Always so tactful," I said, turning my attention toward Thorgana's mansion and changing the subject before he could respond. "Looks like the new owners have wasted no time starting construction."

"I can't blame them," Garrett said as we watched huge, steam-powered machines with broad shovels dig dirt out of the ground. The large, elegant mansion where I'd stumbled into a trap and nearly died only a few months earlier was completely demolished, the manicured gardens buried beneath piles of dirt as the land was dug up. "This is prime real estate, what with that nice ocean view."

A quick chat with the foreman told us that the new owners were building a luxury-apartment complex. I took down the name of the company, but didn't think I'd be digging much further—Thorgana was obviously not hiding out back here. With this possibility crossed off our list, we got back on the bike and headed to the Enforcers Guild.

"There is a new captain in charge, correct?" Garrett said as we prepared to go inside. He craned his neck a bit, studying the dingy grey facade, and I wasn't surprised that he looked thoroughly unimpressed. The building was well past its glory days, and it should have been renovated a few decades ago. Recalling it had been on Kardanor's list, I frowned. I'd have to make sure it got bumped up on the priority list—schools and hospitals were important, but the Guild needed to continue to function no matter what, or there would be no one around to help maintain order during a calamity.

"Yes, the former captain has just retired." I lowered my voice as we walked in through the entrance. "This one is the acting captain, technically speaking, but unless he seriously screws up, I'm sure his position will become permanent soon enough."

I walked up to the sergeant's desk and asked one of the trainees manning it to inform Acting Captain Skonel that we were here to see him. The trainee, a stocky male human who looked like he'd just turned twenty, took in Garrett's seal of office, worn on the front of his burgundy robes, then snatched up the phone and made the call. My sharp ears picked up Skonel's voice easily, as well as the annoyance in it, but despite his clear reluctance to interrupt whatever he'd been doing, he told the trainee to send us up.

We rode the elevator to the fourth floor in silence, and while Garrett seemed at ease, my stomach tightened with nerves. Captain Galling could be stubborn and unreasonable at times, but my years of experience with him had taught me which buttons to push. I had no such knowledge when it came to Wellmore Skonel. He had a good reputation as a solid enforcer who respected and upheld the law, but I knew better than most that reputations didn't always reflect a person's true character.

"Captain Skonel will be with you in a moment," the receptionist said when we stepped into the modest waiting area. She gestured to the beat-up leather waiting chairs. "Please make yourself comfortable. Would you like anything to drink?"

I was going to decline, but Garrett asked for a cup of black tea with cream, so I got one for myself too. It was a good thing, because Captain Skonel kept us waiting far longer than necessary. My nose and ears didn't pick out another person behind his office door, so either he was truly buried in paperwork, or he was deliberately letting us stew.

Finally, after a good ten minutes, the door opened. "Sorry to keep you waiting," Skonel said briskly as he strode out to greet us. "I was on an important call."

I narrowed my eyes at the lie. Once upon a time, I would have called him on it, but we needed Skonel to talk to us, and catching him out would only put him on the defensive. I caught

Garrett's hazel eyes, and could see he didn't buy the excuse either, but he shook the captain's hand anyway.

"You've come a long way, Director Toring," Captain Skonel said once we'd settled into the office. I immediately noticed that Captain Galling's photographs were gone, and that the shelves had been militantly organized. The cot in the corner was also gone, replaced by a comfortable-looking chaise. "What brings you out to our fair city?"

"My office has received intelligence that Thorgana Mills, the Benefactor, may be lying low in Solantha," Garrett said.

"Is that so?" Skonel sat up straighter, his brow furrowing. "Why hasn't the Enforcer's Guild been notified? My office has the right to know if a notorious terrorist is hiding out in our city."

"I'm informing you right now," Garrett said coolly, and I had to hide a grin. For once, it was nice to see his snooty behavior directed at someone other than me. "I didn't want to send any information over regular channels, in case it was intercepted. The last thing I need is for Thorgana to discover we are hunting her."

"Understood," Skonel said with a stiff nod. He turned his glittering gaze on me, and it was clear he wasn't happy I'd been genned in on this before him. "I assume you will be working with us now, to apprehend her?"

"As needed," Garrett said, his voice still chilly. "Lord Iannis has assigned Miss Baine as my liaison, and since she is a licensed enforcer, I assume that is sufficient for now. If we need more resources, she will contact you to arrange it."

A muscle twitched in Skonel's jaw. "This agency is not at your beck and call—"

Garrett stood up, bracing his palms on the edge of the desk. The air in the room was suddenly suffocating, charged with power, and Skonel leaned back, his eyes wide. "We do not have time to sit around here having a pissing contest about jurisdiction," Garrett hissed, his eyes blazing with cold anger. "The Minister of the Federation personally sent me to Canalo to apprehend Thorgana Mills. He is the highest authority in this nation. Do you wish to take it up with him?"

A lesser man would have started babbling apologies, but Skonel simply held Garrett's gaze for a long moment. "I do not wish to supersede the Minister's orders," he finally said. "I just wish to be kept informed. Thorgana Mills is a dangerous criminal who, from what we've seen in the past, is not afraid to maim or kill large numbers of innocent people to get what she wants. I need to be kept abreast of her activities so I can ensure the safety of our citizens."

"Of course," Garrett said smoothly. He sat back down in his chair, his expression placid once more. "I will endeavor to keep you informed. But so far, we know very little, only that she is likely hiding out here." He gave Skonel a quick rundown of what we did know—that she'd broken out of the prison on purpose, and that she was supposedly heading to Solantha for revenge.

Captain Skonel was stroking his jaw when Garrett finished, his strong features tight with concern. "Revenge could mean any number of things," he said. "Obviously, Miss Baine and Lord Iannis will be prime targets, but so is the Enforcers Guild, as well as any of the Shiftertown inhabitants who turned on her in the end."

"Have you heard any rumors about secret weapons or viruses?" Garrett asked. "Presumably, Thorgana will want to make a big splash when she makes her move. We have reason to believe she may have a few tricks up her sleeve—something her tame scientists might have been working on before they were captured."

"I'm afraid not," Skonel said. "I'll make sure the crew foremen keep their eyes peeled for anything like that though."

"Make sure they report any mysterious illnesses, or strange magical phenomena," I said. "Anything that could seem like a symptom of a virus, or a malicious spell. Thorgana is not above fighting fire with fire—she's still allied with Argon Chartis, as far as we know."

"An excellent point," Garrett said, his lips thinning. "I will never understand why such a brilliant mage chose to ally himself with that deranged woman. She will try to kill him at the first opportunity."

"I agree," I said. Thorgana's hatred of mages was all-inclusive —there was no way she would be content to share power with Chartis. She probably already had a plan in place for how to get rid of him once she didn't need him anymore.

"There was one strange phenomenon recently," Skonel said thoughtfully, drawing our attention back to him. "There have been several reports of fires started here and there, mostly in the Rowanville and Port areas. Nothing serious, and all small, isolated incidents."

"Interesting. A street vendor came up to me the other day and told me someone had set his cart on fire." I briefly recounted the story to them. "Could there be an arsonist on the loose?"

"If there is," Garrett said, "that doesn't necessarily mean they're using magic. And I doubt Thorgana would bother herself with such petty mischief. Setting small fires is too low key for her."

"That doesn't sound like Thorgana," I agreed, "but if someone is going around setting fires, it should be looked into immediately. The last thing we need is an arsonist wreaking havoc while we're preparing for an earthquake."

"Of course. I already have a crew on it," Skonel said tersely, and it occurred to me that he probably thought I was stepping on his toes. Who was I, a low-ranking enforcer, to give him orders? "You should pass the details from the market vendor to them, so they can investigate it with all the rest."

"Yes, Captain," I said, and he looked slightly mollified by my response. "By the way, I heard an interesting rumor at Captain Galling's farewell reception that I've been meaning to take up with you."

"I don't have time to discuss rumors, Enforcer Baine," Skonel said irritably, his back up once more.

"You'll discuss this one," I said firmly. "It's been brought to my attention that the Enforcers Guild has been paying higher bounties to mages, and selectively giving out end-of-year bonuses to the foremen and their cronies. Is this all true?" I demanded.

"Well, yes," Skonel said, sounding flustered. "The system has been in place for decades, maybe even more than a century. I've only held this office for a handful of days, and the bonus system is hardly top of my priority list."

"It should be," I said evenly, holding back the temper simmering in my chest. "It wasn't a big deal for Captain Galling when everyone was in the dark about it, but now that word is getting out, tensions in the Guild are rising. We need to be a unified front, Captain, and that's not going to happen if the establishment keeps showing everyone that inequality is acceptable."

"If you come up with a better system, I would be happy to discuss it," Skonel said stiffly, his cheeks coloring. "But to take the bonuses away now would lead to even more discontent and morale issues. We can't just rip the current system out from underneath them without replacing it with another."

"An excellent point," Garrett said before I could argue with Skonel that it wasn't *my* job to come up with another system—that was his responsibility! "We appreciate your time, Captain, but we really must be going now." He gave me a warning look, his eyes brimming with impatience.

"Of course," Skonel said, standing. "Let me show you out."

"Thanks for the support," I muttered as we got into the elevator.

"I'm sure the issue is important, Miss Baine," Garrett said in a tone that suggested the exact opposite, "but it has nothing to do with finding Thorgana, and I didn't come all this way to sit in his office while the two of you come up with a new bonus system. We must move on."

"Fine." I clenched my jaw and stared straight ahead at the elevator doors, refusing to look at him. I knew part of the reason his words rankled was because he was right, but I still didn't like the way he'd undermined me.

On our way out, I stopped by the sergeant's desk again. "Hey. Has Annia Melcott reported back in for duty yet?"

The trainee shook his head. "Sorry, Enforcer Baine. She's still in Southia, as far as I know."

"Thanks," I said, swallowing my disappointment. I really hoped Annia would come back soon. I'd expected her to return at the same time I came back from Garai, but even her mother hadn't heard from her in a few weeks. I told the trainee to send word to me at the Palace the moment she returned, then headed out the doors after Garrett. Hopefully, she'd be back in the next few days—she would be a real asset to the investigation. And it would be nice to have a true friend around, instead of being forced to chauffeur a man who might very well be the death of my fiancé and one of my closest friends.

11

By the time we stopped outside Boon Lakin's house in Shiftertown, most of my grumpiness had melted away. Riding on my steambike always lifted my spirits a little, but it was the thought of seeing Lakin again that did the trick. Unlike Skonel and Garrett, Lakin would actually be happy to see me.

"Sunaya," Lakin exclaimed when he threw open the door. His smile dimmed slightly when he caught sight of Garrett, but he didn't shirk away from the strange mage. "What brings you here?"

"Official business, I'm afraid," I said with a rueful smile. "Mind if we come in a minute?"

"Sure, sure." Lakin stepped back, letting us enter his small but cozy house. I hadn't been here since before I'd left for Garai, and was pleased to note he'd added some family photographs to the walls and side tables, from the Jaguar Clan he'd left back in Parabas. Included in those pictures was the smiling face of the little girl I'd rescued from the lab in Osero, and I felt a pang in my chest. I hoped she was doing okay. Those children had been through a terrible ordeal—they'd been lucky to make it out alive, since the scientists were experimenting on them with the deadly diseases they'd intended to unleash on the shifter and mage populations.

Before I could allow myself to sink further into the past, my nose caught the scent of a female jaguar shifter—one who came around often, I noted. As the Shiftertown Inspector, Lakin had regular visitors, but none with quite as strong a scent marker as this one.

Flopping onto the couch, I looked up at Lakin with a grin. "New girlfriend?"

He blushed. "It's not official," he said, scratching the back of his sandy hair.

I waggled my eyebrows. "Smells pretty official to me. You have to have been seeing her a few months."

"As fascinating as this sounds," Garrett said dryly as he lowered himself on the couch next to me, "I don't believe we came here to interrogate Inspector Lakin on his love life."

"Which I am incredibly grateful for," Lakin said sincerely as he sank into his arm chair. "What *are* you here for? When I heard you outside the door, I thought maybe you'd come to volunteer as you'd mentioned before, but since you've got a mage with you, I figure that's not the case."

I flinched at that. "Shit. I'm sorry, Lakin." I'd completely forgotten about my promise. "I was absolutely intending on doing that, but Director Toring's unexpected visit kind of threw a wrench in my schedule." The two of us got Lakin up to speed about Thorgana's escape and alleged plans, as well as our progress—or lack thereof—on finding her. We discussed various theories as to where she might be hiding and what plans she might be cooking up, but didn't come up with anything new. We were just circling over the same ground, much to my frustration.

"I wish I could be of more help," Lakin said, his blond brows drawn into a scowl. "It's possible that Thorgana only just arrived, and that's why we haven't heard or seen anything unusual yet. I will definitely forward any rumors or info about the Benefactor straight to you—you know that none of us harbor any love for her," he added darkly.

We thanked Lakin for his time, leaving him with a promise I would get in touch with him as soon as I had a spare moment to volunteer. We hit up the Shifter Courier next, followed by the Herald. Everyone we talked to was very helpful, but nobody had any leads, to our mutual disappointment. I'd expected to get something out of the Herald at least—they were still suspect, even though they were under new management, and I wouldn't have put it past Thorgana to leverage contacts in her former media company in some way. But clearly that was too obvious an angle—if she was here at all, she was being careful to fly under the radar.

By the time we finished with the Herald, it was well past two o'clock. Starving, I dragged Garrett to the diner in Maintown where Annia and I had once shared a meal during our very first case together. As we settled into a booth with a street view window and ordered bowls of hot soup and sandwiches, I couldn't help but wish that it was Annia sitting across from me, instead of Garrett. The director was clever and intelligent, but he didn't know Solantha very well. Annia, like me, had grown up here, and her contacts with the city's underbelly were much better than mine. I often consulted with her when I was working on a tough case, and she usually spotted things I didn't.

"There is another place I would like to check out," Garrett said after he'd finished polishing off a grilled cheese sandwich. "Firegate Federal Credit Union."

My brow furrowed. "A bank? Why?"

"Thorgana was using several banks around the country to funnel money through, and Firegate was one of two banks she used here in Solantha," Garrett explained. "The other—"

"Was Sandin Federal," I said, then scooped a huge spoonful of clam chowder into my mouth. It was my third bowl, and I'd already polished off four grilled cheeses, much to Garrett's astonishment. I guessed he hadn't been paying attention to my eating habits in Garai.

"Ah, yes," Garrett said, a small smile playing on his lips. "I'd forgotten you were the one who shut them down."

"Along with Lakin, Iannis, and Secretary Garidano," I reminded him sharply. I didn't like the admiring way he was gazing at me—I strongly suspected Garrett had a little crush on me. I *had* saved his life, risking my own neck to dive into the stormy sea after he'd been thrown overboard, so I guess it wasn't totally weird. But I was engaged to Iannis, and the fact that Garrett, a mage fully capable of controlling his emotions, was letting me see his interest at all was pissing me off. Just because he was getting the chance to enjoy time away from the office, riding around on a steambike with the exotic shifter girl, didn't give him license to be anything less than professional.

"Of course," Garrett said smoothly, as if he didn't notice my warning tone. "I understand that Fenris has also been of help to you during past investigations and missions?"

"His knowledge comes in handy," I said, turning my attention back to my chowder. Garrett had been subtly tossing questions about Fenris to me all afternoon, and I'd deflected them as best I could, refusing to betray that I knew his game. I wasn't going to hand Fenris over to him on a silver platter.

"I imagine it does," Garrett said. "He has decades of it, if that is to be believed. Has he been studying magical lore all his life?"

"I wouldn't know," I said airily, flagging down the waitress to get the bill. "I've known him less than a year."

"Surely, he's told you about his past, though?" Garrett pressed. "The two of you must be well-acquainted, considering you're both shifters living among mages, and so close to Lord Iannis."

"You got any coin on you?" I asked, sliding the bill over to Garrett after the waitress handed it to me. "I figure we're splitting this."

"I'll take care of it," Garrett said irritably, pulling a hefty purse from the magical pocket in his sleeve. "Are you avoiding my question?"

"No," I said simply as I rose from the table. "I just think that if you want to learn about Fenris's past, the best person to ask would be Fenris. I'm not his biographer, you know." Garrett pressed his lips together. "I'm going to the restroom. Meet you outside."

And with that, I sauntered off before I could give in to the urge to grab Garrett by the collar and punch him in his too-shrewd face.

12

A fter visiting the bank, which turned out to be just as fruitless as the other leads, Garrett and I returned to the Palace. Our dinner meeting was in just a few hours, and he wanted to consult with his assistant to see if he'd found anything useful in the magazine archives. Garrett invited me to come with him, but I begged off, claiming I had another matter that needed my attention.

In reality, I just needed a break from him.

"That good, huh?" Rylan asked as I stormed into my suite. I drew up short, surprised to see him sitting on my sofa, reading a book.

"What are you doing here?" I asked, closing the door behind me with less force than I'd intended. "I thought you'd be on guard rotation or something."

"I was," Rylan said, closing the book and setting it aside, "but Lord Iannis sensed you were returning, so he told me to come meet you. I figured this would be the best place to catch you."

"Huh." My hand drifted up to the *serapha* charm around my neck, and I focused on it. Iannis was downstairs in his Guild office. I rarely thought about the charm that bound the two of us, but I wondered now how often he used it to check on me. He must have done so as I was traveling toward the Mages Quarter, and sensed that I was heading back here. "Well, you can go hang out in your own room until dinner if you want."

"Wait a minute," Rylan said. He stood up and snagged my arm as I tried to brush past him. "What are you going to do, lie on your bed and sulk?"

"Do you have a better idea?" I snarled, twisting out of his grip.

"Yes, actually."

His fist swung toward my face with lightning speed, and I barely managed to duck out of the way. "Slow," he accused, side-stepping my return blow with ease.

"What the hell are you doing?" I shouted as he assaulted me with a barrage of blows—blows I was hard-pressed to deflect as a few landed in my midsection.

"Giving you what you really need," Rylan said, tapping the pin on his chest. His tiger-shifter illusion dropped away, revealing his true face, and his yellow-orange jaguar eyes gleamed with challenge. "When was the last time you sparred, Naya? For shame, you're getting soft!"

I *was* getting soft, I realized as Rylan forced me back across the room. Gritting my teeth, I drove my churning thoughts out of my head, and focused my attention on beating back my pompous cousin. As we exchanged blows, attempted leg sweeps, and went for takedowns, a kind of serenity swept over me. I was no longer worrying about Thorgana or Garrett, trying to predict the next assassination attempt, or to steer prying eyes away from Fenris's secret. I was only in the moment, ducking and weaving, punching and kicking, sweat sliding down my skin as adrenaline scorched my veins.

By the time we were done sparring—one win, three losses—there were a few broken knickknacks and a hole in the wall, but overall, I felt a lot better. Panting, I sank down to the carpeted floor and leaned my sweaty head against the wall.

"Much better," Rylan said across from me, his eyes gleaming with satisfaction.

"I guess I didn't realize how much I needed that." I rubbed my flank, which was still smarting—Rylan had gotten me good with a well-placed sidekick. "You're right. I'm not training enough."

Rylan shrugged. "You've been focusing on your magical studies, so it's understandable. You've only got so much time in the day. I, on the other hand, spar with the other guards regularly, and during the months you were gone, I've been teaching Fenris. He's surprisingly clumsy for a shifter," he added, making a face.

I let out a startled laugh. "For real?" I tried to picture the calm, stoic Fenris in workout gear, sparring with Rylan, and failed miserably. "I have a hard time seeing him outside the library."

"Yeah, and that's pretty strange for a shifter as well." Rylan pinned me with a frank gaze, and my insides squirmed. "Sunaya, I know there's something weird going on with Fenris. Ever since that Garrett fellow showed up, his tension has gone through the roof. I tried sparring with him today, and he was just too unfocused and angry."

"By Magorah," I said, feeling absolutely terrible. I hadn't even given a thought to how Fenris would be coping. Yes, he'd made the decision to leave, and he was probably busying himself with preparations for his departure. But he had to be feeling awfully lonely, and even depressed, as he faced such an uncertain future. I would have to go and visit him tonight, no matter what.

"Sunaya," Rylan said gently, as tears sprang to my eyes. "What is going on?"

I blinked rapidly before the tears could slide down my cheeks. "Fenris's story isn't mine to tell," I said, swallowing against the lump in my throat. I wanted to confide in Rylan, but Fenris was a private person, and damn if I was going to betray his trust. If he didn't feel safe in confiding in Rylan, he had his reasons. "All I can tell you is that Director Toring is a threat to him, and Fenris plans to leave Solantha as soon as Garrett wraps up this investigation into Thorgana."

"Well, shit." Rylan looked saddened by the news. "We've only just become friends, and he's the only other shifter besides you who knows the truth about me. I'll miss having him around."

"Me too." I cleared my throat. "In the meantime, I need to keep Garrett busy and away from Fenris, which is pretty fucking stressful because Garrett is like a dog with a really juicy bone."

Rylan frowned. "So Fenris is in trouble with the law, but Director Toring doesn't have enough on him to do anything about it? And you're hoping to keep it that way?" When I nodded, he tapped his chin thoughtfully. "I imagine that wherever he goes, he'll want to lie low, off the government's radar. I might have a few contacts who can help."

"I don't want you compromising your identity," I said sharply, sitting up straight. "I'm already losing Fenris—there's no way I'm losing you too."

"I won't," Rylan promised, giving me a reassuring smile. Scooting over, he wrapped an arm around my shoulder and drew me against him. "I know how to be discreet, cousin. How do you think I've managed to sneak out of so many boudoirs unscathed?"

I snorted at that. "Because you're a shifter and you have super healing abilities?"

"Spoilsport."

We burst out laughing, and I had to admit it felt really good.

Spending time with my cousin had been just the tonic I needed to wash the sour taste of Garrett's suspicion from my soul. Feeling refreshed, we parted ways to clean up for dinner. My heart was lighter now, and I'd be able to approach this meeting with a clear head.

Dinner was in the Winter Garden room again, with Iannis, Director Chen, Cirin, Garrett, Pillick, and Kardanor. Over pasta, meatballs, and minestrone soup, Garrett and I briefed the others on our progress—or lack thereof—on the Thorgana case. We discussed our plans for tomorrow, which mainly included tracking down her known associates and questioning them. If we didn't find a lead soon, Iannis declared, then perhaps Thorgana was not in Solantha after all. Perhaps a new trace would turn up in some other location, prompting Director Toring to move on with his search while the rest of us focused our attention on earthquake preparations.

Garrett did not look happy about Iannis's suggestion, and I wondered if he'd dig up some additional pretext to stay on, if push came to shove. But he wasn't prepared to argue about it now, so he only nodded his agreement.

The conversation quickly moved to earthquake prep, and Chen and Kardanor briefed us on the project they'd drawn up throughout the day, and the results of the spot inspections done by several mixed teams of mages and engineers. "There are four newish schools and a large hospital in Maintown that are in such bad state that we are ordering them to be shut down right away," Kardanor was saying. "Pending structural repairs, of course."

My eyes widened at the thought of all those children and teachers, suddenly displaced. "What's going to happen in the meantime?" I asked. "Those kids can't be pulled out of school for months. Most of them will have working parents. And the hospital patients need to continue receiving care."

"We know that," Chen said patiently. "We have arranged with the Maintown Council to set up temporary facilities in some large cruise ships in the harbor that we have leased for the next six months. It is quite an undertaking, making these vessels suitable as classrooms and hospital facilities, but we are working as quickly as we can."

"Good," Iannis said with a satisfied nod. "I have no doubt you will take care of it, Director Chen." His violet eyes darkened. "I would like to know what is being done about these neglectful construction companies. Have either of you met with them yet?"

Director Chen nodded. "I called the CEOs of Mendle and Gorax to my office, giving them no time to meet with each other beforehand. Mr. Makis and I interviewed them together, and they have been informed that their entire personal fortunes and lives are forfeit if anyone comes to harm as a result of their shoddy and deceitful practices. In the meantime, large fines have been assessed against them—the gold will come in handy for the cost of leasing the cruise ships." Her expression was stony. "I do not think they will presume to get away with such malpractice again."

"You should have seen their faces, Miss Baine," Kardanor said. Unlike Director Chen, he was grinning from ear to ear, and I couldn't help but smile back. "They were sweating and squirming as if their feet were being held to the fire, babbling promises that they'd do their best to make up for the damage." He curled his lip at that. "They should be imprisoned, of course, but their machines and personnel are very much needed, so we let them off with a warning for now."

"*I* let them off with a warning," Director Chen reminded him, her elegant eyebrows arched. "*You* are merely assisting, Mr. Makis—you do not have any authority."

"Of course, Director," Kardanor said cheerfully, completely

unabashed. "And I am more than happy to assist you in any way you might desire."

I choked on my soup, and Director Chen's face flushed. Cirin's lips twitched, and even Iannis looked amused, though he hid it well. Garrett merely looked annoyed, though I wasn't sure if that was because of Kardanor's obvious flirtation, or because he was sitting through a meeting that no longer had anything to do with him.

"What about the Shiftertown construction companies?" I asked Kardanor, sparing Director Chen the necessity of responding. It was clear she had no idea what to say—the idea of a human male flirting with her was evidently so unthinkable that she didn't know how to react. "Did the two of you interview them as well?"

"Yes," Kardanor said, "but that was a much more pleasant experience. None of them have used systematic fraud and shoddy practices like Mendle and Gorax, and most of their buildings are smaller, which reduces the risk to some extent. Still, they have agreed to donate time and effort toward fixing up those buildings of theirs that aren't quite up to code. They've done a couple of projects in Rowanville as well, and those are mostly acceptable."

"That's great," I said, trying not to beam with pride. I was happy to hear that my fellow shifters had not abandoned their integrity, but not at all surprised. Clan meant everything to us, and the idea of constructing unsafe buildings for our own people was abhorrent.

As soon as dinner was over, Garrett and his assistant bowed out, retreating to their quarters for the evening. The bastards were probably going to hold a war council of their own. Glad to be rid of them, Iannis and I bid the others a good evening, then went to find Fenris. He'd elected to dine in his own room tonight instead of joining us. With Garrett in the room, he would have had to face probing questions, or else eat from a doggy bowl in wolf form, which he considered demeaning.

The lingering scent of steak and potatoes met my nose as Iannis and I entered Fenris's room. We found him sitting in his recliner, a plate on the side table next to him that was clean aside from a leftover bone.

"Enjoy your dinner?" he asked casually as Iannis and I sat down on the edge of Fenris's bed—his room was smaller than mine, with only the bed, dressers, closet, and the single chair and table by the fire.

"As much as can be expected," Iannis said. He raised his hands and spoke a spell, causing the walls around us to shimmer a faint blue. "There," he said, lowering his hands. "We can speak safely now." He turned to me, his expression serious. "Has Garrett learned anything that might put Fenris in jeopardy?"

"No, not really." I told them about the brief exchange between Pillick and Janta, and Garrett's not-so-subtle attempts to question me throughout the day. "All he knows is that Fenris was already a scholar before he came here, and judging by his line of questioning, it's clear he has no idea about your past, Fenris. He's just trying to figure out how to use you as leverage against Iannis."

"Charming," Fenris said tersely, his yellow eyes glimmering with banked ire. "This is only more proof that it is better for me to be on my way, as soon as Garrett is gone. I do not want a repeat of this, Iannis," he insisted when Iannis started to argue. "While you and Garrett were out," he said to me, "Harron, his assistant, was questioning the Palace staff. He likely knows exactly when I joined the household, only some four weeks after Polar ar'Tollis disappeared."

"That doesn't mean they're going to connect the dots," I

pointed out. "Like I said, I don't think Garrett has made the leap."

"Yet," Fenris said darkly. "Director Toring is an intelligent man. It will come to him eventually. I can only hope that by the time it does, he is already back in Dara."

"Agreed," Iannis said, and then changed the subject. It was clear Fenris was only going to be gloom and doom about the situation, and there was no point in discussing it further. "I have been debating what to do about Father Calmias. It seems there is no changing his mind—he will continue to preach his pernicious views on shifters and mages, and spread what he believes to be the Ur-God's true message. While he does not soil his own hands with violence, he has already caused enormous damage with his gospel of hatred and division."

"Maybe we really should kill him," I growled. "To hell with the consequences. At the very least, it'll buy us some time until they install someone new."

"There is another option, though I never considered using it before," Iannis said slowly, his gaze troubled. "A Tua spell that permanently changes a person's attitude and personality. I could use it on Father Calmias to make him forget all about his genocidal tendencies, and instead replace them with a message of tolerance and unity."

"You're joking," Fenris said, looking as astonished as I felt. "I have never heard of such a spell in my life. Is there a mage equivalent?"

"Not that I ever heard of—and if there were, it would be buried deep down in the forbidden archives somewhere," Iannis said. "Using magic to alter an individual's personality like that is highly illegal, and it goes against Resinah's teachings. The First Mage would never have countenanced such a thing, but the Tua are an amoral race who view humans as their playthings, so they have no such qualms about taking their free will from them.

They often use this spell to make a human fall hopelessly in love with them, which is what happened to my grandfather." His tone had taken on a dangerous edge. "It would be far more ethical to simply kill Calmias, as Sunaya says, than it would be to use this spell on him."

There was a long pause as we mulled over the pros and cons.

"Still," Fenris eventually said, "if such a change can be permanently and seamlessly effected, it would be worth a try. Father Calmias cannot be allowed to continue to agitate the populace, and killing him would only upset the humans further, so it's counter-productive. The idea that you have such a spell that could do this...it's amazing," Fenris added, shaking his head in admiration. The scholar inside him had come out in full force, the prospect of new knowledge banishing the demons gnawing at him.

"The suggestion techniques we mages use are far less effective," Fenris explained to me, adopting his lecturing voice. "They are rarely permanent, and usually produce adverse side effects like stuttering, memory gaps, and cognitive dissonance. His acolytes would suspect us of tampering with his mind if Father Calmias emerged with any of those symptoms, but if his personality could be changed without them, they would have no choice but to accept his change of heart as genuine."

"I am still not certain it is the right thing," Iannis insisted. "There may be far-reaching consequences we are not considering, just as my Tua grandmother did not consider anything beyond her own needs when she ensorcelled my grandfather."

"Yeah, but you wouldn't be alive if she hadn't done it," I pointed out. "And that would be a damn shame. No matter how amoral your grandmother's choice was, good came out of it in the end," I added with a smile.

"Very true," said Fenris.

Iannis's jaw flexed, and he looked like he was about to object.

I placed my hand over his atop the bedspread, trying to calm him. "This isn't the same thing at all," I said, squeezing his hand. "You aren't doing this for selfish or personal reasons, like your grandmother did. *Your* aim is to save lives and bring order to our country. That's a worthy cause, Iannis."

"Besides," Fenris added, "Father Calmias's pathological hatred can easily be viewed as a sickness—he is certainly not right in the head if he thinks his benevolent Ur-God truly wishes the destruction of all mages and shifters. As a healer, Iannis, wouldn't you want to cure him if you could?"

Iannis was silent for a long moment, staring into the fire. "I will ask the First Mage for guidance and sleep on it," he finally said. "A large part of me agrees with you both, but I cannot make this decision hastily."

Maybe not, I agreed silently as we bid Fenris a good night and headed back to our quarters. But he would have to do it soon, now that Father Calmias wasn't on Prison Isle anymore. If Thorgana could be broken out as easily as she had, it was only a matter of time before Calmias's own followers decided to rescue him. And it would be a lot better for us if we could hand him over as a changed man, rather than someone fueled by poisonous hate.

13

The next morning, right after an early breakfast, Garrett and I left to interview our list of Thorgana's associates. I'd half considered bringing a carriage around so Rylan could accompany us, but Garrett had seemed eager to use the steambike again, and I didn't want him to think anything was wrong.

Our first stop was the Mendle family, who had just recently moved into a new mansion in Maintown. It was a ginormous affair of stone and glass, with a huge, cobblestone paved round-about in front, and gardens that stretched around the sides and to the back for who knew how far. Heavy silk curtains hung in the six-by-six casement windows spanning the two stories, and several chimneys jutted from the slate roof. Just how much house did these people need, anyway? Of course, most of the guests who regularly attended the Benefactor's lavish parties lived in opulent style. Maybe they were planning to host similar parties, now that Thorgana was no longer able to do so.

A wrought-iron gate prevented us from parking in front of the door, so I left my bike at the curb, then flashed my enforcer bracelet at the lone guard manning the small booth outside the gate. He let us in immediately, then picked up a phone to let the house staff know we were coming.

"The Mendles must be doing very well," Garrett remarked as we approached the house, skirting around the stone fountain at the center of the roundabout. The leaves on the bushes edging the fountain were turning burnished shades of red and gold. No doubt they grew brilliant flowers during the spring and summer. "This is quite the place."

"From what I understand, they just moved in," I said, trotting up the stacked-stone steps. I reached for the heavy brass knocker, then recoiled with a hiss moments before my fingers brushed against it. "What the fuck?"

"What is it?" Garrett asked, sounding alarmed.

"Silver." I glared at the offending knocker, my fingers twitching toward my crescent knives. Not that I'd be able to cut the knocker off with them, but someone ought to. "Guess shifters aren't welcome here."

"That's right," Garrett said, his gaze lighting with understanding. "You are allergic to silver. I completely forgot." Stepping forward, he grabbed the knocker and rapped sharply on the door.

I glared at him. "Seriously? That's it?"

He turned to me, a puzzled frown on his face. "What? I knocked on the door for you. Isn't that what you wanted?"

"Yes," I said through gritted teeth. I didn't know why I was acting offended that Garrett wasn't showing more consideration for me. We weren't friends. Still, if I pushed emotion aside, it was an interesting tidbit, this knocker. Were the Mendles an anti-shifter family? Had they supported the Resistance in any way?

Approaching footsteps sounded beyond the door, and it opened before Garrett could say anything else. "Good morning," a human male dressed in a dark suit greeted us—the butler. He had thinning blond hair and sallow skin, and there were dark circles beneath his pale brown eyes. "How can I help you?"

"Umm, we're looking for Mr. and Mrs. Mendle." Normally, I would have sounded a lot more official, but the fetid smell of sickness was wafting from beyond the open door, and man, it was *strong*. My skin crawled, and I fought the urge to back away. "Are they in?"

"Mr. Mendle is at the office, and the missus is indisposed, I'm afraid," the butler said. A gust of wind blew past us, and he looked like he was about to topple over. "If you'd like, I can take a message."

"This is a matter of some urgency—" Garrett began, but I cut him off.

"That would be just fine." I took out a pad and pen, scribbled down a note, and handed it to the servant. "Please have Mrs. Mendle call me at her earliest convenience."

As soon as the door closed, I grabbed Garrett by the sleeve and dragged him away from the house as fast as I could without looking like we were running away.

"What are you *doing*?" he snapped, struggling to break my grip. "Why did you cut me off like that!"

I refused to answer him until we were beyond the gates and out of earshot of the guard.

"Didn't you notice how sick that guy was?" I demanded, finally letting go of him. "There's no way we were going in there and interviewing Mrs. Mendle today." I shook my head. "Something was definitely wrong."

"Don't be ridiculous," Garrett said, smoothing the sleeve of his robe where I'd grabbed him. "You're a shifter—you don't succumb to human illnesses. And neither do I. We would have been perfectly safe."

Normally, I would have agreed with him. But... "I just had a bad feeling, okay?" I snapped, folding my arms across my chest.

Damn, did it get colder, or did I just have the chills? "That sickness, whatever it is, was affecting the whole house. Even the butler was barely able to stand, for Magorah's sake. Just because I can't get sick doesn't mean I can't accidentally pass the disease to someone else. There are human children who I help look after. Besides, it won't do any good to interview Mrs. Mendle while she's so ill. She needs to be coherent."

"Very well," Garrett said, but from the sound of his voice, I could tell he was anything but pleased by my explanation. "We'll do it your way and come back another time. But I don't have forever, Miss Baine. As Lord Iannis himself said, if I don't find any leads soon, I'll have to move on."

"I know, and I've been wondering why a man of your importance, with a large and growing organization at his beck and call, would be doing this sort of house call at all. Surely the boss doesn't need to lower himself like this." I arched a brow, deliberately needling him.

"A bit of fieldwork now and then helps keep my skills fresh," he said stiffly. After a moment, he added, "And this case is high-profile enough to merit my personal attention. I don't see why we are even discussing this, not when every minute that passes is so precious. We should be heading to see Mr. Mendle at his office. Not bickering about why I'm here."

"Sure, we can do that. I just didn't want you to feel like I was wasting your precious time." His eyes flashed, and I bit back the rest of my snarky retort. Garrett was right—there wasn't time for bickering.

We got back onto the bike, and drove to Mr. Mendle's office, which was on the other side of Maintown. Unfortunately, he wasn't in—he was out overseeing some emergency repairs—so we moved on to the next people on our list, a banker and his socialite wife, and a rich playboy in the diamond trade who lived in a tricked-out bachelor's pad in Rowanville. Neither of them had seen Thorgana or had any clue about her whereabouts, and as my nose could detect no lie, we had nothing to show for our efforts.

Maybe Thorgana really isn't here, I thought as we rode back to the Palace for lunch. I wasn't too keen on the idea of giving up if there was a chance she was lurking in my city, but if this was an excuse to send Garrett packing, I'd gladly pounce on it. I could always continue sniffing her out after he was gone.

I WAS TEMPTED to go back to my room for a bit of solitude, but I forced myself to follow Garrett straight to the Winter Garden room. *It seems like every meal is going to be a working one these days*, I thought resentfully as I sat down to lunch with Chen, Kardanor, Garrett, and Pillick.

To my surprise, I spotted Fenris curled up on the window bench in wolf form. No doubt he'd chosen to come so he could keep up on developments. The kitchen had sent up shepherd's pie today, one of my least favorite meals, but I forced myself to pile two helpings on my plate and dig in. I would need my strength to get through the rest of the day.

As we ate and talked, I noticed that Chen seemed to have warmed to Kardanor. The two were sitting close together, chattering enthusiastically about the progress they were making on their various projects. At one point, Chen even gave him a rare smile. Her cheeks flushed as her eyes met mine, and I bit back a grin. Oh boy. Director Chen was in *big* trouble.

I was just considering the idea of teasing Director Chen about her new beau when Iannis walked in. My jaw dropped in shock as my eyes flitted from Iannis to his guest—Father Calmias, dressed in a fresh set of white robes, and glowing with inner peace and serenity.

"*Lord Iannis,*" Director Chen exclaimed in horror, shooting to her feet. Fenris and I exchanged a glance. Could it be...? "Why have you brought Father Calmias in here, with no restraints?"

"There is no need to fear," Iannis said, pulling out a chair for himself and another for his unorthodox guest. "Father Calmias has renounced his previous gospel. He is being released today as a free man." He looked over the room. "Now be seated."

"That's outrageous," Garrett said, staring at Iannis as though he'd lost his mind. He remained standing even as the rest of us took our seats. "Father Calmias is indirectly responsible for hundreds of casualties."

"For which I will spend the remainder of my life repenting," Father Calmias said gravely. I nearly fell out of my chair at the profound sorrow in his voice, which my nose told me was absolutely genuine. "I have done terrible things in the name of the Ur-God, things I now realize must have been planted in my head by some evil spirit."

"And how did you come to this realization?" Garrett probed, sounding highly skeptical.

"The Ur-God came to me in a dream last night." Father Calmias lifted his face to the ceiling, a misty sort of awe in his eyes. "He showed me a grand vision, where the three races existed together in harmony, and taught me that my real purpose was to help guide my parishioners toward peace, rather than turning their hearts against their neighbors." He bowed his head in shame. "I cannot believe it has taken me all this time to see the path to true wisdom."

"*By the Lady,*" Fenris said to me in mindspeak, sounding astonished. "*He really went through with it! That Tua spell works even better than I imagined!*"

"*He must have,*" I agreed, turning my attention to Iannis. His eyes were twinkling with delight despite the calm mask he wore. "*When did you do the spell on him?*"

"*This morning,*" Iannis said, "*after I came back from the temple. It would seem that you and Fenris were right to insist—the change is remarkable,*" he admitted reluctantly. "*But we shall see what happens.*"

"Father Calmias," I said, deciding to test out his new personality, "I attended one of your sermons in Maintown, not long before you were imprisoned. It was very interesting, and I'd like to ask you about some things that were said."

"I'm sure I said many things of which I am now ashamed," Father Calmias said heavily. He clasped his hands together atop the table and met my eyes. "Please ask whatever you wish, child."

I cleared my throat, trying not to be thrown off by his drastic change in attitude. He seemed wise and gracious now, almost grandfatherly. "I overheard some members of the congregation gossiping about secret weapons being developed by the Resistance. Do you know anything about this?"

"Other than the viruses?" Calmias asked, and I nodded. He hummed under his breath for a moment, thinking. "I'm not sure —I was never personally involved in any of that, though I heard many things. A few of my parishioners were indeed Resistance members, but the viruses were the main thing they had up their sleeve. If they are still around, I will talk to them about letting go of any malicious intentions, and returning to a normal life."

"If you are serious about peace," Iannis said, "you should gather your parishioners and give them the same message. Do a radio broadcast and tell them about your vision from the Ur-God. If you do not spread the message far enough, there will continue to be unnecessary loss of life."

A tremor shook the walls as he spoke, and Father Calmias paled a little, gripping the edge of the table.

"Yes, of course. You are right, Lord Iannis," he said faintly when the shaking had subsided, his eyes wide as he looked around in shock. "It would seem that the Ur-God agrees. I shall follow your suggestions immediately."

"Are you certain there was no other weapon in the works?" I pressed. "Nothing else that Thorgana might be planning to use against us now?"

"Well, the viruses were never delivered to Solantha's Resistance chapter," Father Calmias said, eyes far off in thought. "And when they field tested the few vials they did have, they found that the viruses were insufficiently powerful to cause a real epidemic. Only a few dozen mages and shifters died, and the improved versions they were waiting on never arrived. As you can imagine, the Resistance soldiers administering the tests were very disappointed. So you should be safe on that front."

"Thank you, Father. You have no idea how much that gladdens my heart," I said, letting out a sigh of relief.

"Wait!" Father Calmias exclaimed, jerking upright in his chair. "I do remember one other thing. There *was* another secret weapon, of which Thorgana showed me pictures once, that was said to be very effective. She called it the Magic Eraser, or the Eraser for short."

My mouth went dry.

"The Magic Eraser?" Iannis demanded. "Surely that title is a misnomer. There is no device that can erase magic."

"This one can," Father Calmias insisted. "Or at least, Thorgana seemed to think so. It certainly doesn't look magical, though—the pictures showed a strangely shaped metal object, about the size of a human skull. Thorgana said it is very heavy, and that placing it close to a mage for a mere twenty minutes results in irreversible erasure of his or her magic. The older ones die soon after, since the magic is what unnaturally prolongs their lives."

"Preposterous," Garrett exclaimed, his eyes wide with anger

and alarm. "If such a metal existed, it would be strictly regulated, perhaps even banned by the Accords."

"It could be a new discovery," Iannis said thoughtfully, rubbing his chin. "The humans have always been more interested in technology than we are. As unlikely as it may seem, they may have found some naturally occurring metal capable of such devastating power."

"Are there any other side effects?" Director Chen asked Father Calmias. Her face was paler than normal, and I could smell the shock and unease coming off her. "Any kind of warning sign that would tell mages if the object is near?"

Father Calmias shook his head. "It is noiseless and odorless. Thorgana said that the victims feel a terrible nausea, but only once the damage is done. By then it is too late. She also said—" and here, his gaze turned to me, "—that if used on a shifter, it results in them permanently being fixed in their current form."

I gaped. "You mean if it was used on me in panther form, I would never be able to change back into a human?"

"Yes," Father Calmias confirmed, nodding.

"It's impossible to say how it might affect you," Iannis said, eyes full of worry, "seeing as how you are both shifter and mage. Maybe it would be worse, or maybe it wouldn't affect you at all." His eyes hardened as he turned back to Father Calmias. "What happened to this Magic Eraser? Why hasn't Thorgana put it to use yet, if it was so effective?"

"The research team never managed to replicate their one working prototype," Father Calmias said, staring down at the table. "Apparently, the material is exceedingly rare, and there must have been an accident with the viruses they were also working on, because all the members of the team suddenly died from some kind of infection." Iannis and I exchanged a look —*that* didn't sound ominous. "I think the prototype would have been sent to Thorgana, but I have no idea if she ever received it or not. It has been some time since we last spoke."

We questioned Father Calmias about the weapon a little bit more, but once it was clear he didn't know anything else, we sent him on his way with an escort. No doubt there would be a celebration at his release—at least until his followers got to hear their pastor's new gospel. I wondered if they would accept it, or if they would turn on him. I hoped it was the former—we really didn't need them to seek out some other bigot catering to their prejudices, even if that was more than likely to be the case. After all, people tended to seek out those who reaffirmed their own biases.

ONCE FATHER CALMIAS WAS GONE, the rest of us immediately launched into a discussion about the Magic Eraser. Garrett and Pillick refused to believe such an object existed, and Director Chen seemed torn. Iannis wasn't willing to dismiss the possibility completely, but I could tell even he was skeptical. It was simply beyond the ability of these mages to conceive that a man-made object could strip them of their power. Kardanor wisely said nothing, keeping his own counsel on the matter.

"Regardless of whether you believe this weapon exists or not," I said loudly, interrupting them, "it doesn't change the fact that Father Calmias definitely believes every word he said to us. Unless Thorgana lied to him about it, and I can't see why she'd spin up a story about such a powerful device, we have to assume this thing exists."

"She could have made it up to convince him and his followers that the Resistance had a good chance of winning," Garrett pointed out. "I'm sure she received lots of funding from Father Calmias and his parishioners. If they thought that the

Resistance didn't stand a chance, they might have withdrawn their support."

That was possible, but it didn't really sound like the kind of thing Thorgana would do. We argued about it for a little while, but in the end, we agreed we should at least assume the object existed until proven otherwise.

"I wonder where such a weapon would best be deployed to do the most harm," Chen said. "Surely it would be Dara, rather than Solantha, since the capital has the highest concentration of powerful mages? Even if Thorgana did flee here, she could have arranged to have the device smuggled into the Capitol building during the next Convention. If she could cripple all or most of the Chief Mages and the Minister in one go, the effect would be devastating."

"I will have the building searched immediately," Garrett said, his face hardening. "Pillick, I want you to take care of tightening security. No human will be smuggling such an atrocious object onto the Capitol grounds, not on my watch." His hazel eyes glittered dangerously.

"I will do the same for the Palace," Iannis said. He reached for my hand under the table and squeezed it a little harder than necessary. "I wouldn't put it past Thorgana to force you to live as a panther for the rest of your days, so try to remain in human form unless you absolutely have to shift."

"I will," I promised, my veins icing at the very thought. Permanently turning me into an animal before Iannis and I were wed would be a horrible vengeance that fit Thorgana's brand to a T. "We should make sure any large or heavy parcels delivered to the Palace are opened and searched before being allowed inside. And all unexpected deliveries should be subjected to an automatic search."

"We'll put a team of human servants on it," Iannis said, nodding. "They won't be at risk."

"Do you think my predecessor is at all aware of this Magic Eraser?" Director Chen asked, her brow furrowed. "I am having a hard time envisioning any mage being okay with the existence of such a terrible device."

"I doubt it," Iannis said. "Argon Chartis may hate the establishment now, but he is still a mage, and he would not want Thorgana to be in possession of a weapon that could destroy him so completely. He is not an idiot—he must suspect that she plans to get rid of him when he is no longer useful, as he is no doubt planning to do to her. He likely thinks that once he is the last mage standing, it will be very easy to do away with Thorgana."

"Yeah, well, if this Eraser thing really exists, then he's gonna be in for a nasty surprise," I said with a grim smile.

"Let's hope Chartis never needs to find out that he does not have the upper hand," Garrett said. "As Miss Baine says, if this thing does exist, we must make every effort to find it and destroy it quickly. Since it will likely be with Thorgana, we can kill two birds with one stone." He smiled fiercely, and I recognized the gleam in his eyes—it was the thrill of the hunt. The bastard was far from ready to give up.

14

Garrett and I had planned to spend the rest of the day going down the long list of Thorgana's associates, but it turned out he had an urgent transmission from Dara to deal with, giving me an unexpected reprieve. I spent an hour on my Loranian lessons with Fenris, then headed down to Shiftertown with Rylan to volunteer, as I'd promised I would.

Lakin was more than happy to see me, and I spent the rest of the afternoon helping him deal with small-claims cases. It was frustrating work, but I was surprised and pleased to see that most of the shifters I dealt with no longer viewed me with resentment. In fact, they treated me with respect, and even a certain amount of admiration in some cases.

More proof that my role in society is changing, I thought as I rode home. And wasn't that the kicker, that I considered the Palace my home? Once, it had been a prison, and I'd been a bottom-rung enforcer, shunned by society. Now I was being viewed as a role model. The weight of that responsibility sat heavily on my shoulders, and I realized I was going to have to be more careful about my reputation than ever. I was, in many ways, the bridge that supported the tenuous peace between shifters and mages right now. If I fell, many others would be affected.

I parked my bike in the garage, then headed up the stairs to my room in the west wing while Rylan went to grab snacks for us from the kitchens. But before I could get far, Garrett called my name, and I turned to see him striding up the hall after me.

"What is it?" I asked, unable to keep the annoyance from my voice. Couldn't he get through a single day without me? I planted my hands on my hips as he came to a stop in front of me, and frowned as I got a good look at him. His eyes were bright, and there was no mistaking the air of buoyancy around him despite the mask of calm he wore. "Did you make some kind of breakthrough?"

"Yes." His hazel eyes darted around, and he lowered his voice. "Is there somewhere we might speak privately?"

Holding back a sigh, I steered him to the sitting room in the east wing, where guests could sit and talk outside of their own quarters. It was a spacious common room of sorts, decorated in pale pink and gold, with small, ornate chandeliers hanging from the ceiling, and thick rugs. There were two groupings of pink-and-gold-striped furniture on opposite sides of the space, each with their own fireplace, and wing-backed chairs with small tables in the center of the room. I elected to sit in one of the chairs, so there was no chance of Garrett sitting next to me, and he followed suit.

"All right," I said, crossing my right ankle over my left knee as I leaned back. "Tell me what you've found."

"Unfortunately, this is not about Thorgana, but Lord Iannis."

Icy fear shot straight down my spine, but I forced my body to remain relaxed. I would not let my emotions betray me, or my friends.

"I strongly suspect there is a dark secret between the Chief Mage and your mutual friend, Fenris, that could have grave consequences for them both," Garrett continued. "And as the Director of Federal Security, I cannot turn a blind eye." He let out a regretful sigh that would have been very convincing if not for my shifter senses, and I had to make a concerted effort not to curl my hands into fists. *The smarmy bastard's enjoying this.*

"Despite my initial misgivings about you, Sunaya," Garrett continued, "I have grown fond of you, and I do not want to see you caught up in ancient affairs that are beyond your control. I promise I will warn you before I act, so that you may make yourself scarce, if you will confirm my suspicions."

"That would be hard to do, considering I have absolutely no idea *what* you suspect," I said, confusion in my voice. "Honestly, I don't know what you're going on about, Garrett. And whatever it might be, I'm not going to believe it. Iannis and Fenris are honest and decent men, and have proven their firm commitment against the Resistance on more than one occasion."

"Oh, I don't suspect them of that kind of treason," Garrett said with an unconcerned wave. "Lord Iannis is a loyal member of the Federation and despises the Resistance scum, no doubt about that. But like other powerful men, he is not averse to bending the laws when it suits his purposes, and I believe he and Fenris have done so in a manner that cannot be allowed to go unpunished."

"If they have, then I know nothing about it," I said firmly.

"It does you no favors to lie to me, Sunaya," Garrett said, his face hardening. "Surely you have noticed that Fenris is a very unusual shifter. My assistant has drawn up a list of the books he has requested over the three years of his sojourn in Solantha, and a most suggestive pattern emerged. His scholarly interests coincide closely with that of a particular fugitive who once escaped me, who was also a noted scholar of magical history. That cannot be coincidence. If there is any chance the two are connected, it is my duty to investigate." He leaned forward a little, his gaze intent. "For your own sake, Sunaya, you must help me uncover the truth."

I laughed in his face, which was better than what I really wanted to do to him. Really, the nerve! This bastard had known me for all of a few months, and he thought I would turn my back on my friends just because I'd once saved his life?

"Garrett," I finally said, adopting a soothing tone—he looked pissed now. "I know that you're stressed, what with the constant setbacks in our hunt for Thorgana, and I can completely understand your need to make some kind of capture or arrest. But Fenris has an annoyingly high respect for law and order—he would never do anything illegal. I think you're letting your suspicious nature carry you away, or maybe you're just grasping at straws for some way to eliminate Iannis as a rival." I allowed my own expression to harden. "I was there when the Minister pitted the two of you against each other, and I saw how much the idea of nabbing the highest office in the land meant to you. If that's your motive for this crazy line of reasoning, that is absolutely despicable on your part, Garrett. I expected better of you."

Garrett flinched at the accusation, giving me a fleeting moment of satisfaction. But he quickly rallied. "You misunderstand, Sunaya," he began, but I rose from my chair, done with this conversation. "Don't walk away from me," he growled as I turned. "We aren't finished here!"

"But we are," I said coldly, spinning around to face him. There was an interesting mixture of guilt and determination coming off Garrett, but I refused to indulge him further. "I saved your life, buddy, and I've made every effort to assist you in your mission here. The fact that you would even try to make me turn against the man I love, a man who has selflessly risked himself for the sake of the Federation time and again, is unspeakably insulting."

I stormed out of the room before Garrett could say

anything else and headed back to my chambers. It wasn't hard to look like I was angry—my inner beast was furious, itching to unsheathe her claws so we could shred that forked tongue of Garrett's. I wanted to silence him for good, before he struck the deadly blow that would spell the end for Iannis and Fenris.

And myself, too, I reminded myself as I flung my door open. I wouldn't let the two most important men in my life go down without a fight, and I didn't see how that would end in anything but death for me. Besides, with the kind of Chief Mage the Minister would nominate in Iannis's stead, Solantha would soon backslide into the same cesspit of hatred and division the Resistance had stirred up before. No, I couldn't allow that to happen. We had to figure out what to do about Garrett.

My front door banged against the wall, and Rylan jumped up from the couch, alarmed. There were crumbs on his livery, no doubt from the half-eaten platter of meat and cheese beside him.

"I wondered what was keeping you," he said as I stalked over to the sitting area. "What the hell happened?"

"Director Toring has happened," I spat, snatching up a cracker. I slapped some cheese and salami onto it, then crammed it into my mouth. "The fucker is closing in on us," I growled around a mouthful of food. Knowing that it was only a matter of time before Rylan found out anyway, I spilled the whole story to him while we finished off the platter together.

"By Magorah," Rylan said, his face stark white. "Fenris told me a little bit about his past, but he left out the fact that he was a fucking Chief Mage, and number one on the Federal Government's Wanted list. We can't wait any longer. We need to get him out of here now."

"Yes." My stomach plummeted into my shoes at the thought, but I refused to cry or howl about it—I didn't have the luxury of emotion. "Let's go talk to Iannis," I said, jumping out of my chair. "He'll have a plan."

We hurried down the hall, clutching firmly to the hope that Fenris had made sufficient preparations, and that Iannis's brilliant mind had already conjured up a foolproof escape plan. Running away at this juncture might be as dangerous as staying, though. Could Garrett have told me what he suspected in hopes of catching Fenris as he sneaked off? He and his cursed assistant would be watching, waiting for the moment to pounce. Unless Iannis ensured they were sufficiently distracted, we were going to need a fucking miracle, and I wasn't sure we had any more of those left.

"Dira," I said, skidding to a halt in front of the Mages Guild reception desk. "I need to speak to Lord Iannis, urgently."

She held up a finger, and I gnashed my teeth, noticing she was on the phone. It seemed like an eternity—though in reality, it was less than a minute—before she finally hung up. "I'm sorry, Miss Baine, but Lord Iannis was called away."

"Called away?" I echoed, my voice sounding hollow to my ears. "To where? Did something happen?" *And why the hell hadn't he told me?*

"A quake triggered a catastrophic landslide in Seros, and he left immediately to assist in the rescue. He asked me to relay the message to you, and to tell you he apologizes for not getting word to you himself." Dira must have noticed the stricken look on my face, because her expression softened a little. "I'm sorry, Miss Baine. He won't be back for at least two days."

Two days. Rylan and I exchanged a look, and I knew he was thinking the exact same thing I was.

We were fucked.

15

I spent a sleepless night in my own bed, tossing and turning as my mind chewed on the various disasters that loomed every which way I turned. The earthquake preparations were moving along, but not as fast as I'd have liked, and Iannis's sudden departure wasn't helping matters. Thorgana was still nowhere to be found, very possibly in possession of a weapon that could destroy magic. And Garrett was sniffing at Fenris's heels like a bloodthirsty hound.

As soon as we heard that Iannis had left town, Rylan and I had sought out Fenris. He'd been in his room, buried in spell books as he continued his search for spells that could help us with the earthquake prep. He'd found a few small ones, but nothing terribly helpful. And his mood had only grown darker when we told him what Garrett had discovered.

"I'm not leaving," he said to us when we were finished. "Not yet," he amended when I opened my mouth, flabbergasted, to protest. "Doing so right after Garrett warned you, Sunaya, would not only be an admission of guilt, but it would also implicate you. I would like to bid farewell to Iannis if at all possible, and I want to make a few more preparations."

"Fuck the preparations," I snarled, grabbing him by the front of his tunic. "We can send you whatever you might need. Why are you being so blasé about this? This is your life on the line!"

"So it is," Fenris growled, knocking my hand away. His yellow gaze simmered with a multitude of emotions—anger, despair, defiance. "And as it is my life, I think I should be allowed to decide what to do with it. I am not ready to leave yet, Sunaya." He crossed his arms over his chest. "If I change my mind, I will let you know."

I wanted to shout at him that he was being stupid, but the implacable look on his face stopped me dead in my tracks. Nothing I said to him would matter.

"Fenris," Rylan said in a soft voice, drawing Fenris's hard gaze away from mine. "The offer I made you earlier today still stands. I have contacts in the South, and the Midwest. Both can help you resettle."

Fenris nodded. "I may take you up on it. But for now, I must get back to my books." He squeezed my shoulder, his face softening. "Don't worry so, Sunaya. I have lived long and seen much in my lifetime. Enough to know that, even if I die, this will not be the end for me." The look he gave me was hardly a consolation. I could barely imagine my life without Fenris in it. He was such an intrinsic part of my inner circle that the idea of being without him very nearly broke me.

Still, this wasn't my choice and I had to respect his, if only because I knew he'd respect mine if our positions were reversed. So I'd hugged him hard and held back the tears long enough to make it back to my room before dissolving into a heap on my bed. Why was life so fucking unfair? Why did Fenris have to face the death penalty for doing what would be a good deed in any sane person's book? He deserved so much better. Was the Creator going to strip all my friends from me, one by one? Noria was slaving away in the mines, Annia was off in Southia, Roanas was dead. Who was next?

My alarm woke me barely an hour after I'd finally managed to fall asleep, and I seriously considered smashing it to bits. But Garrett had a few more interviews to do this morning, and I couldn't allow him to go nosing about my city unaccompanied. So I showered, dressed, and put my game face on. I wasn't going to let him see how much our conversation last night had shaken me. That wasn't just because doing so would piss me off. If he knew how much he'd affected me, it'd make his bloodhound senses go into overdrive, and that must be avoided at all costs. No, it was much better to point him in Thorgana's direction and let him have at.

I was just on my way out the door when the telephone in my sitting room rang. I debated ignoring it, but I so rarely received calls in my room—what if it was Iannis?

"Hello?" I said, snatching it from the receiver and trying not to sound like death warmed over.

"Naya!" Comenius's frantic voice burst from the speaker. "I need your help. Rusalia is missing!"

Shock and dismay jolted my system, driving the last vestiges of sleep from me. "I'm on my way," I said. "Give me fifteen."

I slammed down the phone, then went across the hall and banged on Rylan's door.

He opened it, still rubbing the sleep from his eyes with one balled-up fist. When he opened his mouth to ask what in the hell I was doing there, I waved off his words with one hand.

"I need you to meet Garrett and Pillick in the Winter Garden today and go with them," I ordered. "I've got an important errand to run, and I don't want that asshole tramping around Solantha unaccompanied."

"What errand?" Rylan demanded. "And who's going to protect you if I'm not by your side?"

"Com's daughter is missing. I'll take Fenris—he'll be protection enough," I said sternly when Rylan looked like he was about to protest. "He needs to get his grumpy tail out of the Palace for a little while anyway, and this way I can keep an eye on him. It's not like I can send *him* with Garrett."

"Fine. I'll tell them you were called away on an urgent enforcer matter. But be *careful*, Sunaya." He grabbed my upper arm as I was about to turn away. "For both your *and* Fenris's sake."

I nodded, then dashed down the hall toward Fenris's room. Part of me worried Garrett would think I was dodging him after our argument, and while he was half right, I would have to risk it. Comenius was more important than Garrett's feelings.

Fenris didn't answer when I knocked on the door, so I unlocked it with a spell, then kicked it open.

"What?" he snapped, shielding his eyes against the light as I stalked in. He was in bed, his naked form covered by the sheets, and by the looks of things, he'd been cuddling a book. Weirdo. "Can't a man get some sleep around here?"

"Not these days," I growled, shutting the door behind me. "Comenius's daughter has gone missing, and I need an escort so I can go help him. I've unloaded the escort duty for Toring on Rylan in the meantime. I'd really appreciate it if you came with me," I added, softening my voice. "I don't have anyone else to turn to. Please."

Fenris sighed. "Of course I'll come." He sat up, the sheet sliding down to his hips, and I raised an eyebrow as I noticed how much more defined his pecs and abs were now. "What is that look for?" he asked, a little irritably.

I grinned despite myself. "Nothing. You're just looking a little ...scholarly these days." My gaze went back down to his abs.

"My eyes are up here," Fenris said dryly, and when I met his gaze, I was relieved to see he looked amused. "My sparring sessions with Rylan have motivated me to take better physical care of myself. I was tired of getting beaten so easily."

"I'll say." Lips twitching, I turned around and opened the door. "Cover those muscles up and meet me outside. The last thing I need is all the women in Solantha throwing themselves at you while we're out today."

Fenris snorted as I shut the door behind me, and I grinned again. But my amusement faded when I reminded myself that, pretty soon, the women in Solantha would no longer have the opportunity to throw themselves at Fenris. He was leaving, and I needed to enjoy what little time I had left with him. Even if the world seemed to be crumbling around us.

COMENIUS WAS an absolute wreck when we arrived—his clothing rumpled, his hair sticking up in all directions from having run his hands through it so many times. His cornflower-blue eyes were frantic as he paced back and forth in his living room. Elania was gone—her shop was opening in ten minutes, and she needed to see to her customers. But she'd left soothing chamomile tea for Comenius before she left, and had made breakfast for Fenris and me to eat while Comenius filled us in.

"I keep thinking about how I could have done better with her," Comenius said, still pacing. "How I could have been more tolerant and more understanding. But Rusalia is so outrageously rude all the time that I couldn't go on ignoring her bad behavior. She insulted Elania to her face last night after refusing to help her in the kitchen, so I sent her to bed without dinner. Elania and I were up late discussing how to deal with her constant tantrums, and she must have overheard our angry words. I woke up this morning to a note on my nightstand from Rusalia, and my bedroom window open." He scrubbed a hand over his face. "She must have climbed down the fire escape."

"I'm so sorry, Com," I said, not sure what else to say. I wasn't used to dealing with belligerent children—I likely would have lost my temper with her much earlier, if I'd been in Com's shoes. "Can I see the note? Maybe she left some clue."

Comenius dug it out of his tunic pocket and passed it to me. "It's in Pernian," he said when I smoothed out the wrinkled piece of paper. "She merely writes that she hates Elania and me, and that she is leaving and will never return." A tear slid down his stubble-roughened cheek.

"Oh, Com." Abandoning my half-eaten breakfast, I rose from the kitchen table and enfolded him in a hug. "It's going to be okay," I said, hugging him tight. "We're going to find her, even if I have to tear the city apart."

"Don't lose hope," Fenris said gruffly. "She's not the first child to have run away, and since she does not know the city at all well, chances are good we'll be able to track her down quickly."

Comenius nodded, returning my embrace. His shoulders loosened slightly, but I knew he wouldn't fully relax until his daughter was returned, safe and sound. Releasing him, I forced him to sit at the kitchen table and help us come up with a list of places to look for her. Unfortunately, we couldn't think of where to begin—the school had been shut down for structural repairs, and Rusalia hadn't been around long enough to make any friends.

"She's refused to go to the replacement school on the cruise ship," Comenius said tiredly. "She claims she cannot understand the lessons, her classmates are all horrid, and the teachers don't want her around."

Big surprise, I thought, but I didn't say it aloud. "We'll have to track her the old-fashioned way, then. By scent," I explained at

Comenius's confused look. "Do you have a piece of clothing she's recently worn, that Fenris can sniff? He hasn't met her yet."

Comenius retrieved the girl's nightgown, and Fenris changed into wolf form before taking a good sniff. Shifters could scent things better in animal form, and we decided it was best that I stay in human form since Rusalia didn't know Fenris. Com was clearly torn about staying behind, but we convinced him that given her hostile mood, it might be easier for us to approach her and convince her to return. She'd recognize me on sight, at least, even if she didn't like me. Besides, if she changed her mind and returned home, she should not find the door locked. Promising Com that we'd update him as soon as we could, Fenris and I went out to the fire escape, hoping to pick up her scent from there.

"She did indeed use the fire escape to leave," Fenris said, his bushy wolf's tail high in the air as he sniffed the ground. *"Let's hope she did not go too far."*

Leaving the steambike parked outside Comenius's shop, I followed Fenris on foot. A few shoppers gave us strange glances —it wasn't unheard of for shifters to walk around in wolf form, but it was a little unusual to see one sniffing around the way Fenris was doing. We followed Rusalia's scent all the way down to Market Street, then promptly lost it amongst the crowds of people and the delicious scents of roasting meat and baked goods.

"There are too many other scents here." Fenris shook his great wolf head. *"I do not think I will be able to pick up her trail again."*

"Dammit." I pursed my lips, scanning the crowd, but I didn't see any sign of Rusalia here. Had she come down this way to filch something to eat off one of the food carts, or seek shelter in a toy shop somewhere?

"Miss Baine!" someone called. I turned to see Lamar, the ham and sausage vendor I'd met with the other day, hurrying up the sidewalk toward me. "Have you made any progress in your search for that pesky arsonist?"

"I turned the case over to a unit in the Enforcers Guild," I said, and immediately felt guilty for the way that sounded. "The new captain put together a crew specifically to investigate the fires."

"Well, they're not working fast enough," Lamar groused, folding his beefy arms over his chest. "There was another incident early this morning—this time at Alice's cart! All of her divine cinnamon buns, completely ruined."

Fenris and I exchanged a glance. *"We don't have time for this,"* he warned.

"Yeah, but I can't just dump this again." I turned back to the vendor. "Take us to the cart."

Lamar escorted us to the remains, which were little more than a charred pile of wood and the strong scent of burnt sugar and bread. "My poor cart," Alice moaned, rocking back and forth on her heels. She was a pretty blonde human, dressed in a pale yellow frock with a white apron. "I've had it for ten years, and it's never failed me. I don't know how I'll replace it."

"Sunaya," Fenris said, his voice urgent. He had been sniffing the remains, but now he lifted his head, as if he'd caught something. *"Rusalia was here. I would bet my tail on it."*

"Shit." My stomach plummeted straight into my toes as the truth began to dawn on me. "Did either of you see a little blonde girl hanging around here when your carts were set on fire?" I asked both vendors.

Lamar shrugged. "I don't know. There are many little blonde girls in Rowanville. I see dozens of them every day."

"I might have," Alice said suddenly, her eyes bright. "She was standing over by the produce cart, eyeing an apple. I remember because I warned Prickett, the owner—she looked like she was about to steal from him." Her face paled. "Do you think she set my cart on fire because she was angry with me?"

"I don't know," I said, but I had a feeling that was exactly what happened. By Magorah, I should have considered this. Rusalia was an angry, confused child with two magical parents. Of course there was a strong likelihood that she, too, had magic, and she was about the right age for it to manifest. "But I'm going to find out."

Energized by the promise of a lead, I questioned the other vendors who had been hit by the arsonist, with Fenris in tow. A few of them confirmed they'd seen a little girl shortly before the fire had started, and they directed us further up the neighborhood, to where other businesses and individuals had been victimized. Pretty soon, Fenris and I found ourselves a few blocks away, in a residential neighborhood.

"Hang on a second," Fenris said, coming to a stop outside the chain link fence of a school. *"Is this not where Rusalia would have gone to school?"*

"Shit. *You're right.*" Stuffing my hands in my pockets, I surveyed the three-story, rectangular brick building, which boasted a small playground and a track field. *"Could she be hiding out here?"* The wind shifted, and Fenris and I both stiffened as we caught her scent.

"She's definitely in here," Fenris said, taking off toward the entrance. I sprinted after him, knowing his instincts were taking over—he was on the hunt. My blood hummed in my veins in anticipation—there was no doubt Com's daughter was hiding out in this abandoned building, the only place she could go to be alone. Why hadn't we thought of this sooner?

The gate and entrances were all locked, with not a single guard stationed on the premises, but magic enabled us to get inside fairly easily. We moved slowly through the empty halls, and I took care not to let my boots ring out against the vinyl-tiled floors. If Rusalia was here, we didn't want to startle her.

A normal human would have been forced to check all the rooms—and even though this was a simple elementary school, there were still over fifty of them. Luckily, Fenris had latched onto her scent strongly, and he led us straight past the classrooms, toward a door at the end of the hallway that led to a basement. My hair stood straight on end as I caught the scent of smoke—something was burning down there.

"Rusalia?" I called, summoning a flame to my hand as we descended the stairs. The bluish-green fire illuminated the large, rectangular space, crammed with old filing cabinets and shelves full of supplies. Rusalia was huddled in a corner, her hands hovering over a small fire—she was burning textbooks, I realized, to keep warm.

"*You*," she shouted, jumping to her feet. Her blonde hair fanned out behind her, and I noticed she was dressed in a simple sweater and pants—not nearly enough to stay warm in this weather. There was no central heating turned on in the school right now; she had to be freezing. Her eyes widened at the sight of Fenris, still in wolf form. "Stay back!"

She hurled a ball of flame at us, but before it could hit, I countered with a spell Iannis had often used during our training sessions. With a flick of my wrist, I formed a bubble around her fireball, cutting off the oxygen completely and extinguishing the flames.

Rusalia snarled in fury and hurled more fire at us, but I'd done this dance before, and managed to quickly counter her attacks. Fenris deflected a few of them too—even in wolf form, he was more than able to use simple magic like this.

Still, I could tell this was going to get worse before it got better. Rusalia was going to keep flinging around fire until either someone really got hurt, we set the building on fire, or she passed out from exhaustion. Neither of those three options were good.

"Fenris, I'll cover you, just try and get to her," I cried, stepping forward and bubbling another fireball.

"Fine," he growled in mindspeak as he leapt over the stack of books Rusalia was using as kindling. She screamed, summoning more fire, but before she could fling it, the big wolf landed on top of her, knocking her down. As her hands smacked into the ground, the look in her eyes made my blood run cold. Fenris was so close to her that if she hit Fenris with those flaming hands, there'd be nothing I could do to stop her.

"Don't you *dare*," I shouted, taking a step forward and lifting my own hand. Magic crackled at my fingertips as I glared at her. "We're not here to hurt you, but if you try to harm my friend, I will knock you out myself." I lifted a hand, magic crackling at my fingertips, and she blanched.

"L-leave me alone!" she wailed, tears running down her face as the flames wreathing her hands vanished into the ether. She tried to squirm out from beneath Fenris, but he simply sat down, putting his not-inconsiderable weight on her chest.

"Fenris," I chided, drawing closer. "Get off the poor girl. We don't want to crush her." I put out the fire Rusalia had started, then used another spell to heat up the air until it was comfortably warm. "Is that better?" I asked as she scrambled away from the wolf and scrunched herself into the far corner, arms wrapped around her knees.

"I..." She frowned, confused. "Did you make it warmer in here?"

"Yep." I sat down on the hard floor in front of her, wanting to make myself more approachable. "One of the perks to being a trained mage."

She turned up her nose at me. "A *partially* trained mage."

I arched a brow, refusing to let her bait me. "Kid, I don't

think you're in a position to make cracks like that. You're in big trouble right now."

She folded her arms across her chest and glared at me. "What else is new? Nothing I do is ever good enough, not for Ma, and not for Pa either. Why should I care about what other people think?"

I let out a breath—I understood that sentiment very well. I'd had a similar outlook about my aunt, especially during the last few months I'd lived with her. But now wasn't the time to share that with Rusalia. "It would be one thing if you'd caused an accident or two at home," I explained as patiently as I could. "But you've hurt a lot of other people, setting their carts and other belongings on fire—those are crimes, Rusalia. We're not going to be able to sweep this under the rug."

Her chin began to quiver. "Will they send me to jail?" she asked, her cornflower-blue eyes—Comenius's eyes—wide with terror.

I shrugged, pretending not to feel pity for her. "Probably not. But someone's going to have to pay for all those damages, and that someone is going to be your dad. And I can tell you right now he's going to have a very hard time coming up with the money for that, after being away from his shop all those weeks to bring you back here. Also, it's illegal for the inhabitants of Witches' End to harbor mage children, so Comenius may be forced to hand you over to the Mages' Guild. That, or he'll have to send you back to Pernia."

"*No*," Rusalia cried, tears spilling down her cheeks again. She threw herself to the ground, clutching at my ankles. "Please, please don't send me back there. I have no one there."

"Then why are you so mean to your father?" Fenris demanded, and I started—he'd changed back into human form. I always envied how he was able shift without the usual fanfare because I never noticed when it happened. "He is your only family, is he not?"

"Y-yes," Rusalia mumbled into my boots. "It's just...it's been so hard to trust him. Ma always told me he was a bad man, and he just *left* me with her."

There was so much vitriol in that last statement, such a sense of deep betrayal, that I couldn't help feeling sympathy for the little girl. Burying a hand in her tangled locks, I gentled my voice. "Why don't you tell us what happened, Rusalia? From the beginning."

And so she did. Slowly, painfully, Rusalia told us in a tearful voice about how her mother raised her, neglecting her for days at a time, and then taking her out for ice cream and lavish shopping trips where Rusalia could buy any toy her heart desired. The inconsistent behavior had confused Rusalia—she'd been punished for imagined slights, then rewarded spontaneously and without rhyme or reason. Eventually, the poor child had given up on figuring out what her mother wanted and how to predict her moods.

The woman had also drilled into Rusalia's head that her father, Comenius, was a deadbeat who didn't care about her. When Rusalia did something wrong, her mother would rail at her, shouting she was just like her useless, hateful father. As Rusalia grew older and began acting out more, her mother started spending less time with her, punishing her more frequently.

"I...I think I killed her," she said in a hollow voice, a faraway look in her eyes. She was leaning against Fenris now, who had joined us on the floor, and his arm was around her. "The day she died, she'd locked me up in my room for smashing one of her potions. She was in her potion workshop in the backyard, and all I could think about was how much I hated her, and then...

and then..." She hiccupped, her eyes filling with tears again. "The workshop caught on fire."

"And you were in your room?" Fenris asked, not a shred of judgment in his voice. When she only nodded, he said, "It takes very strong magic to start fires from a distance. And strong magic is very hard to control for a beginner."

"He's right," I said, meeting her tearful gaze. "I had a lot of trouble controlling my magic at first, too. Whatever might have happened to your mother that day, it wasn't your fault. It was an accident."

"It *wasn't*," Rusalia wailed, throwing her head back and tearing at her hair. "I hated her so much then. I just wanted her to die! And she did! It's all my fault!"

She collapsed into a puddle, weeping. Fenris reached for her, intending to console her. Just as he touched her shoulder, a powerful vibration, stronger than any of the ones we'd felt previously, rocked the earth beneath us. The basement walls shuddered, and something above us groaned.

"W-what is that?" Rusalia whimpered, lifting her tearstained face from the earth. The sound of something heavy collapsing sent a burst of fear through me.

"We've gotta get out of here." Heart thundering in my chest, I scooped Rusalia into my arms and turned toward the exit. "Fenris, let's go!"

Another tremor, even stronger than the last, shook the walls and floor as we ran for the stairs. I nearly tripped as I fought to keep my balance with the child in my arms, and that was when the quake chose to strike with full force. The three of us went crashing into the back wall as the very ground churned beneath our feet, and the sound of the roof and walls above the earth tumbling down sent a flash of horror through me. Magorah save us, we were about to be buried alive!

"*Shield*," Fenris cried as a huge chunk of the basement roof caved. He threw himself atop Rusalia, who'd fallen to the floor, and we both shouted the spell the Garaian Emperor had used during his trials to stop that wall from falling on him.

A blue shield burst into life overhead. Chunks of concrete bounced off it and rained down around us. Only we hadn't quite been quick enough because one of those chunks struck me in the left shin. Sharp agony radiated through my leg as the bone fractured, ripping an involuntary scream from me.

Fenris cried out in pain as well, the scent of his blood filling the air. I twisted toward the sound frantically, trying to stamp down my own pain and see what had happened to him and Rusalia.

And that, of course, was when the lights went out.

16

Between Fenris and I, we managed to stop the worst of the rubble from falling on us. But even with the two of us working together, we weren't strong enough to put up a shield to cover all three of us completely without using up every ounce of magic we had. As a result, a huge chunk of concrete had fallen on my exposed left leg, crushing it. Fenris had been hit by debris before the shield had come down fully—his left sleeve was shredded where rubble had hit him, and his hips had been crushed by a steel girder. It was a miracle Rusalia hadn't been hit by it, and I couldn't believe Fenris was conscious enough to continue powering the spell.

"*Nooo*." Rusalia sobbed beneath him. To our horror, a huge ball of flame burst into life within our shield. Fenris used his magic to snuff it out immediately, but it was too late—I'd felt the huge whoosh of air as the flame had immediately begun sucking on oxygen.

"Put her to sleep, then heal yourself," Fenris ordered. His dark hair was matted with sweat, and his jaw clenched with effort. "I will focus on maintaining the shield as you do."

I did as Fenris said, pulling Rusalia from beneath his torso before she was suffocated, and using a sleep spell to render her unconscious. As for my leg, I judged the severity of the break as best I could, then decided I wouldn't heal it completely. I had little experience with healing as yet, and doing so would be another huge drain on my magic. Fenris, hurt even worse than I was, didn't have enough power to hold the shield for long, and I needed to heal him, too. Instead, I staunched the blood flow, then used my power to give a little boost to my shifter body's natural healing process. On its own, my leg would heal fully in a couple of hours—now it would be within the next sixty minutes.

Unfortunately, I didn't think we had that much time.

"Okay," I said, turning back toward Fenris. "Let's get this heavy bastard off you."

"No," Fenris snapped, but it was too late—I was already lifting the girder off, using a combination of magic and my own shifter strength. Despite his protest, he sagged in relief when the weight was off him, and his face relaxed some. Panting with the exertion, I dropped to my knees next to him.

"Stop," he barked when I reached out to touch him. "You don't have enough energy to heal me and tunnel your way out of here. Conserve your strength."

"How the hell am I going to get us out of here, if half your body is broken?" I argued. Another tremor hit, and we flattened ourselves against the ground as more debris came crashing down. "By Magorah," I growled through gritted teeth. "That's all three floors on top of us." I diverted my power back toward the shield, relieving Fenris of the burden somewhat. If the spell failed, we were all doomed.

"Half the city will be tumbling down right now," Fenris ground out through clenched teeth. His face was white with pain. "Kardanor and Director Chen did not have nearly enough time to quake-proof all the buildings on their list, and there were many more they'd written off completely. This will have been one of those. I doubt anyone will be able to find us—they won't think to look in the rubble of a condemned building," he added bitterly.

"Iannis will be able to find us eventually with my *serapha* charm," I said, reaching up to touch it with my hand. I closed my eyes and activated the charm, pinpointing his location. "He's still at least a day away," I said, sighing heavily.

"We can't rely on Iannis," Fenris gasped. "We'll need to move some of the debris aside to make an escape shaft. I know a spell that would work perfectly, but I am too weak..."

"Let me try." Ignoring the pain in my leg, I scooted myself up into a sitting position, then held my hands out and concentrated on the wall of debris. Raw magic poured out of me, and I used it to push as hard as I could, but it was no use—the wreckage was too heavy. Panting, I shut off the magic before I used it up—I couldn't risk the fragile barrier above me failing.

"I could try transmogrifying it—" I began, but Fenris shook his head.

"That would take too long, and use up too much magic." Gritting his teeth, he hauled himself forward a few painful inches and grasped my hand. "I'm not going to make it, Sunaya. You should take the girl and leave me."

I recoiled, his words a physical blow. "No! I can't leave you here to die. What kind of person do you think I am?"

"A compassionate one," Fenris said fiercely, his yellow eyes glowing. "And one who has responsibilities that are far more important than keeping me alive. I should have died three years ago, Sunaya. I've been living on borrowed time, and we all know it."

"That's bullshit," I growled, tears in my eyes. But before I could convince him—and myself—that he was wrong, he pulled me down on the ground next to him, close enough to embrace me.

"Hush," he chided, cupping the back of my head as he leaned my cheek against his broad chest. His heartbeat was surprisingly steady despite the danger and his wound—had he truly accepted his fate? "Let me give you one last gift."

Magic surged through me, fast and furious and so powerful that I gasped. My body went rigid as I was bombarded with an onslaught of impressions, thoughts, words, feelings. *Memories,* I thought numbly as I struggled to keep the wave of sensory input from overloading my mind. But it was almost impossible, and the best I could do was fashion a sort of vault inside my head, then open the door and allow the new memories to rush inside it.

As soon as it was over, the door slammed shut, and I sagged against Fenris, breathing hard. He was panting, too, his strong body shaking from the effort.

"What..." I took a second to catch my breath, still reeling, "What the hell was that?"

"The knowledge transfer," Fenris said, sounding oddly at peace. He lifted my chin to look in my eyes, and I was surprised to see a small smile on his dirt and sweat-smudged face. "All of my memories and knowledge about magic are now yours, too, Sunaya. All the Loranian lessons of a lifetime that I won't be around to give any longer. You now know everything you need to get yourself, and the girl, to safety."

I eased open the vault door a crack, startled to realize he was right. A spell to safely create a tunnel through the debris and up to ground level sprang straight to my mental fingertips. It was a complex spell, not something I would have been able to master the first time around as an apprentice, but with Fenris's knowledge inside me, I knew I could do it with ease.

"This is great," I said, hope easing the crushing weight on my chest. "I can get us all out now. You're coming with us." I struggled to my feet, mindful of my healing leg.

"No," Fenris said, ignoring my outstretched hand. He looked exhausted, his normally tan skin pale and dark smudges under his eyes. "I am too weak, and one of us needs to maintain the shield while you cast the spell. You cannot do both, Sunaya."

"Fine." A tear escaped my right eye, but I pushed the emotion away—I couldn't afford to let it distract me. Clearing my head, I focused my attention on the debris, then called up my magic and spoke the Words of the spell. The power sank into the pile of crushed stone and metal, which began to groan as it was shifted and manipulated. I held my breath as another tremor shook the walls around us, and I wasn't sure if it was from the quake or the spell. Long, agonizing minutes passed before the debris and dirt finally stopped shifting, and then the magic pouring out of me abruptly stopped, the spell completed. A wave of dizziness passed through me, and I had to catch myself to keep from stumbling sideways—I'd used a lot of magic just now, and I was dangerously close to burn-out.

"Take Rusalia," Fenris shouted, grabbing my leg to get my attention. "Take her and go!"

"I'm coming back for you," I growled, dropping down to my knees. I wrapped my arms tight around Fenris in a brief hug, then pulled Rusalia onto my back and climbed into the makeshift tunnel. It wasn't large enough to walk upright, and with the burden of the sleeping child and the agonizing pain in my leg, it was slow going. Even so, I pushed myself as fast as I could. There was no telling how long I had, and I was determined to get Rusalia out. I wouldn't let Fenris's sacrifice be in vain, and I wouldn't fail my promise to Comenius to bring his daughter back safely.

When I finally burst out into the open, a rush of cool air slapped me in the face—a welcome reminder that I was alive. Taking in deep gulps of air, I set Rusalia down in the schoolyard field, then shifted into panther form to heal myself. The process was slower than usual, and it took even longer to change back into human form—I was running really low on magic.

Once I was done, I turned back toward the building. The roof of the school had caved in completely, and the outer walls had collapsed inward—a complete shambles. Maybe there was still enough time, maybe I could still get Fenris out. He was badly hurt, but Iannis could heal him once he got here. He *had* to heal him. Trembling, I took a step forward, but then another quake hit, nearly as strong as the first. The tunnel collapsed inwards, buried completely by the rubble I'd managed to push out of my way.

"*No*," I screamed, falling on the mound of dirt and concrete. Frantically, I began to dig, but the sound of a small explosion stopped me in my tracks, and I ducked as a flaming hunk of metal came flying my way. To my horror, I realized the entire block of buildings south of the school was on fire, and the wall of flames was rapidly heading in our direction. The irony didn't escape me that it was Fenris who had warned of the likelihood of fires being caused by the quake, and a stab of pain went through my chest. He would never get to see that he'd been proven right.

"Fuck," I swore, remembering Rusalia, who was lying defenseless on the ground. Abandoning the caved-in tunnel, I rushed over to her, then undid the sleep spell.

"Wha..." she mumbled, sitting up and rubbing her eyes. Any vestiges of sleep quickly disappeared as she beheld the ruins of the school and the state of her dirty, torn clothes. "What happened?" she shouted, jumping to her feet. Her eyes nearly popped out of her head at the sight of the huge flames, which were spreading quickly toward us. "Oh no, I burned the school down!"

"No, you didn't," I snapped, grabbing her by the arm. "You're not that powerful yet, kid. Now get on—we've gotta run."

I hauled Rusalia onto my back, piggyback style, then sprinted for Witches End as fast as I could. I tried not to think about the fact that I was leaving Fenris's body behind, and focused on avoiding the very real pitfalls—the sidewalks and streets had cracked open in places, exposing water mains below, and there were more buildings on fire. Luckily, most of the shops and homes in Rowanville seemed to be holding up, but several had collapsed, and there were plenty of people screaming and crying in the streets. The scents of blood, fear, and despair told me that there were injured and dead amongst them, but there was no time to stop and help. I had to get Rusalia home safely first.

"Thank Magorah," I said aloud as Witches End finally came into view. The pier, and all the shops lining it, were still standing strong. Magic shimmered along the thresholds and roofs, and I knew that whatever protection spells the residents had put in for this situation had been activated.

"Comenius," I yelled, banging on his apartment door. "Com, I've got her!"

"Pa," Rusalia sobbed as soon as a very harrowed-looking Comenius opened the door. She threw herself into his arms, and he gathered her tight against him. "Pa, I'm sorry!" She began sobbing in Pernian, burying her face against his abdomen.

"Shh, shh," he soothed, picking her up. He tucked her tearstained face against his chest and carried her to the couch. I followed him inside. Elania was sitting in the living room, looking incredibly relieved. There was a tender look on her face as she watched Comenius settle on the couch, rocking his crying daughter in his arms while murmuring assurances to her in their mother tongue.

"I am so glad you found her," Elania said to me, tears in her dark eyes. "Comenius was terrified that she might have been hurt in the quake." She paused, her brow furrowing. "Where is your wolf-shifter friend?"

Grief hit me with the force of a train, and I collapsed into a chair. "He's dead," I said, and the words sounded like they were coming out of someone else's mouth. There was no way I was sitting here, so completely calm, talking about Fenris's death. I should be screaming, crying, tearing my hair out. Cursing the gods above for their cruel machinations. Instead, I was just sitting here, my strength completely sapped, so weighted down by grief I wasn't sure I'd be able to get up again.

How could he be gone?

"Dead?" Comenius echoed, finally tearing his attention away from his daughter. He looked stricken at the news. "What happened?"

I explained how we'd managed to track Rusalia to the school, and how the quake had hit after we'd found her in the basement. Silent tears ran down my cheeks as I described Fenris's selfless sacrifice, how he'd chosen to give me his knowledge and memories so that I might get away with Rusalia, and how it had weakened him so much that he hadn't been able to follow us through the escape tunnel. By the time I got to the part where the tunnel had collapsed, my entire body was shaking, my cheeks raw from scrubbing away at the tears that wouldn't stop coming.

Elania silently put a heap of sandwiches before me, and I devoured without tasting anything. I had no appetite, but I was running on fumes and my shifter body was crying out for fuel. "I'm so sorry, Naya," Comenius said. He set a now-sleeping Rusalia aside, then knelt in front of my chair. "I know how important Fenris was to you. We shall all miss him."

He took me into his arms, and I buried my face against his chest, still tearstained from Rusalia. He rubbed my back in slow circles as I gulped in shuddering breaths, trying to get myself under control. His woodsy, herbal scent soothed me, and after a few long moments, the tears finally stopped.

"I know this is hard," Comenius said, his words gentle but firm as he lifted my head. "But we don't have time to grieve now. The city needs every able-bodied mage, and the only reason I stayed here was in case you and Rusalia returned. Now that she is home, you and I must go out and assist in whatever way we can."

I nodded, letting Comenius help me to my feet. He was right. Fenris might be dead, but there were plenty of others still alive who needed our help to stay that way. Squaring my shoulders, I shoved all my pain into the vault filled with Fenris's memories, then slammed it shut. There would be time to grieve later. Right now, it was time for action.

17

The first place we headed was the Enforcers Guild, to see where we might be most needed. To my relief, the building had weathered the quake with only minor damage. Captain Skonel was running a tight ship, efficiently dispatching crews to deal with the terrified citizens and prevent any looting. Two foremen from the smaller crews were helping him organize, and a quick talk with them confirmed they were indeed following Chen and Kardanor's plan to the letter. Tents were already being set up outside the city for temporary shelter, as well as improvised hospitals. The crews were herding homeless citizens to the tents, but there weren't nearly enough hands available to search through the wreckage for survivors, so Comenius and I were dispatched to Maintown to assist with that.

"By Magorah," I said, after I'd brought my steambike to a halt just two blocks away from the Maintown border. We'd cut through Shiftertown to get here, and while there were some collapsed buildings and road damage there, it was nothing like Maintown. The whole damn place seemed to be on fire, acrid smoke billowing from crumbled buildings. Screams and sobs carried to us on the wind even from this distance. It was worse than anything I'd ever seen before—far worse than even the damage the Resistance had done during the Uprising.

"It's a good thing I brought supplies," Comenius said, hefting his brown leather bag full of potions and bandages. "I fear they won't be nearly enough."

We walked the rest of the two blocks, and Rylan met us at the border. His usual smirk was nowhere to be found. In its place was a hard, implacable gaze. "This is unconscionable," he growled, his rage barely leashed. "Those cheap bastards, Mendle and Gorax, should be castrated, then drawn and quartered, for this."

"That would be a good start," I agreed, letting my own rage come to the surface. It was better to feel anger than grief right now, I decided. Anger would fuel me, push me to work harder to save the survivors. Grief would only hold me back.

Rylan smiled grimly at that. "I've already checked in with Kardanor," he said. "He and Director Chen are running the show down here, and making quite a good team, too. He said to report to Foreman Chabot—she needs help digging out survivors in the Coldwater Shopping District."

Comenius and I followed Rylan in the direction he'd mentioned, but we didn't make it there. There was catastrophe everywhere—children trapped in burning buildings, women and men lying in the street with broken limbs as they waited for mages to triage and move them to the hospitals, and we ended up helping along the way. Rylan jumped into one of those burning buildings to save a child, while I used my magic and brawn to help clear rubble away that was trapping another family inside their home. Comenius was roped into helping at the nearby hospital tent to mix up pain-killing potions. It wasn't that there wasn't anyone helping—in fact, there were hundreds of shifters, humans, and mages working side by side to save the survivors. But for every one helper, there were fifty citizens who needed saving.

Unfortunately, not everyone I pulled from the wreckage could be saved. I had to force myself not to get emotional whenever I pulled the bodies of dead children from the rubble, which was far too often. I nearly broke down when I unearthed the corpse of a pregnant woman who looked to be only a few weeks away from her delivery date. But I managed to hold it together, to shove my grief and rage into the box that held Fenris's memories, and keep slogging through.

Eventually, I ended up in the hospital tent too, healing broken limbs and internal bleeding. The mages running the tents seemed surprised and impressed at the skill and speed with which I healed my patients, but they didn't question me about it. Which was good, because how could I tell them that my newfound skill and knowledge was unearned? That it had been given to me by a mage who wasn't even my master, a mage who everyone had considered a shifter? The memory-sharing spell was only supposed to be used if a master was passing away before his student could complete their apprenticeship, and in these times of peace, that was incredibly rare. Acquiring wholesale knowledge this way when everyone else had to work for it was considered cheating.

I wasn't sure how long I toiled away in the tents, but eventually I had to stop and refuel. All the magic I'd used to heal bodies and clear away rubble was taking a heavy toll. Sitting in a corner of a tent, I wolfed down a stack of ham sandwiches as fast as I could, not wanting to sit around too long. There was still too much work to be done.

"Miss Baine?" someone asked, and I jerked my head up to see Director Chen staring down at me. Her silk robes had been replaced with utilitarian brown wool, her long hair was pulled up into a no-nonsense bun, and her ivory skin was smudged with soot and blood. "Thank the Lady I've found you. Lord Iannis has returned."

I shot to my feet, my exhaustion forgotten. "He has? How?" In all the commotion, I hadn't thought to check my *serapha* charm, and as far as I'd known, there had been no point. He'd been a day away this morning, and I hadn't thought he would make it in time to assist today.

"He has been experimenting with creating *gulayas*, using that new method from the diary he found on that deserted island," Chen said, lowering her voice. "He took one with him on his trip, and he used it to get back as soon as he got word about the quake. He's been leading the firefighting for the past hour, and the flames are almost completely subdued now."

"That's great." Touching my *serapha* charm, I confirmed that Iannis was indeed back in Solantha, and though he seemed tired and strained, he was healthy. "I'll go find him. Thanks."

Using my *serapha* charm as a guide, I picked my way through the rubble-strewn streets toward Iannis. He was a couple of blocks west, at the town center, putting out a fire in the town hall. I leaned against the remnants of a street lamp and watched as he and, to my great surprise, Director Toring, worked together to staunch the flames licking the roof of the building. The other buildings on either side of the town hall were partially charred and still smoking, but their fires had been put out safely.

"You've been busy," I said, strolling up to the two mages once they'd gotten the fire under control. I would have volunteered to help, but I was still recovering from the healings I'd done, and the two of them hadn't seemed to need my help anyway. Like Chen, Iannis and Garrett were dressed in simple robes rather than their usual finery. Both their faces were black with soot, but I grabbed Iannis and kissed him anyway. He tasted like ash and blood, but also himself, and as he wrapped his strong arms about me and crushed me tight against him, an indulgence he rarely allowed in public, the knot of grief and pain inside my chest loosened a bit.

"I'm very glad you're safe," he finally said, pulling back. He pushed a curl out of my face with a blackened finger, no doubt streaking soot across my forehead. But I didn't care. After this hellish day, I needed to feel his touch, hear his voice, see those brilliant violet eyes staring down at me as they did now, still so full of vitality despite the grueling, draining work. "I felt your pain, and I was worried that something had happened to you. Are you all right?"

I swallowed hard against the sudden ball of tears in my throat, eyes stinging again. "Fenris is dead," I choked out.

Iannis's face went deathly pale beneath the soot. "What?"

"Dead?" Garrett echoed, scowling. "What do you mean, dead?"

"I mean he's no longer living in this world, you asshole!" I took a step toward him, fangs bared, and Garrett recoiled in shock. He wasn't used to seeing me this feral. Iannis braced a hand against my forearm, and the only reason I halted was because he was as much leaning on me as he was silently telling me to stop.

"Why don't you sit down?" I said heavily. We sank onto the cracked marble steps in front of the town hall, and I relayed the story to Iannis, leaving out only the part about Fenris gifting his knowledge to me. By the time I was done, my eyes were burning with unshed tears, and my heart felt like it had been repeatedly run over by a steamtruck. By Magorah, how could he be gone? How could I have let him die?

A long silence settled over the three of us when I finished. Iannis's expression was like stone, but I knew that was because we were in public—the anguish coming off him, which I could feel clearly through the *serapha* charm, was so great that it made mine feel paltry in comparison. Fenris had been his friend far longer than mine.

"You did not fail him," I said firmly in mindspeak, sensing what Iannis was thinking. *"He left this world knowing how much you loved him."*

"He wouldn't have left this world at all, had I not convinced him to stay the first time he announced he was leaving." Iannis's eyes burned with restrained emotion, and I had to struggle to keep from hugging him again. *"He could be a thousand miles away by now, living his own life."*

"Well, that's very convenient," Garrett said skeptically, interrupting our silent conversation. "For Fenris to die just as I was preparing my arrest warrant for him. How do I know that you aren't lying, and that he didn't escape in the confusion?"

"You bastard—" I snarled, but stopped myself before I lunged for Garrett again. Fenris wouldn't want me to get myself into hot water after all he'd done to save my life. *Fuck.* Taking a deep breath, I sat back down, then said, "If you doubt me, I will take you to the place where it happened. We need to recover the body anyway."

"Sunaya," Iannis said, putting his hand on my arm. He turned to Garrett, his voice full of reproach. "Now is hardly the time to squabble about such a petty—"

"No," I said, my voice hard. I got to my feet and pinned Garrett with an icy stare that could give Iannis a run for his money. "If taking time away from helping the sick and the dying is what we need to appease Director Toring's sense of *justice,*" I spat the word, and his eyes flickered, "then that's what we'll do."

"Very well," Garrett said, his tone chilly. But I could tell I'd thrown him off balance, and that he was no longer so sure about the move he'd just made. "Lead the way."

Since the roads had been completely torn up by the quake, we were forced to traverse the town on foot. To prevent ourselves from being constantly accosted, we disguised ourselves as humans, but it was incredibly hard to ignore the pain and suffering going on and continue forward. There were so many times I wanted to stop and help, to dig out more survivors, to heal more broken limbs. But Fenris's body was still buried beneath that school, and I would not leave him there to rot. He deserved better than that.

"Here we are," I said bitterly as we stopped outside the cracked sidewalk in front of the school. Someone had put out the fire, but the damage had been done. I stalked across the once-grassy field, now charred to ash, heading toward the side of the school where I had created that tunnel. The entire building had been reduced to rubble.

"Miss Baine," Garrett said, his voice subdued. He hurried to catch up with me, pulling at my sleeve. "Miss Baine, I see now. There is no way anyone in that basement could have survived. I believe you."

"Don't touch me, you self-serving prick." I smacked his hand away, staring straight ahead so that he wouldn't see my tears. "You wanted to see proof. I'll get you proof. Fenris's body is buried down here."

"Sunaya," Iannis warned as I sank to the ground in front of the pile of debris blocking the tunnel I'd dragged Rusalia through. The tunnel I'd made using Fenris's knowledge.

"Fenris's body is down here," I repeated, refusing to look at him. "We can't leave him there." Calling up a spell from my dead friend's memories, I turned toward the tunnel and attempted to excavate it again. My magic burrowed into the ground as the spell yanked on it and, for a moment, I thought it was going to work. But something inside me snapped, like a wire stretched too taut, and I gasped as piercing pain sliced through the center of my body. The spell shut off abruptly, and my inner muscles began to seize up as intense heat radiated throughout my skull.

Suddenly, I couldn't draw breath; it was as though all the oxygen had been sucked out of the air around me...

"Sunaya," Iannis shouted, his voice rife with fear. Strong arms came around me as I toppled sideways, and that was the last sensation I felt before the blackness claimed me.

18

When my eyes opened again, I found myself lying on the sandy beach of the island I'd once been stranded on, staring up at the cloudless blue sky. The white sand was powdery beneath my skin, and the warm water lapped gently at me, like a pet dog trying to rouse its master from a slumber.

But I couldn't get up. Exhaustion had settled into my limbs, so pervasive I could barely keep my eyes open. The only reason I was even awake was because I was struggling for breath—my lungs felt like they were collapsed, and no matter how hard I tried, I couldn't suck in enough air.

Writhing in the sand, I tried to roll over, hoping a change of position might help. But my arms and legs were leaden, and I only seemed to dig myself further into the surf, closer to the tide that no longer seemed quite so gentle. The waves were growing larger, more menacing, the sea turning its hungry gaze toward me. It had deemed me not worth saving, and instead intended to drag me beneath its depths so I could join the myriad souls it had carried to the afterlife.

"Relax," a female voice, low and musical, said. A warm hand

settled on my damp shoulder, and I turned my head to see an exotic, caramel-skinned woman with golden eyes and flowing mahogany hair crouching next to me. Her teeth gleamed white in her dark face as she smiled down at me, and I stared dumbly up at her, struck by her beauty. She was otherworldly, her presence gentle but powerful. Somehow, I knew I was in the presence of a powerful spirit. "You are not going to die."

The knot of anxiety in my chest loosened a little, and I nodded. The woman pressed a dark green leaf to my lips, and I opened my mouth. As soon as it touched my tongue, a wave of cool, soothing energy rippled through me, soothing my raw nerves. Power hummed in my veins, and I sucked in my first real breath as my magic flared back to life.

"Much better," the woman said, nodding in satisfaction. She pressed her slender hand against my brow...

And then I opened my eyes to see Annia leaning over me, her dark eyes warm as she pressed her own hand against my forehead.

"By Magorah." I shot upright, nearly slamming my forehead into Annia's nose. "Annia, you're back! How long have you been here? How long have I been out? What's going on?" Heart thundering, I looked wildly around me. I was in the Palace infirmary, and I wasn't alone. Dozens of metal-framed beds were filled with other patients, mostly mages, but a few shifters and humans, too. I'd never seen the place so crowded.

"Slow down, champ." Annia laid her hand against my shoulder and pressed me back into the pillows. "You've been out a few hours, about the same length of time I've been back. Was a real shock to return home to this shit show." Her elegant features drew tight as she surveyed the room. "I was on a boat for the last couple of days, so I had no idea what I was coming home to."

"I'm so glad you're here." Tears sprang to my eyes, and I sat up so I could hug Annia, hard. Seeing her back, alive and well, was the balm my soul needed after this horrific day. Pulling away, I studied her, wanting to make sure that she really was intact. Her normally fair skin was a little darker, tanned by the tropical Southian climate, and her dark eyes seemed older, almost ancient. There were secrets lurking in those eyes— stories I would pull out of her when things settled down.

"I see you've been shopping," I said, my eyes dropping to her collarbone. A gorgeous, antique-looking torque of solid gold lay against her tanned skin, with a fiery gemstone in the center. It smelled strongly of magic, and I frowned. "What is that?"

Annia sighed, looking decidedly unhappy for someone who loved clothes and jewelry as much as she did. "It's a long story," she said, settling back into her chair.

I pursed my lips, remembering the woman from my dream, and how she and Annia had both touched my forehead. "Did you do something to heal me?" I asked, lowering my voice a little so the others wouldn't hear. "A strange woman appeared in my dream, and she gave me something that restored my magic."

Annia shrugged. "You might have gotten a little boost, yeah."

I stared down at the torque, then back up at Annia again. That ancient presence that lingered in her eyes...was that Annia, or the woman I'd seen in my dreams? Now that I was paying attention, there was a subtle aura of power around Annia, similar to what I'd sensed from the spirit. And it was emanating from that torque.

"Who was the woman in my dream?" I asked slowly, sinking back against the pillows again. What kind of adventures had Annia gotten herself into, to come back with a goddess, or at the very least a powerful spirit, attached to her?

"Her name is Garalina, and she's a friend, of sorts." Annia smiled, but it didn't quite reach her eyes. "Like I said, it's a long story, and one I'd rather tell in private."

"Of course," I said, understanding. We were sitting in Solantha Palace, the seat of the Mages Guild, and Annia might very well be in possession of illegal magic.

Certainly, whatever spirit resided in that torque was incredibly powerful. I had no idea how the mages would react if they learned that Annia, a human enforcer, was walking around with the equivalent of a mage hanging around her. I'd have to discuss it with Iannis, once I learned more about what happened to my friend. And I'd extract a promise from him that, no matter what, he wouldn't interfere with Annia.

"I hadn't planned to come back for another few weeks," Annia said. "I wanted a little more time to deal with my new... condition. But Garalina said I was needed at home, so I hopped on a boat a few days ago. I can see that she was right," she added, her eyes somber now. "Did the quake take you guys completely by surprise?"

"Not completely, but almost. We've been preparing over the past week, but we didn't have nearly enough time to protect the citizens and buildings." I briefly explained to her about our meeting with Kardanor, the truth about Mendle and Gorax's practices, and what limited preparations we had been able to make.

"I can't believe those bastards were able to get away with this for so long," Annia seethed, her dark eyes glittering with restrained fury. "My mother lives just a block away from where the worst of the fires and collapses are. Our house was built by a reputable company, and my father made double-damn sure it was quake-resistant, so she's fine. I checked on her before I came to find you, and I'll go spend the night with her after I volunteer for a few hours. They need all the help they can get out there."

"I should go back out, too," I said, sitting up again. I didn't want to sit here, alone with my thoughts, while my friends were out there working their asses off. I needed to keep busy, or I'd break down in tears again.

"Oh no, you don't." The doctor chose that moment to bustle into the room, much to my consternation. He was a tall, lean mage with silver-streaked chestnut hair and wire spectacles, dressed in blue-and-white robes. "You just suffered a massive magical burnout, and you nearly died. I cannot allow you to go back out there."

"Burnout?" I echoed as the doctor fussed about me, checking my heartbeat, peering into my eyes, and feeling my forehead.

"Yes, you silly girl." The doctor clucked his tongue, then pressed his thumbs against my forehead and spoke a Word. A jolt of magic went through me, and I jumped back with a yell.

"What the fuck was that?" I demanded, wrapping my arms around myself.

"I was testing to see how much magic you still had left." His eyes narrowed. "Come closer. I need to test you again."

"You're not doing that to me again," I snarled. "My magic is fine."

"It certainly seems to be," the doctor said, looking both amazed and irritated. "Which doesn't make any sense at all. You suffered a level-two burnout, which means you exhausted your magic so completely you almost snuffed it out. Lord Iannis healed you as best as he could before he had to leave, but still, you should have been unconscious for days."

Annia and I exchanged a look. "Maybe my shifter healing allows me to recover faster," I said, shrugging.

"Hmm. Whatever the reason, you are very lucky indeed," the doctor said, not entirely convinced. "Most of the mages in here are suffering from similar levels of burnout, and it will take them several days to recover. There are even a few who have lost their magic completely."

My eyes widened. "Does that happen very often, in situations like this?"

"No," the doctor said, his mouth tightening. "It is very rare, actually, because mages will usually faint in time to prevent such a calamity. I've never seen this many cases of total burnout."

Alarm bells went off in my head. "How many cases do you have?"

"Three. Why?"

"Take me to them." I threw off the bedsheets and swung my legs over the side. The room spun a little, and I gripped the headboard—I might have gotten my magic back, but I was still physically weakened. "Annia, help me up."

"What do you want to see them for?" the doctor demanded as Annia slung my arm over her shoulder and gently helped me stand.

"Stop arguing and just show me." I gave him my best death glare. The doctor complied, though not without a scowl of his own, leading me to three beds on the far side of the room. Two men and one woman lay prone in their beds. Their faces were nearly as white as their bedsheets, their breathing so slow I could barely detect their heartbeats even with my sensitive ears.

"By the Ur-God," Annia said, pity in her voice. "They look like they're ready to be embalmed."

"No kidding." If not for my keen nose, I would have thought they were dead, too. "Where were these mages found when they collapsed?" I asked the doctor.

"They were excavating a building in Maintown somewhere." He picked up the clipboard sitting on the side table next to one of the pages, scanned the sheet there.

"The Mendle mansion, actually." His lips twisted in a mockery of a smile. "That is some cruel irony—you would think the Mendles would have quake-proofed their own mansion, at least."

"By Magorah." Icy horror filled my veins, sending a burst of adrenaline through me, and I whirled toward the doctor. "We need to send a message down there right now. No other mages should go near that mansion, or shifters, for that matter!"

"Naya, what's going on?" Annia asked urgently. "What have you discovered?"

"Hang on," I snapped. *"Iannis!"* I called, using my magic to boost my mindspeak signal. *"Iannis, I know where Thorgana and the Magic Eraser are!"* There was no answer, and I gnashed my teeth. He was too far away. Drawing on Fenris's knowledge, I conjured three ether pigeons, then sent them off to Iannis, Chen, and Garrett—with the message I knew where Thorgana was, that I needed to see them immediately, and that they needed to keep mages and shifters away from the Mendle Mansion at all costs, because I strongly suspected the Magic Eraser was in there.

"Are you going to tell me what's going on?" Annia demanded when I'd sent the pigeons off.

"Yes," I said tiredly. "But let's head back to my room. I'd rather not have an audience."

Over the protestations of the doctor, Annia led me back to my quarters, flagging down a servant to bring me food along the way. Stretched out on the couch, I devoured a huge platter of chicken wings, followed by a small mountain of pork ribs, and filled Annia in on Director Toring and his mission to find Thorgana. I also told her about his history with Fenris, and that he'd been a hand's breath away from making an arrest before the accident today at the school. My entire body seemed to ache with grief as I retold the circumstances of Fenris's death, and how I'd passed out while trying to unearth his body, but I didn't cry this time. My eyes burned, but my tear ducts had nothing left to give.

"I'm so sorry, Naya," Annia said, tears in her own eyes. She scooted closer to me on the couch, then put my head in her lap so she could stroke my hair. "I can't believe he's gone. I wish I'd gotten here sooner, so I could have seen him one more time. I wasn't close with him like you were, but we did go through our own adventures together while rescuing Iannis, and in Osero."

We sat in silence for a long moment, simply relishing each other's company. Despite the restlessness I could sense in Annia, and the shadows in her eyes, I could tell she was happy to be back home again. Even if home had somehow turned into hell.

The door banged open, and Iannis rushed in, still soot-stained and disheveled. From the way his hair was flying about him, and the flush in his cheeks, I could tell he'd used his super speed to get here.

"What happened?" he demanded, kneeling by my side. His worried gaze searched my face as he felt my forehead. "Are you all right? Why aren't you in the infirmary?"

"I'm a lot better," I said, taking his face into my hands to get his attention. "My magic is back."

Iannis went completely still, and I could feel his magic probe me, much more gently than that damned doctor. "How is that possible?" he asked, wonder in his voice. "You should have been out for days."

"I'll explain later," I said, pushing myself upright. "We have more important things to worry about."

"Indeed," Iannis agreed. He sat down on the couch next to me. "I gave orders to cordon off the ruins of the Mendle Mansion, and to set up wards so that no mages or shifters can come near it. Why do you suspect the Magic Eraser is in there?"

The door flew open again, and Director Chen and Garrett hurried in. "Where is Thorgana?" Garrett demanded, his eyes bright and hard. He looked around the room, as if expecting her to materialize in my suite.

"I don't know," I said. "She could be dead, or she might have escaped when the mansion collapsed. But I'm pretty sure she's been staying with the Mendles. Don't you remember how sick the butler was when we came to visit, and how the wife was sick, too?"

"Yes." Garrett frowned, taking a seat along with the others. "But what does that have to do with the Magic Eraser? They were humans."

"Father Calmias said that the team developing the Magic Killer all died from some mysterious illness," I reminded him. "What if the Magic Eraser isn't just harmful to mages? What if it emits something deadly that gradually kills humans? Thorgana might have brought it into the Mendle household unaware of its effect, and ended up slowly poisoning them with it."

"That would be quite ironic," Director Chen said, "as terrible as that sounds."

"And quite problematic, too," Iannis said. "If neither humans, shifters, or mages can get near it, how are we to safely dispose of it?"

"I think humans *can* get near it," Annia said, drawing all eyes to her. "They can probably risk small amounts of exposure without being affected too badly. I ran across a primitive tribe in Southia with a similar object," she explained when Garrett looked like he was about to argue. "The tribe kept it in a sacred cave far away from the village, and the men they set to guard it watched it from a distance. They would bring it out only if they were attacked by another shaman, which was very infrequent as they'd developed quite a reputation. I managed to get into the cave and have a look at the object—it was about the size of a melon, and metallic looking. Absolutely nothing grew in or around that cave. Nothing," she repeated gravely.

We all fell silent for a moment. I wondered if it had been Garalina, rather than Annia, who'd had this experience. Did that mean her kind of magic was safe from the stone's effects, or just that she had not lingered long enough? How long ago had that been, and could it be the very same stone?

"And you experienced no adverse effects?" Iannis asked.

Annia shook her head. "No, but the object did give me a very bad feeling. I don't think anyone should remain around the Magic Eraser for long, but a team of humans should be able to go in and get it out. I volunteer to lead it."

"Very well," Garrett said. "But since this concerns the Benefactor, I shall supervise."

Iannis's eyes flickered with annoyance, but he didn't object—this was Garrett's mission. He turned to Director Chen. "Can you find out if any of the Mendles survived, or if a woman matching Thorgana's description has been seen in any of the shelter or hospital tents?"

"Yes." Director Chen rose from her seat. "I will get on that immediately."

"Good," Iannis said. "Miss Melcott, go and pick a crew of five able-bodied humans you trust. They shall be well compensated. Director Toring and I will accompany you to the site, but keep at a respectable distance, to make sure that everything goes smoothly."

"I'm coming, too," I said, rising from my seat, but Iannis pressed a hand against my thigh, pushing me back down with annoying ease.

"You will do no such thing," he said sternly. "You're still too weak from your latest near-death experience, and I don't want you going anywhere near an object that could potentially destroy your magic, or your ability to shift."

"*I love you too much to let you put yourself in harm's way so soon after losing Fenris,*" he said to me in mind-speak, his mental voice raw. "*Please, Sunaya. Do me this favor and stay home. I need you well rested for what's ahead.*"

I sighed, letting out the anger that had instantly bubbled up inside me. "Fine. But you all had better come back safe and sound. I can't afford to lose you either," I told him. "If you weren't the Chief Mage, I'd tie you to the bed and never let you leave."

"Under normal circumstances, I would be very excited about that prospect." Iannis pulled me against him for a brief kiss. "Send word if you need anything or have any other ground-breaking epiphanies."

"I will," I said, leaning back against the couch. Annia and Garrett made their goodbyes, then left along with Iannis. I closed my eyes, hoping to calm the anxiety bouncing around my nerves. As soon as I did, exhaustion hit me. Guess I was more tired than I thought. Mercifully, I slipped into a deep, dreamless sleep. I had good friends I could trust, and for just this once, I would leave the rescuing to them.

19

A few hours later, I was woken by a phone call from Dira. She informed me that Mr. Mendle had been found, and Iannis wanted to know if I felt well enough to sit in on the interrogation. I was still a little tired, but the food and sleep had helped a lot, so I washed up and changed out of my hospital gown, then went down to the Mages Guild.

"They're in the conference room, Miss Baine," Dira said when I walked in.

"Thanks." I headed down the hall, then knocked on the door.

"Come in," Iannis called. I opened the door to see Mr. Mendle, a rotund, middle-aged man, sitting in cuffs on one side of the table. His fine clothes were torn and soot-stained, and I noticed that beneath the dirt, he was sporting a sallow complexion and thinning hair much like his butler had been. Iannis sat on the other side, dressed in fresh clothing, and Garrett stood in the corner. His face was ashen, and such potent fury blazed in his eyes as he glared at Mendle that I had no doubt he was the reason the man was sweating bullets in his chair.

"Pillick was found unconscious, not far from the mansion," Iannis explained in mindspeak as I shut the door behind me. *"He was helping those other mages with the excavation, and he ended up affected as well."*

"Oh." I struggled to keep my expression calm even as I felt a strong wave of pity for Garrett's assistant. I hadn't liked him, but he didn't deserve this fate. "Hello, Mr. Mendle," I said aloud, taking a seat next to Iannis. I put the emotion aside and focused on our suspect. "You're looking much better than the rest of your family."

Mr. Mendle's stiffened. To my surprise, tears rolled down his round cheeks. "My family is *dead*, you callous girl," he spat. "Crushed when the house collapsed. They were too ill to get out."

"I'm sorry to hear that," I said, and I did mean it. "I'm sure your wife and children didn't deserve to die, just like many of the other citizens who were crushed by buildings today didn't either." My heart clenched at the thought of Fenris's body, squashed beneath the weight of that elementary school, and I had to shove the image away before I was overwhelmed by emotion again. That school, too, had been built by the man before me. His criminal greed had contributed to Fenris's death.

Mr. Mendle clenched his bound hands, but said nothing. What else was there to say when you knew you were responsible not only for the deaths of your fellow citizens, but your family as well?

"I understand that you were in your office during the quake?" Iannis asked, bringing us back on track. His face was expressionless, his tone businesslike. "Do you spend much time there?"

"Nearly all of it," Mr. Mendle confirmed. "Running a successful business is very time consuming."

"That explains why you're not as sick as the rest of your family was," I said.

Mr. Mendle glanced sharply at me. "What do you know about my family's illness?"

"Director Toring and I passed by your home a few days ago to question you and your wife," I said. "You were at the office, and Mrs. Mendle was too sick to receive us. Your butler looked ill too—exhibiting the same symptoms you are now. And I overheard you and your wife, at Captain Galling's farewell reception, talking about the hair loss afflicting your whole family." I leaned in closer when Mr. Mendle said nothing. "I know that you've been harboring Thorgana Mills in your home, Mr. Mendle, so don't try to deny it. Did she bring a strange object into your house at any time?"

"I'm not sure," Mr. Mendle said, looking taken aback. "She did receive a mysterious package a few days after her arrival, not long before she became sick. Are you saying this package is what made my family ill?"

"Yes," Iannis told him. "It is a special weapon called the Magic Eraser, and it looks like it harms humans as well. Shifters have been affected too—a bear-shifter volunteer who helped excavate your home can no longer change out of his human form."

Fuck. Shock and anger filled me at this unexpected announcement, and Mr. Mendle cringed as I glared at him. "I assume Thorgana was ill, too, possibly even sicker than the rest of you?"

"Yes." Mr. Mendle's lips thinned. "If she hadn't been crushed in the quake along with my family, she probably would have been dead within a few weeks. Even the finest doctors, who I brought to the house in secret, couldn't figure out what was wrong with her."

Relief and disappointment swamped me all at once as Mr.

Mendle confirmed my suspicion—that Thorgana had died. I would have liked to look her in the eye one last time, to let her know that despite everything she'd done, she hadn't beaten me. But it was better this way. There would be no more arrests or escape attempts. She was gone for good.

Garrett took command of the conversation then, and extracted the names of the doctors and other accomplices. Mr. Mendle was too broken to resist, and it didn't take much effort to get him to agree to sign a full confession. He didn't bother begging for clemency—the man had to know he only had a swift trial and execution to look forward to, at best. With nothing more to be gleaned from Mr. Mendle, Iannis had him escorted to Prison Isle, then left for a meeting with the Council and Director Chen. Before he left, he informed me that Annia was at home with her mother—she and her crew had success-fully retrieved the Magic Eraser from the ruins. It was being held in a building on the outskirts of the city, well away from the Mages Quarter and Shiftertown. Iannis and the Council were going to put their heads together to figure out the best way to destroy the thing without getting close enough to it to compromise their own magic. And Rylan was still out in the city, helping in Shiftertown now. I didn't see any reason to call him back—with Thorgana dead, Father Calmias no longer spouting evil nonsense, and the city so thoroughly distracted, I doubted I was in any particular danger behind the Palace walls.

Back in my room, I stripped off my clothes and changed into a simple silk robe, then grabbed a novel off the shelf to read. My mind was too restless to sleep—I needed a distraction. But before I could settle down with it, someone knocked on my door.

"Garrett?" I asked, catching his scent immediately. What the hell was he doing here?

"May I come in?" Garrett asked, for once sounding quite hesitant. "I won't take too much of your time, I promise."

I scowled, tempted to turn him away. But my heirloom ring remained cool to the touch, a signal that he meant me no harm, and besides, I was curious as to what he had to say.

"Make it quick," I said, opening the door. "I was about to take a nap."

Garrett stepped inside, barely bothering to glance at me. He sank into one of my armchairs, looking absolutely defeated, and dropped his head into his hands, startling me. I'd seen him angry plenty of times, but never despondent. What was going on?

"I thought you'd be happier," I said, sitting down on the couch, "now that Thorgana has been taken care of, and the Magic Eraser found. Isn't that what you wanted?" *Aside from arresting Iannis and Fenris,* I thought bitterly, but I didn't say it aloud.

"Yes," Garrett admitted, lifting his head. "But I cannot help thinking that if we had gone inside the Mendle Mansion that day instead of leaving them alone, we would have apprehended Thorgana sooner. Poor Harron wouldn't be lying in a hospital bed, his magic stripped from him."

"Oh." My insides squirmed with guilt—I'd completely forgotten about Pillick. "I'm sorry about your loss, Garrett," I said after a moment of tense silence, in which I was certain Garrett was harboring blame-filled thoughts about me. "But we have no idea what would have happened if we'd entered the mansion that day, especially since we didn't even know about the danger. It's very possible the Magic Eraser would have stripped both of us of our magic while we were waiting to talk to Mrs. Mendle. *We* could very well have ended up on those hospital beds instead of your assistant."

Garrett's lips thinned. "I suppose we'll never know either

way." His eyes glittered with a combination of self-loathing and grief that made him more human than I'd ever seen. "I don't know what I'm supposed to say to him," he finally said. "He will no longer be able to work in my office now that he is not a mage."

"Why the hell not?" I asked, my annoyance rising. "It would be ridiculously unfair of you to fire him, especially since he was injured on duty."

"Do you think I don't know that?" Garrett threw his arms up in the air. "I just don't know *what* to do with him!"

"Here's a thought," I said, suppressing my dislike of Harron and forcing myself to be objective. "Why don't you create an elite squad of human agents and put Harron in charge of them? The biggest problem our country is facing, as evidenced by how easily Thorgana was able to turn humans and shifters to her cause, is that you mages keep looking down at the other races as inferior, excluding them from important positions even though this is their country, too. Harron might not have his magic anymore, but he still has all his knowledge, and his nose for scandal." Garrett opened his mouth, but I kept talking, my enthusiasm growing for the idea. "It might be easier for a human unit to liaise with the various Enforcers Guilds across the Federation than for mages. Remember how Captain Skonel reacted to you when we visited him? And speaking of sharp noses, why not have a shifter unit too? The Garaian Emperor employed an entire unit of lion shifters as his personal guard. I'd be surprised if they don't also serve as an informal spy unit."

"That all sounds very unusual," Garrett said, looking bemused. "But unconventional ideas might just be what we need right now. And you are right—it would be a shame to put Harron out to pasture when he could still be of use. I will consider it, and discuss it with the Minister."

"Great. Let me know if you need my help." Not that I particularly wanted to keep working with Garrett, especially in light of his recent actions. But I was beginning to see that it wasn't always possible to crush your enemies outright—sometimes you had to work with them. And if Garrett could convince the Minister to bring more humans and shifters into government positions, it would be a huge step forward for the Federation.

"Very well." Sighing, Garrett sat back in the chair. "I am sorry, too, that Fenris did not survive," he said somberly. "I know he was a good friend to you. But perhaps it is best that he did not—I meant it when I told you that I was very close to arresting him. I have strong evidence that he was likely not Fenris at all, but Polar ar'Tollis, the former Chief Mage of Nebara. Their interests and knowledge were far too similar, and eccentric, for me to write it off as simple coincidence. But," he added with another sigh, "there is no way I will ever be able to prove it, now that Fenris is gone."

A burst of anger filled me at Garrett's callous pronouncement, but icy fear followed on its heels. Fenris might be gone, but Iannis was not. If Garrett *did* find a way to prove that Fenris was Polar, he could still go after Iannis for performing that illegal transformation spell.

While Garrett stared bleakly at the grate, lost in his own thoughts, I quickly sifted through Fenris's memories, searching for something I could use to deflect suspicion. Images of the two of us talking rushed past, of spending nights by the fire out in the wilderness of Mexia, and of fighting Resistance soldiers. I forced myself not to get caught up in them. I could feel Fenris's fond regard of me, his almost fatherly affection, and my heart ached for the loss once more. Thankfully, his earlier memories of Polar were quite different, and I was able to put my emotions aside and sift through the events that had gotten him exiled in the first place.

"You were right to be suspicious of Fenris, but your

reasoning is completely off base," I said at last, and Garrett's eyebrows winged up. "Fenris wasn't Polar—he was Polar's son."

Garrett nearly fell out of his chair. "That's ridiculous," he sputtered, looking at me as though I were insane. "Polar wasn't married, and I never heard that he had any children. Believe me, I investigated his past in great detail. And even if he had been married, it would never have been to a shifter."

"Well, you missed one secret," I insisted, thankful Garrett did not have a shifter nose—the lie I was spinning was outrageous, but no more so than the truth. "About forty years ago, Polar had a one-night stand with a wolf shifter female that resulted in Fenris. The wolf shifter refused to keep the cub because he was a hybrid. Since Polar couldn't acknowledge him without causing scandal, he entrusted him to Mendir ar'Tollis, Polar's cousin, to be raised discreetly." There was a little truth sprinkled in there —Mendir actually *was* Polar's cousin. He'd been a reclusive mage who lived near Nebara's chilly northern border, and his scholarly tastes had run very similarly to Fenris's.

"Mendir?" Garrett's brow contracted. "I have been to his estate in my search for Polar. The old fellow died a couple of years before the scandal, and the place was empty. But I talked to the neighbors, and there was no mention of any wolf shifter."

"He was very eccentric and reclusive, from what Fenris told me. He made Fenris hide in the library on the rare occasions he admitted visitors. Fenris told me all about how he had to hunker down behind the big green leather sofas as a cub."

Garrett blinked as that particular detail, which would have been impossible for me to know under normal circumstances, struck home. "Unlike me, Fenris only had a tiny bit of magic," I continued before Garrett could ask any awkward questions, "but he was still brought up as a mage, and he became Mendir's research assistant when he was older. He also corresponded with Polar about their research. When Mendir died five years ago, he inherited his mountain property, but it was very lonely up there, so Fenris took discreet trips to the city to visit his father."

"No wonder you two were close, then," Garrett said, sounding astonished. "You were both shifter-mage hybrids."

"Yep." My throat tightened a little—there was truth to that, even if not quite in the way I was spinning it for Garrett. "After Polar got into trouble—"

"Trouble," my ether parrot squawked, materializing on top of Garret's head again.

"Dammit," Garrett shouted, flailing his arms about in an effort to dislodge the bird, and giving me more time to think up a logical conclusion to my story.

"Get over here," I told the bird, holding out an arm.

"Here," Trouble cried, launching himself off Garrett's head. He landed on my forearm with a flap of his wings, sending a little hum of magic through me. "As I was saying," I continued, stroking the parrot's ghostly head, "once Polar got into hot water, he wrote to Iannis and asked him to take Fenris in, knowing that once he died, Fenris would have no one. Iannis agreed, and he and Fenris became good friends. You know the rest," I finished with a glare. "And before you ask, Fenris had no contact with Polar while he lived here. He once told me that he suspected Polar had gone to Faricia."

Garrett was silent for a long moment, clearly weighing each aspect of the story I'd just spun from him. "It is plausible, what you say," he finally agreed. "I did not know Polar very well, but he was a mage through and through. It would be unthinkable for one of us to live as a shifter, even to escape certain death. Had such a transformation even been possible, submitting to it would not have been in character. Despite the evidence pointing in that direction, I found it hard to believe that your Fenris and

Polar could have been one and the same. I'm glad you finally saw fit to explain about his peculiarities."

I was silent, resolutely repressing a tiny spark of guilt at misleading him. There was no point in feeling remorse—Garrett could never learn the truth, or Iannis would be at risk once more. "Now he is dead, I am no longer bound by my promise to keep his secrets," I finally said.

"In any case, I shall no longer be devoting so much time to this matter," Garrett said, smiling thinly. "I may have become a little too obsessed with this case, to the detriment of my career."

"Maybe you could stop attacking my fiancé, too," I suggested dryly, "and just focus on being good at your job, if you want the Minister's position so badly."

Garrett's face flushed. "I *am* good at my job," he said, drawing himself upright. "And I am not afraid to do whatever is required to move up in the ranks. But," he admitted, softening a little, "these past few days have shown me that Lord Iannis is a very good Chief Mage indeed, who went far beyond what most of his peers would have done to save and protect his citizens. It would be a disservice to the people of Canalo to remove him. So you need not fear on that count." He stood up, then bowed low. "I must go check on Harron now. Good evening, Miss Baine."

He walked out, taking all the fear and anxiety I'd been experiencing over the last few days with him. Sighing, I settled back into the couch, feeling both relieved and sad. My lies had been spun too late to do Fenris any good, but with any luck, they would at least save Iannis from further persecution.

20

I wanted to tell Iannis about Garrett's change of heart right away and make sure he'd back up my story, but my *serapha* charm told me he was still in meetings. So instead I called my social secretary, Nelia, to my quarters, and the two of us spent the rest of the evening rearranging my schedule for the next month. Nelia raised a brow when she noticed how much I was cutting down my magic lessons, but she accepted the current state of affairs as a necessary excuse. I was determined to spend more time volunteering, not just in Shiftertown, but in Maintown as well. The city would need all the help it could get to recover from this new catastrophe, and I wanted to be down in the trenches with the rest of the workers.

When we were finally done, I dismissed Nelia for the night, then crawled into Iannis's bed to wait for him. He came in at around two in the morning, waking me from a sound slumber as he settled his weight onto the edge of the mattress.

"How'd it go?" I asked sleepily as he stroked my hair. I rolled over, and even in the dim light, I could see the exhaustion and stress etched into his handsome features. "That bad?"

He sighed. "We had to break it to the three local mages and

Pillick that their magic was irretrievably gone. And that bear shifter as well. It was harrowing."

I swallowed against a sudden lump in my throat at the thought of that poor shifter. I couldn't imagine what he and his family were going through right now. I would have to visit him, to express my condolences and offer what assistance I could.

"The Council is very unhappy that we have not found a magical method of dealing with this Eraser," Iannis went on. "The object is simply too dangerous for any mage to attempt approaching it or touching it with their magic. We have no idea what might happen."

"So what did you decide?"

"We considered calling in the best human scientists in the country to come and study the Magic Eraser, so that they might come up with a better solution. But as you might expect, the Council is uneasy about having such a dangerous object in our midst, or letting human scientists handle such a weapon. If they managed to duplicate it, after all..."

"I can't blame them. Better to destroy or get rid of it, if at all possible." Gently, I grabbed Iannis's forearm and pulled him down on the bed next to me. "Garrett came to see me, and he was devastated about what happened to his assistant. I was surprised he felt so strongly about the guy. But he gave me some good news, too."

"Oh?" Iannis's eyebrows rose. "Is that meddlesome bastard finally leaving?"

Grinning, I told him about the conversation I'd had with Garrett, and the elaborate story I'd spun about Fenris's past. By the time I finished, Iannis was looking decidedly amused.

"That was some very quick thinking, *a ghra*," he said, dropping a kiss onto my forehead. "And your suggestions about creating human and shifter task forces were also quite inspired. I will be surprised if the Minister allows it, but he may come around to the idea in time."

"He'd better," I growled. "We can't afford any more of this class bullshit. It's time for us all to start working together."

"I agree." Iannis wrapped his arms around me and pulled me close. I snuggled against him, listening to his steady heartbeat. "I still can't believe Fenris is gone," he whispered. His salty tears scented the air, and my throat swelled with grief all over again. "He only lived here for three years—a blink of an eye in a life as long as mine. Yet, now that he is gone, it's as if something vital has been torn from me." He swallowed. "I'll always miss his counsel, his steady presence, and his loyalty. I don't think I told him enough how much I valued his friendship."

"I know." I wrapped my arms around Iannis, hugging him tight. The mental vault I'd stuffed all my Fenris-related memories and emotions into finally burst open, the tears coming fast and furious now. I started to tell Iannis to about Fenris's gift to me, but my throat seized up in another swell of grief. That discussion could wait for another day.

When tomorrow came, we would have to put on brave faces and deal with the world again. But for now, we clung to each other all through the night, mourning the loss of our beloved friend.

THE NEXT MORNING, Iannis went to his office to deal with the Magic Eraser's disposal, while Rylan and I had a quick breakfast before meeting Annia in the lobby. Dressed in her enforcer leathers, with her sword strapped to her belt and that mysterious, powerful aura around her, she looked ready to kick some serious ass.

"Wow," Rylan said, looking her up and down with undisguised admiration. "You look...different."

"It's the tan," Annia said with a wink, turning away. "A couple of months of sunshine can do wonders for a girl."

Rylan smiled, but he didn't look entirely convinced. We followed Annia down to the kitchens, where Mrs. Tandry was running an assembly line, wrapping and packing up boxes of meat, bread, and cheese to take to the survivor tents on the outskirts of town. We'd already agreed beforehand to come and help, so we pitched in, then got all the boxes out to the delivery area, where they were loaded onto a giant steamtruck.

"It's definitely not just her tan," Rylan said in mindspeak as we rode alongside the truck in a smaller vehicle. He was staring at Annia unabashedly as she looked out the window at our ruined city, lost in thought. *"Something fundamental about Annia has changed. She seems older somehow...and sexier."*

I rolled my eyes. *"I think the word you're looking for is 'powerful'."*

Rylan's expression didn't change, but I could practically feel him grinning on the inside. *"So what? Power is sexy, right? And she's definitely got some serious...something, about her. But she doesn't smell like a mage. What's happened?"*

"You'd have to ask her," I said evasively. The high neckline of Annia's leather jacket covered her torque, so I figured she didn't want to advertise it. *"She mentioned something to me about some unique adventures, but she was pretty vague about it. I don't think she's ready to share yet."*

"I'll get it out of her at some point," Rylan said, his eyes gleaming at the challenge. He was looking at Annia like she was a fine sirloin steak that he couldn't wait to sink his teeth into.

"Oh yeah?" I dug my elbow into his ribs, just enough to make him flinch. *"And what about Nelia?"* I bit back a grin as Rylan's cheeks reddened.

"What are you two talking about?" Annia asked.

"Nothing," we said in unison.

Annia arched a brow, and Rylan's face flushed even further. "Just a personal problem," he amended with a sheepish smile. "You know, shifter stuff."

"Mmm-hmm." Unconvinced, Annia turned her dark gaze back to the streets, and I tried not to laugh. If Rylan wanted a challenge, he'd sure picked the right person—Annia was just as big a flirt as he was when she wanted to be, but she was also a very tough nut to crack if she wasn't interested. And though I'd seen her eyeing Rylan once or twice, she rarely dated outside her own race.

We rolled to a stop in the Shiftertown Town Center, and the three of us got out to say hello to the volunteers who were already assembled to unload the truck. The volunteers were mostly shifters, but there were some humans, too. To my surprise, I recognized them from Father Calmias's congregation. Had he already begun talking to his followers? I wondered if he'd been out volunteering in Maintown yesterday—I'd been too stuck in grief and despair to notice. Or perhaps he'd fallen victim to the quake, like too many others.

We got the supplies off the truck in short order, and the volunteers behind the tables set up in the square handed the food to the lines of people waiting. Annia and I helped them dole out pre-portioned packages of varying sizes depending on the family, and I took the time to say a few words to each mother, father, or child who came up, asking how they were coping. Most of them sported bruises and stitches of some kind, and there were more than a few with serious injuries. I made a mental note to come back tomorrow and set up a makeshift clinic in the square, and to rope a few other mages into helping out. We couldn't heal everyone, but we could at least alleviate some of the worst injuries.

Out of the corner of my eye, I watched a middle-aged woman with a nasty burn on her forearm approach our table. As Annia handed her a basket of food, she casually brushed her hand against the woman's arm. The scent of magic stung my nostrils, and Rylan, who stood watchfully nearby, stiffened. To my astonishment, the woman's burn healed completely. Her eyes widened, and she opened her mouth to thank Annia, but Annia only winked, pressing a finger against her lips. Understanding, the woman smiled, then melted away into the crowd, taking the evidence of what Annia had done with her.

My eyes met Annia's, and she shrugged a little before turning to help the next person in line. I forced myself to focus my attention on the next person waiting for food in my own line —a fourteen-year-old boy—but even as I made small talk with him, my mind was still stuck on Annia. That spirit, or goddess, or whatever she was, clearly wasn't limited to what she could do in dreams. Annia could wield her magic, just like any mage! I'd never heard of such a thing before. Carefully, I creaked open the door to Fenris's memories to see if there were any records of humans acquiring magic that way. But nothing popped out, so I guessed it must be very rare.

I'd love to discuss what it means with Fenris, I thought, and a pang of agony hit me in the chest. By Magorah, everything was going to remind me of him. It had been that way with Roanas, my mentor, for a good few months, before the pain of his loss began to fade into something like acceptance.

A couple of hours later, the crowd finally began to thin out. As we handed out the final packages of food, I noticed a wizened old man loitering nearby, shooting me a look of abject hatred. He was dressed in a navy-blue tunic, his skin sallow and wrinkled, his head completely bald. As soon as he noticed me staring, he averted his face. Shrugging, I turned away. My ring was only moderately warm, so he wasn't much of a threat, whoever he was.

"Look again," Annia said in a low voice that sounded a lot like the exotic woman in my dreams. She leaned in close, her shoulder brushing against mine, and I caught the scent of dragon fruit and chilies. "That man is an enemy."

"Rylan," I murmured, making a subtle gesture for him to come forward. "Come with me a sec."

I stepped out from behind the table, and slowly approached the old man. As soon as he saw me coming, he tried to hurry away, but his decrepit form and withered limbs didn't allow him much speed.

"Hang on there," Rylan said, appearing in front of him in an instant. "We just want a quick word."

"By Magorah," I breathed as the man's scent hit me. Beneath the stench of decay was a very familiar male scent, one that made my blood boil. "Argon Chartis, it's you, isn't it?"

"Yes," he spat, whirling about to face me. Up close, I could see the remnants of what used to be his handsome, if cold, face, buried beneath age and illness. His thick chestnut hair and smooth skin were gone, and in their place was a bitter old man. "Are you happy to see me brought so low, Miss Baine? Why don't you get it over with and arrest me?" He shoved his wrists at me. For a moment, I was tempted to do as he said and cuff them.

But I could sense absolutely no magic coming off him, and somehow it seemed wrong to chain such a sorry creature, even if he had committed horrendous crimes.

"So what the hell happened to you, then?" I said instead, crossing my arms over my chest. "Did Thorgana's Magic Eraser get to you?"

"Yes," he hissed, his eyes narrowing. "I met with her at the Mendles' house, and she nearly killed me with that damned thing. At first I didn't realize why I was weakening, but once I figured out that blasted metal object was the cause, I dragged myself from the house as fast as I could manage." He clenched his jaw. "I was only there for around thirty minutes, but that was enough time. I have no magic left."

Rylan and I exchanged a horrified look—thirty minutes? That was all it took to strip the magic from a powerful mage like Chartis? "Prove it," I said, grabbing his gnarled hands. Had the lack of magic accelerated his aging process? Speaking the words of the testing spell, I pushed my magic into him, searching for that glowing core inside all mages. But there was only a wasteland inside of him, devoid of all but the tiniest spark.

He's dying.

"I believe you," I said softly, pulling away. "You can go now."

Argon stared at me. "You're not going to arrest me?"

"What would be the point?" I shook my head, motioning for Rylan to return to my side. "I don't see why we should waste an executioner's axe on you."

I walked away as Argon sputtered, feeling both triumph and pity. Yes, maybe arresting the former Director of the Mages Guild and putting him on trial was the right thing to do. But it seemed more just to let him live out the rest of his numbered days, knowing he was reduced to the very thing he loathed—a mere human.

"You were right," I said to Annia as we rode back to the Palace in the steamcar. "He was an enemy, even if he didn't mean me any harm just then. How did you know?"

Annia's eyes flicked to Rylan, and they assessed him for a moment. "I get...feelings, sometimes," she said. "Not quite premonitions, but more like a really strong gut instinct."

It was clear she didn't want to say more in front of Rylan, so I didn't push. When we got back to the Palace, Annia and I went to meet Iannis and Director Chen in the Winter Garden for lunch. A somber mood settled over our group as we sat down and ate, and even though Iannis led the discussion as normal, going over our accomplishments for the day so far, and our plans for the week, there was a tinge of sadness to his gaze that was barely noticeable unless you knew what to look for. Subdued, I told them about my encounter with Chartis among the homeless in the tent city.

"So Argon Chartis has been turned into a powerless old man?" Director Chen asked, sounding incredulous. "I'm not sure the Council will agree with your decision to let him go, Miss Baine, but I understand why you did it."

"My nose told me he has only days to live," I explained. "Two or three weeks at most. I don't think it's worth the effort to arrest and prosecute him under the circumstances."

"As Sunaya said, Chartis is already suffering the worst punishment that could be imagined for a mage," Iannis said as he forked up some salad. "A quick death would be almost too merciful for that traitor. There is little point in wasting resources on indicting him, when we have so many other things to worry about."

I was about to ask Chen where Kardanor was—he'd attended our other working lunches—when the door opened and a servant hurried in. "Lord Iannis," he said breathlessly, pulling a letter from his breast pocket. "Urgent news from the mines."

Iannis took the letter, his violet eyes scanning it swiftly as he unfolded it. "There have been cave-ins at the prison mines," he said, his voice tight. "Over three hundred dead."

"No!" Annia jumped to her feet, her face white. "Noria. Is Noria alive?"

"I don't know," Iannis said gravely. "The message doesn't list the names of the victims."

"I need to go there," Annia said, her voice trembling. Her

eyes were diamond hard and bright, her skin stretched too tight across her face. "I need to see my sister, make sure she is safe."

"Of course," Iannis said. He pulled a piece of stationary and a pen from his magical sleeve, and quickly began writing. Glancing over his shoulder, I saw that it was an order to the mine overseer that Annia should be admitted immediately, and allowed unrestricted access to her sister. It also said that all mining must be suspended until the place was certified safe, and that a representative from the Guild would be coming out to inspect the place soon.

"Take this," he said, handing the order to her. His official seal was stamped on it—a magical ink that shimmered across the bottom of the page and could not be covered up or removed. "Go and see Dira, inform her that you have access to any form of transportation you may need."

"Thank you." Annia stuffed the letter into the inside of her jacket pocket, briefly exposing the torque around her neck. My throat swelled again, and I swallowed back the emotion. Was I about to lose another friend? Noria had left for the mines, hating my guts after we'd made the very tough decision to prosecute her for joining the Resistance. I hated the idea of that bright spirit going to her grave with that same hatred in her heart.

"Please," I said, throwing my arms around Annia in a hug. "Tell Noria I love her and I'm thinking of her. That we all are," I said.

"I will," Annia told me. She hugged me hard, then spun on her heel and ran out, leaving me behind with a heart so heavy I couldn't do anything more than stare after her and wonder if she would return.

21

O*ne week later*

"No," I said from my seat on the couch, making a slicing motion with my hand. "Mrs. Gorax should definitely *not* be on the list. Strike the name off. I know the company helped with the repairs, but they're responsible for much of the damage in the first place, and Mr. Gorax is in prison. They don't deserve to be honored."

"Very well." Nelia made a scratching motion with her pen, then pursed her lips. "What about the Tomlinsons? They donated over five hundred loaves of bread from their bakery."

Holding in a sigh, I continued going through the guest list Nelia had drawn up for the reception we were planning. Everyone had been working around the clock to repair the damage from the quake, and Iannis had decided a morale booster was needed. But I was having trouble looking forward to the party, what with Annia gone again and the loss of Fenris still so recent and raw. I was still waiting to hear if Noria had survived the cave-ins.

To keep my mind off Fenris's death, and Noria's fate, I'd thrown myself into the various recovery projects, organizing volunteers to help with the food deliveries to the tent city set up on Solantha's outskirts. Shiftertown was almost completely cleared, having been the area least affected by the quake. Most of the displaced shifters had already moved back into the city and started work on repairing their streets and what damaged buildings they did have. Maintown was another story entirely— only a third of the buildings were currently inhabitable, and most of the survivors were still living in tents.

Bodies were still being dug out of the ruins, though we hadn't found Fenris's yet. There were mass graves dug and filled daily, since the few cemeteries were insufficient for this sudden influx. Once we'd finished clearing out the city and tallying up the dead, we would hold a memorial for all the quake victims. I didn't know how I would be able to face it, but I knew I had to. I was a public figure now—I couldn't just hide in my room and cry.

One body that *had* been recovered from the rubble was Thorgana's, as well as the rest of the Mendle family. I'd gone to inspect her crushed remains myself, to make sure it wasn't a fake, and I'd been relieved to confirm that it was indeed her.

Iannis had recruited Noria's former boyfriend, Elnos, to help figure out how to dispose of the Magic Eraser, since he was a mage with a background in science. He was still chewing on the problem, but in the meantime, he'd ordered the deadly object to be enclosed in a thick lead casket and kept in a location far away from the city. The lead seemed to lessen the harmful effects of the object, though it was still inadvisable for mages to get within five feet of it. Garrett had stayed for a couple of days, wanting to see if the scientists would make a breakthrough, but once it was clear they needed more time, he and Harron packed up. They'd left by dirigible this morning, to both Iannis' and my great relief.

A knock on the door interrupted my discussion with Nelia, and I caught Kardanor's scent. "Come in," I called before Nelia could answer, much to her annoyance. I gave her an apologetic smile at the interruption, but I wasn't about to turn Kardanor away.

"Good morning, Miss Baine," Kardanor said with a smile as he let himself in. He looked as dashing as always, though there were a few patches in his red coat and the pants beneath looked like they'd seen better days. "I hope I'm not interrupting?"

"No, no, we're about done." I sat up, then gestured for Nelia to put her things away. "Why don't you go take an early lunch, Nelia? We'll pick this up later."

"Yes, Miss Baine." Nelia gathered her things up, looking somewhat disappointed, though she tried to hide it. Her entire face had lit up when Kardanor walked in, and I fought the urge to roll my eyes at her fickle affections. I was tempted to tell her not to bother, since Kardanor had his sights set on a certain female mage, but I decided not to break the bad news just yet. At some point, she'd have to learn to guard her heart better.

"What can I do for you?" I asked him once Nelia had gone and he'd settled himself in one of my chairs.

"I hate to ask you this at all," Kardanor said, scratching the back of his head. The tips of his ears reddened, and I was startled to see embarrassment in his dark blue eyes. "But I was wondering if you might be able to use your magic to make me look a little more...respectable, for Thursday night's reception."

I frowned. "What's wrong with the way you look now?" I gestured to his face. "Have you not noticed the way women look at you every time you walk by?"

Kardanor gave me a sheepish grin. "It's not my face or form I'm worried about, Miss Baine, but my attire." He gestured to his shabby clothing. "My house was damaged by the fire, and the few decent outfits I have here in the Palace positively reek of soot and dust, after all the rescue work. The senior mages here are always so elegant, not a hair out of place..." He trailed off as a dreamy look entered his eye, and it wasn't at all hard for me to guess who he was thinking about. "Anyway, I hear I am to be mentioned in the Chief Mage's speech, and I would prefer to look less shabby when every eye is on me, however briefly."

"Wait a minute," I said slowly, anger building inside me with each word that came out of his mouth. "Are you telling me that you're living in poverty right now?"

"I wouldn't say that," Kardanor said quickly. "My home is still standing, if damaged, which is much better than most Maintown residents can say. But yes, I am just about broke now, because the bank where I keep my account has not yet reopened since the quake."

"Well, we can't have that," I said briskly, standing. "I'll have Nelia get you fitted today, and arrange for proper evening wear in time for the party. And I will make sure you are compensated for your time and hard work."

"Oh, I don't want to trouble you—" Kardanor began, shooting to his feet as I strode past him. "Have I offended you in any way?"

"Of course not." I opened the door, then turned to smile at him. "I just remembered I have something I need to speak to Iannis about. Nelia will come to your rooms at three with a tailor in tow. We can't have our favorite architect showing up for the reception in rags."

I showed Kardanor out of my quarters, then strode off toward the Mages Guild in search of Iannis. By the time I reached the lobby, I was positively fuming. Dira glanced up as I stormed in, a startled look on her face, and asked if everything was all right. Ignoring her, I bulldozed straight through the small crowd milling about the lobby, following the tug from my *serapha* charm.

The door to the council room opened before I reached it, and the council members spilled into the hallway along with Iannis, Director Chen, and Cirin.

"Miss Baine," Cirin said, starting at the sight of me. I could tell he was taken aback by my expression, as were Chen and Iannis. "Is everything all right?"

"I need to speak with you three," I said tersely. "Immediately."

"Very well," Iannis said cautiously. "Please excuse us, Councilors." He stepped past them, and they watched, wide-eyed, as the four of us filed into Iannis's office.

As soon as the door was shut, I rounded on them. "Do you three realize," I said in a deceptively calm voice, "that Kardanor, the very man who is responsible for saving thousands of our citizens, and who has worked tirelessly since I first brought him to the Palace to help with the earthquake plans, has not a coin to his name, nor a stitch of clothing beyond what is on his back? And that we have not thought to do anything about it?"

I turned my glare on Director Chen, who had worked with him the closest, and she recoiled. "Mr. Makis is welcome to as much gold as he needs," she said. "I had no idea he was in such dire straits, or I would have offered him money myself."

"He would never embarrass himself by asking you," Iannis said. "He is a proud man, and an idealist—not one seeking material reward. And he fancies you, besides."

Director Chen's ivory cheeks turned an interesting shade of pink. "Well, then, how are we to help him if he will not accept our money?"

"We don't have to give him charity," I said. "Name him Secretary of Planning and Reconstruction, and give him a proper salary. Magorah knows he's the most qualified person for the job, and there's work enough to keep him busy for years to come."

All three mages looked astonished by this idea, and began talking at once about how unprecedented it was. But Cirin pointed out that it was only custom, not law, that all secretaries be mages, and they agreed there was nobody else more qualified or motivated to take the position than Kardanor.

"He is already doing the job anyway," Director Chen said. "He's been going over plans with me to put in a better system that will ensure the building codes are not circumvented or ignored again, and I would be hard-pressed to find someone with more enthusiasm for the task. We may as well give him the title, as Sunaya suggests, and see that he is handsomely compensated for his hard work."

"I will speak to him about it," Iannis decided. "And if he is agreeable, I will announce the appointment at the reception."

"Thank you." I beamed, pleased with how quickly we'd come to a decision. Kardanor had saved all our asses, and he deserved way more than an honorable mention in Iannis's speech.

"Should I also confirm Captain Skonel tomorrow night?" Iannis asked me. "I have not had much time to observe him, but he seems quite competent. In times like these, it would be best to have a permanent captain, rather than an acting one."

"I have no objection to that," I said. "He worked very hard to prevent looting during the aftermath of the quake. But we need to do a major overhaul on how the Guild is being run. There are some practices I'm not happy with that are causing a lot of discontent amongst the other enforcers."

"Very well," Iannis said. He dismissed the others, and we spent the next half hour discussing my concerns about the bounties, the extra bonuses, and the crew system in general. These were small issues in the grand scheme of things, but solving them might allow the Enforcers Guild to fight crime smarter and more effectively. And as Iannis and I discussed the pros and cons of possible solutions, I couldn't help but think that Fenris and Roanas would be proud if they could see how far I'd come.

22

The next day was a whirlwind of activity as Nelia and I worked our asses off to prepare the Palace for tonight's reception. We decided to go with dawn colors for the décor—gold, royal purple, and deep and pale pinks—to symbolize that we'd overcome adversity, and that our city had risen again to a new dawn. The dead had been buried, the streets had finally been cleared of rubble, and the city was ready to rebuild and move on.

To my relief, just about everyone we invited had accepted despite being given such short notice. By the time the last guests trickled in, the ballroom was absolutely packed with guests—more full than I could ever remember seeing it. However, the conversation was subdued, rather than deafening. There was an air of muted pride and a sense of accomplishment, mixed with lingering grief and exhaustion, which wasn't surprising as there was still a lot of work to do. The mage, shifter, and human council members were all present, as well as those humans and business owners who had risen to the occasion and provided exemplary service.

Solantha's respective neighborhoods were hosting their own

celebrations, and the entire city was sparkling with celebratory lights, the air filled with music and the sound of the occasional firework exploding. We hadn't allowed the citizens to light their own, due to the recent fires, but city officials had decided to put on a show, and we could see brilliant displays exploding over the bay from the windows lining the ballroom's far wall.

"I am very glad you are around to organize these affairs now," Iannis said in mindspeak as he surveyed the crowd. His hand slid beneath the hem of my reddish-gold silk gown, and sizzling heat rushed through my veins as he squeezed my thigh. *"Perhaps I should put you in charge of them permanently."*

I stifled a groan. *"This isn't exactly what I had in mind when I agreed to become your wife,"* I said to him.

"But you're so very good at it," Iannis said, winking.

One of the Maintown councilmen approached Iannis, engaging him in conversation before I could respond. Done with my food, I wandered down to where Comenius and Elania were sitting, only a few tables away. Rusalia was there as well, and they sat with Kardanor, chatting very enthusiastically together. Rylan, once again in guard uniform, stuck close to my side—he considered the crowd a risk to my safety, no matter how carefully we had vetted the guest list.

"Naya!" Comenius greeted me with a big hug. "I'm so happy to see you are looking well."

"You look beautiful," Elania said, beaming at me. She was dressed in a gorgeous black velvet gown with a halter top, her hair done in one of its trademark updos, and glittering onyx jewelry at her ears and throat.

"Thanks." I smiled back, then turned to Rusalia. "I love your dress." It was pale blue taffeta, and with those blonde curls and large eyes, she looked very pretty.

"Thank you." She smiled shyly, ducking her head a little. There was no hint of anger or resentment in her little face—she seemed like a normal ten-year-old, her eyes bright as she took in the splendor around her.

"Have you been treating your pa well?" I asked, leaning forward a little so I could meet her gaze.

She nodded. "I've been listening, and doing all my chores. Right, Pa?" She looked at him from beneath her lashes.

Comenius gave her a fatherly smile and patted her blonde head. "Yes, Rusalia. You have been doing much better since you came home...though we've still had a few fire-related accidents."

As if on cue, Rusalia's half-eaten steak burst into flame. She yelped, and I snuffed it out before anyone could notice. Even so, the smoke rising from the charred meat drew some curious glances from the guests at nearby tables.

"You, young lady, will be taking lessons in magical control here in the Palace for the next few weeks," I told Rusalia. "Starting tomorrow morning at nine." She stared at me, completely tongue-tied for once. "Is that understood?"

She nodded, her eyes wide.

"Do you mean it?" Com asked gratefully. "It would be a great help if you could arrange for a tutor, since her magic is too strong for Elania and me to reliably control."

"She'll soon learn to do that herself," I assured him. I was planning to teach her basic control myself, now that I had Fenris's knowledge to draw upon, but I couldn't tell him that in front of this crowd. Later, she would be able to do an apprenticeship in the normal way, but those usually did not start until the mid-teens. Mage children normally learned basic control and simple spells from their own families long before their apprenticeships began.

"Are you all right otherwise?" I probed, lowering my voice. "All those market carts that were set aflame...my offer for a loan still stands, you know."

"Thanks," Com replied, smiling, "but I'm fine. We've come to an agreement that allows me to pay the debt off in kind. Healing potions are very much in demand just now."

"You weren't joking about the magic," Kardanor said, looking bemused. "Let's get you another steak." He leaned over and snagged the attention of a waiter, pointing at Rusalia's plate.

"You're looking quite handsome tonight," I told him, admiring his dark red suit. He wore a crisp white shirt and a dark grey waistcoat beneath his well-cut jacket, and the golden chain of a pocket watch, tucked into his pocket, glittered in the light.

"Thank you. Nelia helped me pick the outfit," he said. "Your assistant has excellent taste in fashion."

We talked for a few more minutes before I moved on to the Shiftertown Council table. "Sunaya," Aunt Mafiela greeted me warmly. She stood up and enveloped me in a hug, her floral perfume tickling my nose. "You have done a wonderful job organizing this reception." Her eyes glowed with affection as her gaze turned to Rylan, who bowed his head. They couldn't embrace, not while he was still in disguise as my bodyguard, but their eyes said all there was to say.

"Thank you," I replied, grinning at the unwonted praise. It was still weird to be the recipient of such approval from her, but I was slowly getting used to having a normal relationship with my aunt.

"Yes, this is quite splendid," the tiger-clan chieftain said. His orange eyes gleamed as he looked me up and down. "Perhaps you should help organize the Shiftertown Gala next year."

"Somehow, I think Sunaya would rather jab a fork into her eye," Lakin said, grinning. "I'm sure Lord Iannis had to twist her arm to get her to agree."

"Not exactly," I protested. "I was happy to do it for such a special occasion." But really, I hoped people wouldn't keep suggesting that I organize their events. With my luck, Iannis would make me the official event coordinator.

I stopped by a few more tables, including Captain Skonel's, to thank him for all his hard work. He was sitting with his deputy and several crew foremen, and though he was still a bit haughty, he treated me with respect, as did the others.

"You should come back up here," Iannis said. *"We are about to begin the speeches."*

I returned to our table. Rylan pulled out my chair, then hovered close behind me while I faced the crowd. Iannis stood up, tapping his wineglass with his fork for order. He used magic to amplify the sound, and the rest of the room fell silent.

"Citizens," he said in a sonorous voice that carried easily throughout the room. "It gives me great pleasure to stand here with you all tonight. I am proud of each person here—you all have shown remarkable fortitude and courage these past few days, during Solantha's most trying times since I became Chief Mage. Tonight, we are here to honor you."

He raised his glass, and everyone drank. Enthusiastic applause broke out, and I was pleased to see there wasn't a single resentful person in the room tonight. Everyone was in good spirits, despite all three races rubbing elbows at the tables. The only thing that would have made this more perfect were if Annia and Noria were sitting with Comenius, and Fenris was up at the high table with us. But I was determined not to let those losses dim my mood. I'd spent enough time with my grief—tonight, I would celebrate with the others.

Iannis continued with his speech, calling up various members of society to present them with medals and flowers to thank them for their service. He also called up Captain Skonel and confirmed his appointment as Captain of the Enforcer's Guild, which was met with ecstatic applause from the enforcers present. I was pleased to see that they were enthusiastic about the appointment—it was important the Guild be happy with their choice in captain, and not just the Chief Mage.

"Kardanor Makis," Iannis finally called as we drew to the end of the ceremony. "Please come forward."

Kardanor flashed a grin at Director Chen from his chair, then assumed an appropriately serious expression as he approached Iannis to receive his prize. Iannis placed the medal around his neck, and Director Chen handed him the bouquet of flowers, as she'd done for the others. I wondered if anyone else noticed the flush in her cheeks when Kardanor's hand grazed hers, or if they just credited it to the booze, which was flowing very freely tonight.

"Mr. Makis is perhaps our most important guest here tonight," Iannis said, addressing the crowd. "Without his knowledge of architecture and building codes, and his persistence in bringing the compromised structural integrity of many of our buildings to our attention, we would have suffered far more casualties than we did. Even now, he is working tirelessly on plans to rebuild the city so that it can better withstand any future quakes and fires. To that end, I have officially appointed him as Secretary of City Planning and Reconstruction."

There were a few gasps at this unorthodox pronouncement, mostly from the mages in the room. But they were drowned out by the thunderous applause from the rest of the guests. This went on for several minutes, with much cheering and whooping, before the crowd finally quieted down enough for Kardanor to give a short acceptance speech. During the speech, he thanked Iannis, and promised the citizens of Solantha that as the first human Secretary, he would make them proud. Afterward, he took his seat in between Cirin and Chen's empty chair, and I noticed Chen was smiling brightly at him.

"I have another announcement," Iannis said once the noise had died down again. "There are certain members of the Resistance who, after learning the true nature of their organization and their leader, gave their loyalty to the Federation and put themselves in great danger to help secure our country's future. One of these men is Rylan Baine, a son of the Jaguar Clan. He has worked tirelessly to save lives in the past few days, risking his own neck repeatedly in rescuing victims from dangerously damaged buildings. As a reward, I now pardon him for all crimes against the State of Canalo, and I release him from his service to the Palace. Please come up, Rylan."

The crowd gasped as Rylan stepped forward, then tapped the pin on his lapel to undo the illusion. A lump swelled in my throat as I watched him accept his medal and flowers, and I rushed over and folded him into a tight hug.

"Congratulations," I whispered fiercely. "And don't be a stranger."

"I'll visit often, I promise," Rylan said. He hugged me back, then went to Aunt Mafiela, who was standing now, tears streaming down her face. The crowd erupted into deafening applause as Rylan embraced his mother, lifting her feet off the ground. As I looked around the room, I caught sight of Nelia sitting a few tables away, and I had to bite back a laugh. She looked flabbergasted, and not entirely pleased, about Rylan's sudden transformation. I had a feeling Rylan wouldn't need to end the romance between them—she would be the one to kick him to the curb.

"Now for my last announcement tonight," Iannis said, and the room went quiet again. He turned to look at me, and I froze at the twinkle in his violet eyes. "I am instituting a committee to reform the Enforcers Guild organization and pay structure." Many of the enforcers cheered at this, though there were some folded arms and glares from a few senior foremen. "It is important that everyone is fairly compensated, and that all crimes are appropriately investigated irrespective of bounty size. After due consideration, I am naming Sunaya Baine as chair of this committee, and she will choose six other members to help her, two from each race. They have six months to come up with a plan."

My mouth dropped open in shock and horror, and it took a supreme effort to replace my expression with a pleased smile. Thankfully, the crowd was already applauding again, giving me time to regain my composure. But as I came up to accept my flowers from Director Chen, I shot Iannis a veiled glare from behind my smile. There would be hell to pay for this later.

You're not a simple enforcer anymore, a voice that sounded a lot like Resinah echoed in my mind, and I bit back a sigh. But as I turned to the crowd to give my acceptance speech, I caught Captain Skonel's eye, sitting in the back, and had to hide a grin at the look of sheer horror on his face. He looked disgusted at the idea that he would have to defer to me now. On the other hand, my friends and family were on their feet, clapping and cheering, their faces shining with love and pride.

I'm not just an enforcer anymore, I told myself, at peace with the idea now. *I'm a champion for these people. For my friends, colleagues, and the underdogs of our city.* And with that in mind, I squared my shoulders and prepared to give them one hell of a speech.

23

I spent the rest of the reception talking and drinking with the guests, congratulating those who had received medals and promotions, and accepting congratulations on my own appointment as graciously as I could. But the moment everything was over, and Iannis and I were back in his suite, I rounded on him.

"How could you stick me with a huge responsibility like that in front of a *bajillion* people?" I shouted, jabbing him in the chest with a finger. "Without even asking me first!" Now that I no longer had an audience to hide from, all the outrage and shock at being blindsided came pouring out of me. I fisted my trembling hands at my sides and glared up at him, resisting the mighty urge to punch him. "Do you think that just because I'm your fiancée, you can just tell me when and where to jump, and I'll obey without question?"

"No," Iannis said calmly, completely unfazed by my anger. "But now that you no longer require frequent magic lessons, you'll need something else to keep you occupied. And you really are the perfect person for this particular job. You brought up some excellent ideas about restructuring the enforcer pay system when we talked the other day. Nobody else would approach the problem with as much verve and insight as you."

That took the wind right out of my sails. "What...what do you mean I no longer need magic lessons?"

Iannis smirked. "Did you really think I wouldn't notice Fenris had gifted his knowledge to you? I knew for sure when you sent me that ether pigeon the other day, after you had so much trouble with them earlier." He shook his head. "It would be just the kind of thing Fenris would do with his dying breath —he would have considered it sacrilegious to waste all the knowledge he'd gained over a lifetime of study without passing it on to someone."

"Oh." I let out a little sigh. "So, do I seem...different, to you, at all? Like I've become more like Fenris?" I had been worrying about that possibility, putting off confessing to Iannis what we'd done. I didn't *feel* any different, but knowing I had all those extra memories might seem weird to Iannis.

Iannis shook his head. "You are still my Sunaya." He took me by the shoulders, drawing me closer to him. "Still the same passionate shifter-mage hybrid I fell in love with," he added, smiling softly. "And now that Fenris has given you such a precious gift, I see no reason why we must waste the scarce time we have together with basic training and Loranian grammar."

I arched a brow, even as the pain of Fenris's loss lanced through me. "Is that your way of saying we're going to have more sex instead?"

Iannis threw back his head and laughed, his broad shoulders shaking. *By Magorah*, I thought, watching the way his teeth flashed, and how the firelight flickered across his sculpted face. He really was such a beautiful man.

"No," he finally said, stroking the pad of his thumb along my cheekbone. "Though that is certainly an enticing thought. But we will be able to move onto more advanced lessons. Fenris's repertoire of spellcraft was impressive, but I am three times his age and have far more practical experience." His expression sobered then, and he searched my gaze. "How have you been dealing with Fenris's memories? It can't be comfortable, having the sum of someone's life experiences crammed into your consciousness."

I shrugged. "I've put them in a sort of box so that they don't pop up unexpectedly. At first, it was overwhelming every time I opened the box to reach for a spell, but it's become a lot easier. Now I just leave the box kind of propped open, and whenever I need a spell I don't know, it pops into my mind."

"Excellent," Iannis said, his voice filled with pride. "Someone with a weaker will or fewer memories might have a hard time dealing with such a gift, but it seems you have instinctively figured out how to handle them."

"So, what does this mean, in regards to my apprenticeship?" I asked. "Do we graduate me now, or wait the full ten years?"

"I do not think we need to wait ten years," Iannis said, "but we should keep up appearances for a few years longer. We don't want to risk accusations of cheating, and nobody is supposed to know that Fenris was a mage. Besides, you may have inherited all Fenris's knowledge, but you still need practice in actually applying all those spells."

"Do *you* see it as cheating?" I asked, more anxious than I wanted to admit. "I don't think I could have made it out alive, or saved Com's daughter, without the techniques that Fenris gifted me."

"Both of you did what you had to do." He stroked my hair. "Don't worry about that. Some mages might be suspicious at your sudden advancement, but they cannot prove that you are anything other than a very gifted student."

"Plus, I can always say it's because you are a more than gifted master," I pointed out. "Part of me wishes I could give Fenris the credit." I sighed, sadness filling me again. "He did some great things that we'll never be able to tell anyone about, and it sucks. Hell, we couldn't even bury his body." It had never been recovered, and we could only assume it had burned to ashes in the fire. Iannis had commissioned a gravestone in the Palace cemetery, where Solantha's important figures were buried, but the plot beneath it was empty.

"The only credit Fenris would care about is that which you and I have already given him," Iannis said, pulling me against his chest. "He cared deeply for you, Sunaya, more than you may have realized. It was he who drew my attention to your case and prompted me to bring you to the Palace for further examination. The scholar in him wanted to know how you could have escaped detection for so long, and the shifter in him hoped for a kindred spirit in you."

Tears spilled down my cheeks, and I tucked my face into Iannis's shoulder. "He saved my life that first night in the Palace when the guards nearly killed me," I muttered into Iannis's robe. "He always looked out for both of us."

We stood there for a long moment, grieving in silence and taking comfort in one another's presence. And then, Iannis gently tipped my tearstained face up to his and pressed his lips against mine. I kissed him back on a long sigh, twining my arms around his neck. Desire slowly unfurled its tendrils, warming me up, pushing out the heavy sorrow that had taken up residence inside me. It seemed like forever since Iannis and I had last made love, and I reached for the sash around his waist, tugging it open so I could run my hands over his hard, strong body. He inhaled sharply as I lightly scraped my claws over his pale skin, and then he was working at the ties on the back of my dress, loosening the bodice.

"Yes," I whispered as his hands glided down my exposed back, pushing the skirt of my dress down and baring my body to his hungry gaze. He shrugged his robes off his powerful shoulders, then picked me up and carried me into the bedroom. The satin sheets caressed my skin as he laid me down, and then it was his lips gliding over my skin, sending sparks of desire through me as he gently kissed and nipped, tracing patterns and paths over my curves with his talented mouth. I lifted my head to watch as he spread my legs, then buried his face between them, using that wicked tongue to find my sweet spot. My hips arched off the bed, pressing myself against him, and I buried my fingers in his long, dark red hair as I moaned my encouragement.

But Iannis took it slow tonight, gradually lifting me higher and higher until the pleasure crested, and I cried out his name. And he did it again, and again, and again, drawing out the moment, savoring my moans, my trembles, my need. And when he finally lifted his head again, the hunger in his shimmering violet gaze was tempered by a tenderness so profound I thought my heart might burst with love for him.

"*A ghra,*" he whispered against my lips as he slid into me, the word as much a prayer as it was an endearment. I wrapped myself around him, and we rocked together, holding tight to each other as we gathered our love around us like a kind of armor, a balm that soothed our wounds and strengthened us. I wanted to hold onto this moment forever, to cocoon myself in love and sensation, but need took over, that fierce edge that pushed us faster, made our skin slick with sweat and our lungs short of breath.

"I love you," I gasped, arching my hips as he thrust into me, hard and fast. And then I came again, holding on tight and using Iannis as my anchor as I was tossed into a storm of pleasure.

Afterward, Iannis pulled my back against his chest, then tucked his face into my shoulder and fell asleep. As I listened to his slow, deep breathing, savoring the feeling of being cradled by him, my thoughts drifted back to Fenris again. The pain of his passing was dulled by the afterglow from lovemaking, and with Iannis's love wrapped around me, I finally gathered my courage and checked Fenris's memories from his last few days. I focused on the week before the quake, watching his last conversations with the people he cared about, his long hours in the library and his room, poring through books in search of useful spells, and his sparring sessions with Rylan. It was painful, looking at them, but somehow comforting as well to know that even though Fenris was gone, I would always have him with me.

Feeling sleepy, I pushed Fenris's memories back into the vault, intending to drift off. But one popped back out, and my mental eyes flew wide as I watched it unfold. Fenris was in his room, a stout, waterproof leather pack open on his bed. He was packing clothes, a few knives, his coded research notebook and golden pen, a water filter and canteen, and a heavy purse of gold coins. He put the pack on his back and left the Palace, and I watched him catch a cab all the way to Downtown before trekking far out of the city on foot. Soon, he was in the redwood forest on Solantha's outskirts, a good five miles south of where we'd set up the temporary shelter tents. I could feel his sorrow keenly, but also his sense of acceptance, as he searched the trees for an acceptable hiding spot. He eventually found a trunk that was hollowed out and tucked the pack inside, making sure it was hidden deeply enough that no one passing by could see it.

"Iannis!" I shook him awake, my heart hammering. "Iannis, I saw something in Fenris's memories!"

Iannis listened intently as I told him about what I'd seen. "We have to go and get that pack," I said urgently. "Fenris's most prized possessions are in there. He wouldn't want them to end up in the hands of some random stranger."

"We'll go tomorrow," Iannis promised, kissing the top of my head. "I will make sure Fenris's research notes are properly preserved. And we can donate the gold to the homeless quake victims in his name."

Satisfied, I snuggled back down into the comforters. And, feeling lighter than I had in weeks, I slipped off into a peaceful sleep.

EPILOGUE

The next morning, Iannis and I rose with the dawn, then hopped onto my steambike and headed for the forest I'd seen in Fenris's memories. Disguised as humans, we zipped through the streets, bundled up against the cold. The temperature had dropped another ten degrees, and the rain from last night had crystalized into frost on the windshields and storefronts we passed.

"I now understand why Fenris complained so much about riding with you," Iannis said as I made a hairpin turn down a narrow street. *"You're a daredevil!"*

I laughed. *"Please. You go faster than this with your super speed."* It was hard to believe that this was the first time I'd taken Iannis out on my bike, and it gave me an obscene amount of pleasure that he was clinging to me for dear life, his hard body pressed against me from behind.

"Yes, but at least I'm in control."

Chuckling, I slowed as we approached a stoplight. We were in Maintown, just a few miles from Downtown, which we would cut through to get to the redwood forest south of the city.

"Hang on," Iannis said as the light changed. *"Isn't that Father Calmias speaking?"*

I glanced to the left, and nearly fell off my bike. Right there in the center of an outdoor shopping area, Father Calmias stood on a small stage, speaking to a crowd of several hundred humans. Curious, I guided my bike over to the curb, and Iannis and I took off our helmets so we could listen.

"...we must accept shifters and mages into our hearts, and learn to live with them in harmony," Father Calmias was saying in his deep, resonant voice, and Iannis and I exchanged surprised grins. We listened to him lecture for ten minutes about how the earthquake was a message from the Ur-God, to punish the city for the strife, conflict, and all the hate humans had been spreading through the Resistance. He explained how the Ur-God had appeared to him with a message of love and light, and that it was the responsibility of humans, his chosen ones, to unite the three races so that peace and prosperity would come to all.

Unsurprisingly, his audience seemed confused at his sudden change of heart, and there were some isolated protests at this drastic change of direction. But Father Calmias spoke with such conviction that these were quickly drowned out, and the crowd was soon singing his praises, promising they would live with love and light in their hearts, and set a good example for the rest of their community.

"I am glad now that I decided to alter his mind," Iannis murmured to me, pitching his voice below the cheers of the crowd. "Though I still have strong reservations about the method I had to employ, and I don't plan to use it again if I can help it, in this case it clearly has done more good than harm. I did not realize Father Calmias was quite such a charismatic speaker."

"Yeah. That's why his followers are so rabid, and why he was able to get so much support for the Resistance." I smiled, shaking my head a little. "I know it was a tough decision for you, considering what happened to your grandfather, but I really think you did the right thing."

We moved on then, cutting through Downtown, and soon we were on a rural road that wound up and down a series of hills before taking us into the forest. Redwoods towered all about us as we pulled over to the side of the road, and we stood there for a long moment, soaking in the beauty of the forest and admiring the majesty of the trees.

"This way," I finally said, picking a path through the trees as I drew on Fenris's memory. Fall leaves and brittle twigs crunched underfoot, and squirrels jumped from branch to branch overhead, following us from a safe distance.

Some fifteen minutes later, I finally found the tree—an ancient redwood that had died long ago, its branches withered, its bark dry as dust. Sinking to my knees, I reached into the hollow at the tree's base, fishing around for the pack.

"Well?" Iannis asked after a long minute. "Is it stuck?"

"No." Shock reverberated through me, and I sat back, staring dumbly at the tree. "It's not here."

"Not here?" Iannis echoed. There was a long moment of silence. "Is it the wrong tree?"

I checked the memory again, then shook my head. "No. Someone must have come and taken the pack." I sniffed, trying to catch a scent, but the rain had washed away any smell that might have lingered. "Hold on a sec."

Closing my eyes, I reached for the beast inside me, then changed. The familiar glowing light enveloped my body as I stretched and shifted, bone and muscle cracking and groaning as my body reformed itself. My eyes opened, and I took in a deep breath through my nose, curling my upper lip so the scent gland hidden there was exposed to the air. My sense of smell was much stronger in animal form, and I instantly caught a scent—Fenris's.

"He was here!" I exclaimed, my mental voice vibrating with excitement. *"Fenris was here!"*

"Of course he was," Iannis said irritably. "He came here to drop the pack off. But who took it?"

Ignoring him, I pressed my nose to the ground and followed the scent. It led away from the tree, up a small path, and...

"Where are you going?" Iannis called, rushing to catch up with me.

Annoyed that he wasn't following, I changed back to human form, then grabbed him by his shoulders. "Don't you see?" I said, my voice breathless as I shook him. "His scent leads away from the city, not toward it, and I know from his memories that he didn't go that way when he first came here. Plus, I don't scent anyone else around, which means..."

"That Fenris came here," Iannis finished softly. His violet eyes widened in astonishment. "He came here and got his pack!"

"Yes!" Letting out a whoop of excitement, I jumped in the air, then grabbed Iannis's face and kissed him hard. "He's *alive*," I shouted, breaking into a dance. "Fenris is alive!"

Laughing, Iannis grabbed me by the waist and spun me around, sending the fall leaves around us whirling. The grey clouds above us chose that moment to part, and sunlight shone bright and true into the clearing, lighting up Iannis's face. Tears gleamed in his eyes, and my own eyes stung as joy and happiness filled my body. Flinging my arms around him, I kissed him again, and we toppled to the ground, rolling about in the leaves and laughing like two giddy children.

Fenris had escaped. Somehow, someway, he'd dragged himself out from beneath the wreckage of that building and come to grab his pack. I didn't know how he'd found the energy, but he must have shifted enough to heal himself so that he could escape.

"He'll send a message to us soon," Iannis said confidently, rolling onto his elbows so he could look at me. His eyes were bright, his entire face shining with joy. "He said he would let us know where he ended up, when he told us that he was planning to leave."

"I'm sure he will." But honestly, I didn't care if Fenris never told us where he'd chosen to start his new life. He was somewhere out in Northia's wide-open spaces, safe from Garrett's clutches, free to live his own life, on his own terms. And even though I would always miss him, the knowledge that he was alive and safe was damn well good enough for me.

The End...or is it?

Want to find out what happened to Fenris? Head over to Amazon and grab a copy of FUGITIVE BY MAGIC, Book One in Fenris's Story! Fenris will be getting a trilogy before we return to Sunaya, so make sure you're subscribed to Jasmine's mailing list so you don't miss out on new releases!

Join the mailing list at www.jasminewalt.com/newsletter-signup

Want to keep up with Jasmine on social media? You can find her on Facebook, follow her on Twitter @jasmine_writes, and follow her on Instagram @jasmine.walt. You can also email her at jasmine@jasminewalt.com if you have questions or just want to say hi. She loves hearing from her fans!

GLOSSARY

Alacara: one of the Federation's fifty states, located on the southeastern coast of the subcontinent.

Alarain: a very rare herb native to Garai, that protects against magic. Its sale or export is strictly forbidden.

Allie: baker selling buns and other baked goods in the Rowanville Market.

Annia: see under Melcott, Annia.

Ancestral Spirits: according to Shifter belief, once a being is done with reincarnation, they may become ancestral spirits.

ar': suffix in mages' family names, that denotes they are of noble birth, and can trace their descent to one of Resinah's twelve disciples.

Bai, Asu: Garaian mage, younger sister of Lalia Chen, married to Loku Bai, resides in Leniang City with her family.

Bai, Loku: mage and businessman, resides in Leniang City; married to Asu, the younger sister of Director Chen.

Baine, Sunaya: a half-panther shifter, half-mage who used to hate mages and has a passion for justice. Because magic is forbidden to all but the mage families, Sunaya was forced to keep her abilities a secret until she accidentally used them to defend herself in front of witnesses. Rather than condemn her to death, the Chief Mage, Iannis ar'Sannin, chose to take her on as his apprentice, and eventually his fiancée. She struggles to balance her shifter and mage heritage.

Baine, Mafiela: Chieftain of the Jaguar Clan and Sunaya's aunt.

Baine, Melantha: Sunaya's cousin, daughter and designated successor to the Jaguar Clan's Chieftain.

Baine, Rylan: one of Chieftain Baine's least favored children, and Sunaya's cousin. An active member of the Resistance, with the rank of Captain, he was captured and imprisoned during the uprising in Solantha. His sentence was commuted to bodyguard service for Sunaya, under the guise of tiger shifter Lanyr Goldrin.

Baine, Saranella: Sunaya's late mother and sister to Mafiela Baine, a jaguar shifter who died when Sunaya was twelve.

Ballos, Jonias: an elderly reclusive mage in Solantha, who was involved in Sunaya's early history.

Bao-Sung: pirate, informal master of a small port close to Leniang City in southern Garai.

Barakan, Nimos: a tiger shifter, often found at the Cat's Meow diner in Shiftertown.

Barning, Leo, Rana and **Durian:** a human family living in Solantha.

Benefactor: the name the Resistance called their anonymous, principal source of financial support, before Sunaya unmasked socialite Thorgana Mills as the master criminal.

Bilai: capital city of Garai, seat of the Mage-Emperor.

The Black Curtain: shop owned by Elania Tarrignal in Witches' End, where under-the-table hexes can be discreetly obtained.

Black Market: an area in Solantha where illegal items can be purchased, by night, at the buyer's risk.

Canalo: one of the fifty states making up the Northia Federation, located on the West Coast of the Northia Continent.

Canalo Council, usually just the **Council:** a governmental body composed of eight senior mages, supposed to advise the Chief Mage and substitute for him in case of sudden death or incapacity.

Capitol: building in the capital Dara, where the Convention of Chief Mages meets every other year to conduct government business.

Chen, Lalia: the current Director of the Canalo Mages Guild in Solantha. She immigrated to the Northia Federation from Garai after her apprenticeship, and serves as deputy to Iannis ar'Sannin, the Chief Mage.

Chartis, Argon: former Director of the Canalo Mages Guild, dismissed by the Chief Mage for insubordination and attempts to undermine the Chief Mage's authority. He subsequently joined forces with the Benefactor to avenge his dismissal.

Chieftain: a title used to distinguish the head of a shifter clan.

Calmias, Father Monor: a charismatic preacher in Ur-God temples, with many fanatic followers all over Northia. Currently imprisoned in Prison Isle outside Solantha City.

Canter: an elderly mage often manning the reception at Solantha Palace.

Castalis: a country and peninsula at the southwestern edge of the Central Continent, ruled by a High Mage.

The Cat's Meow: a diner in Shiftertown, owned by the Tiger Clan.

Central Continent: the largest of the continents on Recca, spanning from Garai in the east to Castalis in the west.

Coazi: a group of related tribes controlling large parts of Mexia and adjoining states.

Comenius: see under Genhard, Comenius.

Coracciao: a group of islands in the tropical waters between the Northia and Southia continents.

Creator: the ultimate deity, worshipped by all three races under different names.

Dira: mage, one of the secretaries at the Mages Guild.

Danrian, Warin: regional manager for Canalo of the Sandin Federal Bank, who turned out to be one of the Benefactor's henchmen, coordinating the bank's dodgy credit scheme for shifters. He was also behind the illegal Shifter Royale.

Dara: capital of the Northia Federation, located on the east coast of the Northia Continent.

Downtown: the seamy area of Maintown, especially at night, when the Black Market is operating there. Full of brothels and gaming dens.

Elania, see Tarrignal, Elania.

Elnos: see under Ragga, Elnos.

Enforcer: a bounty hunter employed by the government to seek out and capture wanted criminals. They operate under strict rules and are paid bounties for each head. While the majority of them are human, there is a strong minority of shifters, and even the occasional mage.

Enforcers' Guild: the administrative organization in charge of the enforcers, led by Captain Galling and later, his successor, Acting Captain Skonel. Also, the building from which the various enforcer crews work under their respective foremen.

Faonus: one of the three founding mages of the Federation.

Faricia: a large continent that straddles the North and South hemispheres, located south of the Central Continent's western region. Inhabited by many different nations and tribes; partly inaccessible to foreign travelers.

Fenris: a clanless wolf shifter of unusual antecedents, close friend and confidant of Chief Mage Iannis ar'Sannin and Sunaya Baine. No known last name.

Firegate Bridge: Solantha's best-known structure, a large red bridge spanning the length of Solantha Bay. It is accessible via Firegate Road.

Captain Galling: the human captain of the Enforcer's Guild in Solantha City, appointed by the former Chief Mage and Council.

Garai: the largest and most populated country on the Eastern Continent. Garaians are known for slanted eyes and ivory skin as well as their complicated, rune-like alphabet.

Garidano, Cirin: Finance Secretary of the State of Canalo.

Genhard, Comenius: a hedgewitch from Pernia, owner of the shop Over the Hedge at Witches' End. Close friend of Sunaya Baine, father of Rusalia Genhard, former employer of Noria Melcott, and fiancé of the witch Elania Tarrignal.

Genhard, Rusalia: daughter of Comenius Genhard by his estranged former lover Hiltraud. Came from Pernia to Solantha to live with her father after her mother's sudden death.

Gor, Faron: shifter, Chief Editor of the Shifter Courier, the Solantha newspaper for the shifter population. He provided important information to Sunaya during the investigation into the Shifter Royale.

Gorax: a family of builders in Solantha; Gorax Constructions, their company, has built a large number of edifices in Solantha's Maintown.

Graning, Zavian: mage, currently Minister of the Northia Federation. Elected by the Convention for an indefinite term, he is charged with coordination of governmental business and particularly foreign affairs, between the biannual Convention sessions that he prepares and presides.

Great Accord: a treaty struck by the ruling mages centuries ago which brought an end to a devastating war known as the Conflict. It is still the basis upon which mages rule their countries and territories. All new laws passed must be in accordance with the provisions of the Great Accord.

Gulaya: a star-shaped charm, usually made of metal, that is anchored to a specific location and can take its wearer back there at need. They are rare, and difficult to recharge.

Halyma: shamaness of the hills Coazi and chief shamaness of the entire Coazi tribe, due to her outstanding magic talent.

Hedgewitch: a variety of mage specialized in earth-based magic.

Hennis: a jaguar shifter, butler in the home of Mafiela Baine, the Chieftain of the Jaguar Clan.

Herald, The: the main newspaper in Solantha City, used to belong to Mills Media and Entertainment; it is geared towards the human majority population.

Hiltraud: a Pernian hedgewitch, deceased. She was Comenius Genhard's former lover and the mother of his daughter Rusalia.

Iannis ar'Sannin: Chief Mage of Canalo. He resides in the capital city of Solantha, from which he runs Canalo as well as the Mages Guild with the help of his deputy and Secretaries. Originally a native of Manuc, a country located across the Eastern Sea.

Inara: a state of the Northia Federation.

Janta, see Urama, Janta.

Jeremidah: one of the three founding mages of the Northia Federation ("The Founding Trio") together with Faonus and Micara.

Kalois: a rare foreign plant which masks the smell of silver so well that shifters can be drugged or poisoned despite their sensitive noses.

Kan Zao: a mental and physical martial art tradition from Garai.

Kardanor: see under Makis, Kardanor.

Kazu: mage and general; eldest son and heir of the Garaian Mage-Emperor, later Mage-Emperor himself.

Lakin, Boon: a jaguar shifter from Parabas, appointed as Solantha's new Shiftertown Inspector following Roanas's death. Sunaya and he are friends and occasional allies. It was a case he investigated and discussed with Sunaya, that led to the eventual exposure of the Shifter Royale.

Lanyr Goldrin: supposedly a tiger shifter engaged as guard in Solantha Palace; pseudonym of Rylan Baine.

Leniang Port (also Leniang City): a lawless port city on the south coast of Garai.

Liu: a young Garaian girl of humble origins. She was bought by Iannis and Sunaya during their travels and now works as apprentice cook in the Palace under Mrs. Tandry's supervision.

Lion Guards: a guard unit recruited for the special protection of the Garaian Mage-Emperor, composed of lion shifters.

Loranian: the difficult, secret language of magic that all mages are required to master.

Mages Guild: the governmental organization that rules the mages in Canalo, and supervises the other races. The headquarters are in Solantha Palace. They are subordinate to the Chief Mage.

Magi-tech: devices that are powered by both magic and technology.

Magorah: the god of the shifters, associated with the moon.

Main Crew: the largest group of Enforcers in the Guild. They are generally favored over the other crews and get the most lucrative dockets.

Makis, Kardanor: a human architect specialized in public buildings and safety.

Manuc: an island country off the west coast of the Central Continent.

Melcott, Annia: a human enforcer. She is a close friend of

Sunaya's, and Noria's older sister. After Noria was sentenced to hard labor the Mines, she left Solantha to work for a time in Southia.

Melcott, Noria: Annia Melcott's younger sister. A gifted inventor, who used to work part-time in the shop Over the Hedge, belonging to Comenius Genhard, and had a mage boyfriend, Elnos. She passionately believed in equality between all races, and supported the Resistance, which she eventually joined. After being arrested with other scientists working for the Resistance, she refused a deal and is currently serving a five-year sentence of hard labor in the mines.

Mrs. Melcott: Annia and Noria Melcott's widowed mother, a well-off socialite.

Mendle: family name of the owners of the largest construction company in Solantha, of which Mr. Mendle is also the CEO.

Messindor: pirate mage, almost certainly deceased. Sunaya discovered his diary and other possessions on a deserted island.

Mexia: one of the fifty states making up the Northia Federation.

Micara: one of the mages who made up the Founding Trio of the Federation, together with Faonus and Jeremidah

Captain Milios: commandant of a secret Resistance Camp at the base of the Sarania Mountain Range.

Mills, Thorgana: human socialite, married to Curian Vanderheim, and former owner of a news media conglomerate as well as numerous other companies. After being exposed as the Benefactor by Sunaya, she was imprisoned. Her companies were seized and auctioned off. She may be dead, however, her body was not positively identified after a fire in the Dara prison where she was being held.

Minister, the: the mage who presides the Convention of Chief Mages, and coordinates the affairs of the Northia Federation between sessions, particularly foreign relations. The office is currently held by Zavian Graning.

Mitas, Dr. Elan: a general practitioner of medicine in Dara, member of the Resistance.

Miyanta: daughter and disciple of the First Mage Resinah, from whom the ar'Rhea family traces its descent.

Mogg, Henning: mage, pilot and agent employed by the Federal Office for Security.

Naraka: a country off the Eastern Continent, consisting of several large islands.

Nebara: one of the fifty states making up the Northia Federation.

Noria: see under Melcott, Noria.

Northia Federation: a federation consisting of fifty states that cover the entire northern half and middle of the Western Continent. Canalo is part of this federation.

Osero: one of the fifty states of the Northia Federation, located north of Canalo on the continent's west coast.

Over the Hedge: a shop at Witches' End selling magical charms and herbal remedies, belonging to Comenius Genhard.

Pandanum: a base metal used, inter alia, for less valuable coins.

Parabas: a city north of Solantha, capital of the state of Osero.

Pernia: a country on the Central Continent, from which Sunaya's friend Comenius Genhard hails.

Pillick, Harron: mage, assistant to the Federal Director of Security Garrett Toring.

Polar ar'Tollis: former Chief Mage of Nebara, who vanished after being condemned to death by the Convention.

Prickett: a fruit seller in the Rowanville Market.

Prison Isle: an island in the middle of Solantha Bay that serves as a prison for Canalo's worst criminals.

Privacy Guard: a company that used to lease uniformed guards to governments and other institutions all over the Federation.

Ragga, Elnos: Noria Melcott's former boyfriend, a graduate of Solantha academy and one of the few mages who believes in equality amongst the races. He and Noria worked together to develop new magi-tech devices.

Recca: the world of humans, mages and shifters.

Residah: the mages' book of scripture that holds Resinah's teachings.

Resinah: the first mage, whose teachings are of paramount spiritual importance for the mages. Her statue can be found in the mage temples, which are off-limits to non-mages and magically hidden from outsiders.

Resistance: a movement of revolutionaries planning to overthrow the mages and take control of the Northia Federation, financially backed by the Benefactor. Over time they became bolder and more aggressive, using terrorist attacks with civilian casualties, as well as assassination. They even tried to take over Solantha, when the government was in disarray after they had engineered the Chief Mage's disappearance. Sunaya's discovery that the Benefactor and the human leaders of the Resistance were planning to turn on the shifters once the mages were defeated dealt a blow to the unity of the movement, but its human component is far from completely defeated, and still working on "secret weapons."

ar'Rhea: family name of a noble Castalian family of mages, who trace their descent to the first mage Resinah through her daughter Miyanta.

ar'Rhea, Haman: High Mage of Castalis, a country at the south-western edge of the Central Continent, and Sunaya's long-lost father.

ar'Rhea, Isana: mage, resides in Castalis, Sunaya's younger half-sister.

ar'Rhea, Malik: Sunaya's half-brother, son of the High Mage of Castalis and expected to succeed him at some point.

Rhodea: smallest of the fifty states that make up the Northia Federation, on the east coast of the continent.

Rowanville: the only neighborhood of Solantha where all three races mix.

Rusalia, see under Genhard, Rusalia.

Rylan: see under Baine, Rylan.

Sandia: a large country (and subcontinent) of the Central Continent, populated by many different peoples.

Sandin Federal Bank: a bank with branches in all fifty states of the Federation; its Canalo manager was Danrian Warin. It was shut down after Sunaya brought a scheme of "interest-free loans," financed with illegally mined gold, to the Chief Mage's notice.

ar'Sannin, Iannis: see under Iannis ar'Sannin.

Schaun, Tinari: a young schoolgirl in Solantha, rejected by her human family after she proved to have magic. Subsequently, she was informally adopted by Head Librarian Janta Urama.

Serapha charms: paired amulets that allow two people, usually a couple, to find each other via twinned stones imbued with a small part of their essence. Normally, only the wearer can take a serapha charm off.

Seros: a city located in Southern Canalo.

Shaman/Shamaness: a spiritual leader of the native tribes, highly adept at nature magic, healing, divination and mind magic.

Shifter: a human who can change into animal form and back by magic; they originally resulted from illegal experiments by mages on ordinary humans.

Shifter Courier: Solantha newspaper specifically geared towards the shifter population.

Shifter Royale: an illegal underground betting concourse where kidnapped and drugged shifters were forced to fight against each other, sometimes to the death. Discovered and exposed by Sunaya, with help from Boon Lakin and Annia Melcott, after her cousin Mika had been kidnapped by the organizers.

Shiftertown: the part of Solantha where the official shifter clans live.

Shiftertown Inspector: a shifter chosen by the Shiftertown Council to police shifter-related crime. The position is currently held by Boon Lakin, a jaguar shifter, appointed after the murder of his predecessor Roanas Tillmore.

Solantha: the capital of Canalo State, a port city on the west coast of the Northia continent, home of Sunaya Baine.

Solantha Bay: spanned by the Firegate Bridge, the bay gave its name to the city and port that became the capital of Canalo.

Solantha Palace: the seat of power in Canalo, where both the Chief Mage and the Mages Guild reside. It is located near the coast of Solantha Bay.

South Garaian Sea: local name for the part of the Major Ocean located south of Garai (Note: the Major Ocean is called Western Sea in the Northia Federation, while the Minor Ocean is called the Eastern Sea.)

Southia: forms the Western Continent together with Northia, and is composed of various nations.

Skonel, Wellmore: human enforcer; formerly deputy to Captain Galling, Acting Captain (pending confirmation) after the latter's retirement.

Taili the Wolf: in shifter legend, the very first shifter (a female).

Mrs. Tandry: human, head chef in the kitchens of Solantha Palace.

Tarrignal, Elania: girlfriend and later fiancée of Comenius Genhard; a witch specializing in potions, with a shop in Witches' End, called The Black Curtain.

Talcon, Garius: the former Deputy Captain of the Enforcer's Guild, who pestered Sunaya for sexual favors that she indignantly refused. Sunaya discovered he was in league with Petros Yantz, the man behind the silver murders, and killed him in self-defense.

Teca: the only alcoholic drink strong enough to get shifters drunk, fatal to humans.

Testing: schoolchildren in Canalo used to be tested for magic at least twice during their schoolyears, and a positive result would lead to the magic wipe (often with permanent mental damage.) The testing is now Sunaya's responsibility, and she tries to find better solutions for talented children on a case-to-case basis.

The Twilight: a bar in Rowanville where Sunaya used to bartend.

Thotting, Cerlina: a ten-year-old schoolgirl, who was missing from her home in Solantha. Finding her was Sunaya's very first case as an enforcer.

Thrase, Nelia: a young human, formerly a journalist, Sunaya's social secretary.

Tinari, see Schaun, Tinari.

Tillmore, Roanas: lion shifter, the former Shiftertown Inspector and father figure/mentor to Sunaya. He was poisoned while digging into the silver murders, prompting Sunaya to take over the investigation.

ar'Tollis, Mendir: mage, deceased, an eccentric elderly cousin of Chief Mage Polar ar'Tollis.

ar'Tollis, Polar: a former Chief Mage of Nebara, who disappeared after being charged with a crime against the Great Accord. Subsequently, he was condemned to death in absentia by the Convention.

Toring, Garrett: mage, Federal Director of Security, former Federal Secretary of Justice; an ambitious high official in the Federal government in Dara.

Trouble: a pesky, non-corporeal ether parrot that resulted when Sunaya tried the ether pigeon spell on her own. Appears whenever Sunaya pronounces his name in any context.

Tua: a legendary and highly dangerous race of very long-lived beings with powerful magic, who sometimes cross from their own world into Recca, most frequently in Manuc.

Turain: a small town north of Solantha, where the Shifter Royale took place.

Urama, Janta: mage and scholar, head librarian in the Solantha Mages Guild, foster mother of Tinari Schaun.

Ur-God: the name the humans call the Creator by.

Ursini, Wex: a bear shifter and enforcer.

Vanderheim, Curian: human millionaire and businessman, husband to Thorgana Mills.

Lord Vengar: former Chief Mage of Canalo, immediate predecessor of current Chief Mage Iannis ar'Sannin.

Vance, Eltis: Foreman of the Main Crew, not a fan of Sunaya.

Vestes, Lamar: a ham and sausage vendor in Rowanville Market Street.

Witches' End: a pier in Solantha City, part of the Port, where immigrant magic users sell their wares and services.

Yantz, Petros: the former Chief Editor of the Herald, implicated in the silver murders. A close collaborator of the Benefactor, he found refuge in her Solantha mansion as a fugitive.

Zavian Graning: see under Graning, Zavian.

ACKNOWLEDGMENTS

What to say, what to say? I can't believe we're at the end of Book 7! As usual, writing this book has been an amazing experience, and I couldn't have done it without a number of people who've had my back.

Thank you to Victoria, Lenka, Kaitlyn, and all the other beta readers who took the time to give me valuable feedback. As usual, you've caught plot holes and inconsistencies, and helped take this book from good to awesome.

Thanks again to Mary Burnett, my writing partner. Your fine-toothed comb has made this book shine, and I think we can both be very proud of the seven books we've done together.

Thank you to Judah Dobin, my cover artist and other half, for the amazing cover. As usual, you've outdone yourself!

And thank you to all my readers who've supported me on this incredible journey, and who continue to read and love my books. I really, truly couldn't do this without you, and I'm grateful for each and every one of you.

ABOUT THE AUTHOR

Jasmine Walt is obsessed with books, chocolate, and sharp objects. Somehow, those three things melded together in her head and transformed into a desire to write, usually fantastical stuff with a healthy dose of action and romance. Her characters are a little (okay, a lot) on the snarky side, and they swear, but they mean well. Even the villains sometimes.

When Jasmine isn't chained to her keyboard, you can find her practicing her triangle choke on the jujitsu mat, spending time with her family, or binge-watching superhero shows on Netflix.

Want to connect with Jasmine? You can find her on Twitter at @jasmine_writes, on Facebook, on Instagram at @jasmine.walt, or at www.jasminewalt.com.

ALSO BY JASMINE WALT

Made in the USA
Lexington, KY
05 February 2019